VAGABOND VAMPS

Vagabond Vamps

A Novel

ALICE JUROW

Deco Vamp

This is a work of fiction. All of the names, characters, organizations and events portrayed in this novel are either products of the author's imagination or are used fictitiously. Any historical figures who are named or suggested are treated as fictional characters whose actions are completely invented.

Vagabond Vamps

Copyright © 2024 by Alice Jurow

ISBN 978-0-9977180-3-4 (trade paperback)
ISBN 978-0-9977180-2-7 (ebook)

Deco Vamp
www.vampsof29.com

DEDICATIONS

To my mother, Charlotte Peyser Jurow (1922-1982),
who loved a good read

To all my dear fellow time-travelers (you know who
you are!)

To Charles, for everything

Charroux, France – December, 1929

"I can't stand it!" Sally growled through gritted teeth and angrily ground out her cigarette. She had been pacing the oak floorboards all evening, and now stood staring grimly out the window of the tiny cottage. Snow fell lightly, just visible in the moonless dark.

"What can't you stand?" Lucienne looked up from the antique book she was reading by the fireplace.

"This place! I loved my Grandmère; I always used to love coming here—the quiet, the charm of the country-side—but that was when I could go back to Paris after-ward. Now, no. Two of us, in this tiny village . . . there isn't enough to sustain us. Not to mention boredom."

"I'm not bored. Your grandmother had an amazing library."

Sally turned to her friend. "Yes, she did. But aren't you getting . . . hungry? The butcher doesn't keep much stock and there really aren't enough people here. I know we can't risk Paris, not after what happened, but we

need a metropolis. What about London? I've been practicing my English for years now, you know."

Lucienne hid a smile behind her book. Sally's passionate Anglophilia had not improved her command of the
language, but she persisted in thinking that her ability to
say 'How do you do?' with a firm handshake made her an
international diplomat. Honestly, Lucienne would have
preferred someplace on the continent, Rome perhaps.
But the complicated, intimate, emotionally-draining ritual of the Long Sleep, which she had performed to put
their dear friend Natalie into a thirty-year stasis, left her
too depleted to argue.

"Isn't London expensive?" she wondered. "Do you
think we could sell this cottage?"

Sally looked startled. "We have *some* money, don't
we? We always saved, all the years we were working for
Mlle. Selling this place . . . oh, it would make me sad; I
hope I'll be able to come back here some day."

Lucienne reflected. "Probably just as well. Selling
property is complicated, I think. People might wonder
what happened to your grandmother, why her death
wasn't reported."

Sally smiled, wistfully. "Yes, they might not understand a five-hundred-year-old vamp deciding to open
the curtains and waste away on her sunny bed. Dear
Grandmère. . . .All right then, London! We can hire that
old man with the cart to take our things to the station.
Tomorrow?"

Lucienne stood up and gave Sally a hug. "Not quite tomorrow, darling. We'll need to sort out tickets and plans, pack our things. But all right, soon." She went over to the drinks table, mixed them each a coupe of Benedictine and blood, and toasted, "To London!"

London, February 1930

The trip had been wearying, and once the bellman left, Lucienne flung herself gratefully onto the inviting bed. Nose down, she took a deep sniff of the pillow.

"Mmm, lavender-scented starched sheets, how divine! I wish we could always stay in lovely hotels."

"I don't!" Sally said vehemently. "Apart from our money running out far too fast if we did—what about maids coming in at all hours, people always around? There's no privacy."

"Yes, but one can get a snack at any hour," Lucienne winked. "Always a fresh supply of tasty travelers."

"I prefer to eat out—keep it separate from where we live. Tomorrow we can start looking for a nice quiet flat."

Lucienne sat up with a sigh. "You're right, of course—we can't afford this. Money! Even modest lodgings aren't free. We'll have to get some sort of work."

Sally, sideways in an armchair, stretched her long limbs. "That shouldn't be too difficult. With my English,

I imagine I can get an office job. Perhaps I can learn typewriting." She wiggled her fingers over an invisible keyboard.

"I don't know, darling." Lucienne, a born linguist, once more tactfully kept her estimate of Sally's English fluency to herself. "I don't think that pays awfully well. And do you know what time offices open? Nine in the morning, or perhaps eight."

Sally gasped in horror. "I hadn't thought of that!" She pondered a moment. "I know . . . I could be a chanteuse in a nightclub—the toast of Mayfair! It can't be that hard to learn to sing decently, can it? You'd think I would have picked it up in the last two hundred years."

Lucienne suppressed a shudder. Sally was a passionate jazz-fancier, but her off-key versions of her favorite records did not bear thinking of. "Why don't we go round the couture houses—I know, it's not like Paris, but there are a few at least—and see if they're hiring mannequins."

"Boring. But easy. And we're perfectly qualified. Direct from Paris, rue Cambon, the epicenter of chic . . . and fresh from the collapse of the House of Mlle! We'll be a sensation."

"Careful, darling. We don't want to be too much of a sensation. We're here to be anonymous, remember."

The flat Sally found was rather basic, but by no means the worst one they saw during several afternoons of house-hunting. They had no trouble securing positions as mannequins at the couture house Jean-Philippe—despite its French name, the atelier was run by an English society hostess, who found their Paris credentials unimpeachable. In the reticent British way, no one attempted to pursue the lurid details of the catastrophic 1929 show at the house of Mlle.

"Sally, Lulu, you're up next, better hurry it up a bit . . . Oh, you're dressed! How d'you *do* that?" Margaret looked them over with a bewildered mix of admiration and irritation.

Sally shrugged with Gallic eloquence. (She'd begun to find it useful here to play up her Frenchness.)

"Of course, you're *professionals*." Margaret gave the word an emphasis that made the other young women nearby poke each other and giggle. The other mannequins (who all seemed to have floral names like Daisy, Viola and Hyacinth) were mostly "society beauties," doing a brief stint of modeling to stave off boredom. Sally and Lucienne were able to practically sleepwalk through the job.

After work, they would change and go out in search of nightlife. One breezy May evening found them at the Cafe de Paris in Coventry Street, where they spotted a familiar figure.

Silver-tongued Dolly Wilde was at a loss for words. She couldn't stop staring from one of them to the other. Finally, she burst into laughter and laughed until she was gasping for breath, her eyes wet.

"Well, if this isn't the best surprise of the world," she said at last. "Sally, Lucy—you're here! I wasn't at all sure I'd ever see you again. And where is lovely Natalie?"

"She, erm, had to go away for a bit," Sally said, a little uneasily. "We'll be meeting up again sometime."

"Oh dear, she hasn't gone back to Russia, has she? Isn't it rather unsettled?"

"No, no," Lucienne assured her. "She's visiting family in . . . in Switzerland, I think."

"Well anyway, it's grand to see you, it really is. Shall we have champagne? Or some amusing cocktails?" Dolly looked around for a waiter. "This place is a madhouse tonight; we'll be lucky to get a drink this hour. Meanwhile, you can tell me—what on earth *happened* that night at Mlle's atelier? That fashion show was so bizarre and extraordinary . . . and then when the lights went out . . . it's all a sort of blur. Of course, I may have been several sheets to the wind; I feel I can barely remember a thing. But there were the strangest stories in the newspapers . . . Men bleeding to death? And then, the clothes themselves—she was absolutely prescient—look at what we're all wearing these days . . ."

Lucienne put a light warning hand on Sally's arm, preventing her from blurting out any answers right away. They let Dolly babble on—she appeared, in fact, to be a few sheets to the wind tonight—and she eventually talked herself out, answering her own questions or forgetting that she'd had any.

"So, you're all doing well? That's grand! Welcome to London town—we must see a lot of each other while you're here, before I head back to Paris, anyway. Where *is* that waiter?" She folded back her glove to peer at her small, smart wristwatch. "Heavens, is that really the time? I must be going . . ." And she abruptly gathered her things and tottered off.

They saw Dolly a few more times over the next several months, and each time she greeted them with the same radiant, wide-eyed amazement.

"It is the best lark that you're here, you know! I must introduce you to the Bright Young People . . .only, I'm not on awfully good terms with any of them just at the moment. Perhaps in a week or two." Although she was moderately well-off, Dolly had a few expensive and illegal habits, so that she always seemed to have run through her funds. Her solution was usually to borrow from a friend—who soon became less friendly.

Meanwhile, even with their pay from Jean-Philippe and the modest cost of their small flat (not to mention the absence of grocery bills), Sally and Lucienne were finding London an expensive city. Everyone seemed more worried about money these days, and even with oodles of glamour, it wasn't always easy to find the kind of lavish generosity that had made evenings out in Paris such an effortless pleasure. Sally was particularly miffed one night when an agreeable young swell, whom she'd been dancing with, nibbling and devoting herself to for a few hours, disappeared after a trip to the men's room, leaving her with the bill.

"Cocktails are absurdly expensive!" she told Lucienne the next day.

"Everything is, here," Lucienne sighed. "But the fellow I met last night said that Barcelona is lovely: friendly, elegant and cheap!"

"Does it have jazz and cocktails?"

"Spanish gypsy music and very good red wine."

"Close enough. Let's think about it."

Barcelona, April, 1931

Barcelona was charming. Its narrow streets, tranquil at dusk, were vibrant with convivial pedestrians late into the night.

"People here keep vampire hours," Sally exclaimed in wonder.

"I know—it's perfect here," Lucienne agreed. "This could be *our* place."

They had rented a pleasant room, far below London prices, and immediately found they could spend their nights deliciously mingling with the crowds that wandered from one cozy bar to the next.

"I'm not sure I love the music, yet," Sally whispered as they listened to a flamenco singer in a tiny, dimly lit club. "It's very . . . passionate. Not a lot of swing, though. But I'll give it a chance."

"The Chocolate Dandies were here in '29—remember, they were away for a few weeks? Claude said he quite liked it. And Josephine Baker did a tour here just last year

—why do we always miss her? I can't believe we never saw one of her shows in Paris. So anyway, there must be jazz clubs somewhere. Shall we try another place?"

They finished their rioja and stepped out into the bustling street, interestingly scented with garlic, gaslight and musk. As a pair of dark-haired young men fell into step with them, Lucienne flared her nostrils and nudged Sally.

"Buenas noches," Lucienne said, and raised an eyebrow when the reply was "Bona nit."

The man smiled. "You need to learn Catalan if you are staying here."

"Ah, I'd like that!" Lucienne had switched to French, and he followed, seamlessly. Meanwhile, Sally smiled at the other fellow, and was startled when he lunged, gently but decisively, toward her throat.

"Hey!" She glared at him, letting her fangs show. He backed away immediately, raising his hands in a gesture of surprise and apology. His friend grinned.

"Oho, so you're our sort. No wonder you are so insanely beautiful. Have you been here long?"

"Not long enough to find a decent jazz club. Perhaps you can show us one? I'm Sally, this is Lucienne. We're here from Paris, by way of London."

"I am Guillem; this is my pal, Ferran. You'll have to forgive him; he doesn't know much French, and he likes to bite more than to talk." Ferran smiled, a bit sheepishly. "So, you like jazz, American jazz?"

"Yes, I love it," Sally answered quickly, "but I think of it as not really American, but international. The music of modernity. Don't you like it?"

"I do," Guillem said thoughtfully, "but it is not as dear to me as our traditional music. You should realize you have come at a very exciting time—after years of struggle, we have a Catalan republic!"

"Viva Catalunya!" Ferran exclaimed suddenly. The two of them grew even more animated and began shouting what seemed to be political slogans.

A couple of other men nearby (clearly mortal-smelling) joined in, playfully shoving each other. Sally and Lucienne stepped out of the group and moved on toward the next corner.

"Pleasure to meet you—we'll catch up later!" Lucienne called back to their new friends. Guillem waved distractedly.

Over the next few days, they ran into the local vamps a few times. Ferran remained a bit awkward, as if still embarrassed by his original attack on Sally, but Guillem cheerfully engaged in polyglot chat and even gave Lucienne a small job, translating a Catalan pamphlet into French. With her usual facility, she found the written form of the language close enough to Spanish—with which she had a nodding acquaintance—to manage. She was working on this project when Sally stepped out for a walk, on a pleasantly cloudy late afternoon.

He looks like someone who knows where the jazz clubs are. Sally eyed the young man appreciatively. With his light brown complexion, a jaunty cap atop curly black hair, tight pants and a sort of rhythmic swagger to his walk, he reminded her of some of her favorite musicians. *Maybe he's a drummer*, she found herself thinking, and then realized it was probably the effect of what she was hearing—a regular drum beat coming from the square ahead.

She followed the man around a corner and saw that a couple dozen of his compatriots were there, marching in formation. As her fellow hurried to join them, she realized that what she'd taken for an unusual, rather stylish outfit was the uniform they all wore. *Of course, they're soldiers*, she mused. *Mmm, handsome and tasty-looking.* She stepped into the shelter of an archway to watch them.

"When did you say you were born, miss? And where?"

"Seventeen. . ." Sally began unguardedly and caught herself with a gasp. *What was a reasonable date?* "I mean, the 17th of May, in, er, 1912?" she amended hastily. "In Paris, France."

"1912? You seem uncertain," the officer mused, steepling his fingers and looking at her closely. He was quite handsome, with deepset eyes and a narrow mustache. "I've never known a young woman of not quite nineteen to forget her birth date."

"It's a shortcoming, I know—I've always been horrible with numbers. I just can't keep them straight in my mind, ever since I was a tiny . . ."

"Parents' names?" He cut off her ingratiating prattle.

"Er. Marie-France Lafayette, née Dugarde; Francois Lafayette."

"Marie-France and Francois, eh—very French indeed. And yet they gave you an English name. Occupations?"

"Sir?"

"What do they do?"

"What do they do? My father . . ." *Think, Sally, what would he do now? 'Homme des lettres' isn't considered a modern job—and naturally, this man believes your parents are alive today, not buried in the eighteenth century.* "My father is a teacher of science at a lycée. My mother keeps the house."

"When did you last see them?"

"Please, sir, I don't understand. I've done nothing wrong. And surely my parents, in France, have nothing to do with anything. I am just a tourist here, with a friend."

"What is the name of your friend?"

Sally froze. The last thing she wanted to do was get Lucienne involved in whatever this trouble was. "I'm sorry, I'd rather not say. He's a boyfriend, but he . . . er . . . has a wife."

The officer's eyebrows went up sharply. He tapped his pen and made a brief note. "I see. Well, that's not very savory, is it? I regret, miss, that we may have to detain you overnight for further questioning in the morning."

"Oh no, that's not possible!" Sally gasped.

"It certainly is. Do not be concerned. We have a matron to look after you; you will be perfectly safe." He wrote in his ledger without looking at her. "When did you say your birthday is, again?"

"May 17, 19 . . ." Sally slumped forward, her voice inaudible.

The officer stood up fast and rushed around the desk to her side. "What's the matter?" he said, lifting her chin and peering at her intently.

She latched onto his wrist until he lost consciousness. She couldn't move him back into his chair and had to simply ease him down to the waxed linoleum. Glancing toward the window in the door to be sure no one was near, she tore the last few pages out of his ledger, folded them into her bag and slipped cautiously out.

"Loulou, we have to leave."

"What? We're just getting settled here. I have a translating job starting tomorrow, and I quite like this room." It was indeed cozy, and just outside the wood-shuttered windows was a large balcony filled with night-blooming flowers. Lucienne pushed the casement open and took a deep sniff.

"I know—but for some reason, they think I'm a spy. I've just escaped from the municipal jail. They'll be looking for me, in a couple of hours, as soon as that officer who interrogated me wakes up." Sally read the look on Lucienne's face—exasperation quickly mounting to rage—and extended her hands pleadingly. "It wasn't my fault! I was just checking out some juicy young men in smart uniforms. How was I to know they were on some sort of secret manoeuvre?"

"Oh, Sally . . . they actually took you to jail? Did you attack someone? You know how careful we have to be, especially in a new place. What were you thinking?"

"I didn't do anything! They thought I looked suspicious, and they took me in for questioning. But the officer—cute fellow!—found my answers too evasive and wanted to lock me up there overnight. It wouldn't do!"

As she described her escape from the dreary jail, Lucienne began, methodically, to pack. "Come on, then. We have to go to the bar downstairs. There's a man there who can help us; lucky I chose his neck to nibble this evening."

Cairo, February, 1932

Sally and Lucienne took to Cairo immediately, and the city returned the embrace. Elegant Shepheard's Hotel was a bargain compared with similar establishments in Europe, and the desk clerk (clearly smitten by the two chic charmers with their mountain of luggage) installed them in a luxe suite at the price of a more modest room.

"Mmm. Oriental air!" Lucienne would say, inhaling deeply, each time they stepped out. "Flowers, fruit and offal."

"I feel a bit like Flaubert, don't you?" Sally said. "Like we can wander the back alleys with just a few coins and find willing street boys to bite. Or girls—dancing girls."

"Yes, perfect for the bohemian vampire on a budget," Lucienne deadpanned. In linen suits and veiled, sun-protective hats, they were returning from their daily visit to the souk—spices, copper, carpets, dates, coffee.

"But we shouldn't neglect our fellow hotel guests" Sally noted as they entered the potted-palm-and-wicker-armchair-filled lobby. "Some of them seem quite tasty. Have you noticed those two cute fellows looking us over?"

"Aldo and Giacomo? In the white suits and boaters? Yes, we're joining them for tea, as soon as we freshen up."

"Are we now, Loulou? When did this happen? Never mind, don't tell me—ever since Rome, you speak fluent Italian. I suppose you've already had a long talk about Futurism and D'Annunzio."

"Silly Sally! I know enough of the language to get by, but you've got all the cultural reference points; I'm sure they'll be impressed."

Up in their third-floor suite, they slid out of their walking suits into silky tea dresses and brushed each other's hair—both of them had identical silky black bobs at the moment. A spritz of scent, a nip from their flasks (they'd already located an accommodating butcher) and a touch-up of lip rouge completed their preparations.

"Andiamo," Lucienne said gaily. "Aldo is an architect, and Giacomo . . . a gardener? Gigolo? Honestly, I can't remember, but they'll tell us."

Sally straightened her collar, blew a kiss toward the big trunk in the corner and followed her friend out the door.

The Italians were languid, good-humored and polite. They ordered the full English cream tea, which none of the four of them did more than pick at. Aldo was reasonably conversant in both French and English, so that he and Sally could exchange pleasantries; Giacomo was taciturn in any language. The only time he showed any animation was at the arrival of a lemon layer cake. After an hour, Sally still couldn't tell whether the two handsome young men were merely traveling companions, close friends or a couple.

"But I do like the way they smell, especially that boring Giacomo," Sally told Lucienne as they left the lavish tea room, having promised to meet again for cocktails that evening.

"Boring? I think he's quite remarkable."

"He never says anything."

"Yes, but Aldo says he is a brilliant composer—he's always listening."

"Ah. Still blood runs deep, I suppose."

"What? Does that mean anything?"

"It's an English proverb. Or an English vampire proverb."

"Very amusing, *Miss* Lafayette."

Speaking in English (but not nearly as well as the dragoman she'd employed), Sally rented camels for a twilight expedition to the Great Pyramid. They were bringing along some new friends from Shepheard's, whom they'd spent a few weeks cultivating—a French archaeologist and his wife, as well as the two charming young Italians.

Lucienne supervised the packing of a lavish picnic. "I want to be sure our guests are well supplied with tasty nibbles; it's the least we can do," she winked at Sally. "What shall we bring for them to drink?"

"Lemonade and gin—everyone will like that."

"You don't think the boys will want beer?"

"They might, but I'm not going to drink from a beer-guzzler," Sally said, making a face.

Giza

Aldo and Giacomo were game for climbing a pyramid, but Professeur and Mme Lafont had already done so ("Too many times!"). Cool and mysterious, the interior beckoned.

"The tomb of Pharoah Khafre," the guide said with a flourish as he ushered them in, as if he'd personally arranged it just for them.

Lucienne, Sally and their guests followed him down a passageway, letting their eyes adjust to the dim light. The faint remnants of incised hieroglyphics were barely visible on the stone walls; the vaulted space had a raw, unadorned power.

"The pharoah's interior decorator seems to have left the job unfinished," Aldo remarked in Italian.

The guide moved deeper into the space, raising his lantern and beckoning them forward. "The sarcophagus of the great Khafre. Of course, the tomb has been plundered . . ." He paused and looked the group over sternly, as if they might have been responsible.

"For thousands of years, the pharoah's mummy lay within this sarcophagus. Come closer—you will still feel his presence."

The Lafonts exchanged a look that clearly meant 'what nonsense,' but they all took a few steps closer.

Lucienne and Sally were at the front of the group, and as the guide talked on about Khafre's reign and accomplishments, they caught each other's eyes. Lucienne's nose twitched—she had picked up the scent first—but Sally almost immediately perceived it too. She put a finger to her lips and tapped gently, where a fang would be, and Lucienne nodded.

The light was a bit softer when they emerged, but still glaring after the gloom of the tomb. A bit dazed, they remounted their camels, and their guide led the way to the picnic spot. The sun was setting when they got there, melting into the horizon in a glow of scarlet and violet, and the moon, half-full, was already up, brightening as the dusk dimmed.

Along a sheltered bluff with a magnificent view, Mustafa and his two assistants had already unrolled carpets, lit torches and set out refreshments.

"Perfect! Nothing left to do but make drinks," Sally said. The lemonade and gin had been kept somewhat cool in wet skin bags; Sally mixed with a generous hand for the gin, and soon the party was extremely jolly. The French couple told amusing archaeological stories, they all toasted the old pharoah and Giacomo produced a flute, enlivening the Egyptian dusk with Vivaldi.

Lucienne, sitting close to Mme. Lafont, had whispered something that caused her to throw her head back and laugh; she had leaned in to drink gently from the Frenchwoman's throat, when her eyes met Mustafa's. He was crouching in the shadows beyond the torchlight, and she saw him half-rise and back away.

As the party wound down, all the guests relaxed if not drowsing, Sally looked around for someone to make some coffee, and Lucienne told her, "They've all left—Mustafa and the others."

"What! Our contract clearly included bringing us all back to the hotel!"

"You had a contract?"

"Well, not as such. But we had an understanding."

"Well, he obviously *understood* that we're vamps and decided to vamoose. I think they took some of the camels too."

Sally groaned. "I thought we could just have a lovely time and enjoy ourselves. Come on, let's go count noses."

There were three camels left. "That'll do—we can double up. But we'll have to wait for morning; we can't find our way back in the dark."

"Can we do any better in the daylight? And what do camels need at night—are they all right?" Lucienne wondered.

"They look happy enough." Sally stroked the nearest soft-furred neck. "Hmm, wonder what camel blood is like?"

"Sally!"

"Joking, darling. I'm quite content. Come on, we'd better make sure our friends are comfortable. Hey, what about that tomb—wasn't that extraordinary?"

"I know! I can always tell when there's another vamp in the room, but who would think the scent would linger for three thousand years, when the body's not even there?"

"*There's* something you won't see in the history books: Khafre the Great, the vampire pharoah."

After arranging blankets over Giacomo, Aldo and the Lafonts, Lucienne and Sally rolled themselves together in a carpet against the night chill.

"Just like Cleopatra," Lucienne said, stifling a tiny sneeze. "Ugh, dusty. I hope it doesn't have moths."

"Don't care," Sally said sleepily. She arranged a light shawl over their faces to protect them from the morning light, and they snuggled down together. "I hope Natalie's all right," Sally murmured as she drifted off. She was in the habit of giving the big trunk a caress or a goodnight kiss at bedtime.

They awoke to bright light, cheerful voices and the divine aroma of coffee. Sally scrambled out first, reaching for her veiled pith helmet.

"Shake it out first, in case of scorpions," M. Lafont warned. "Your boots too."

Sally followed his advice, putting on dark glasses as well, and staggered over to where Mustafa and his assistants were dispensing cups of coffee and fresh, hot flatbreads. She lowered her dark glasses to hold his eyes, and he adjusted his turban to hold hers. Wordless but more or less satisfactory information was exchanged.

"I had thought we'd go back to the hotel last night, but how much more delightful to sleep under the moon and stars. Thank you for arranging it." Sally gestured with her cup.

"As long as Madame and her guests are happy, we are happy." Mustafa poured out another fragrant cup, and Sally brought it over to Lucienne.

Cairo

Although their guests thanked them profusely on their return to Shepheard's that afternoon—remarking particularly on the novel excitement of the moonlit night out—it was clear in the days that followed that the Lafonts were avoiding Sally and Lucienne, and even their Italian beaux seemed busy and preoccupied.

"Oh dear. I thought we'd given them such a nice time," Lucienne said wearily, sipping from her flask. It was late afternoon; they were lounging in their room in the dim dappled light of the closed wood shutters.

"Well, that was a poor investment, as it turned out," Sally agreed. "And I had to give Mustafa an extra-large tip, of course."

"I guess it's alley-way snacks in the souk for us. We should probably look for a cheaper hotel."

Sally turned and looked anxiously toward the corner where their large trunk stood. "I don't want to stay anywhere . . . questionable. We have to keep *her* safe."

Soon, however, they were back to seeing Aldo and Giacomo for tea or cocktails most days. A few weeks later, the young men proposed a proper night on the town. Sally and Lucienne dressed accordingly, in cool evening gowns, diaphanous shawls and vivid make-up. They began with a stroll in the Ezbekkiya Gardens, shady and beautiful as dusk was falling, where they drifted off to kiss and nibble among the fan palms. Next, Giacomo insisted they take in a game of jai alai at the Basque Pelota.

"I promise, you won't be bored," he told skeptical-looking Lucienne. "It's a very fast game, the players are handsome—and I've got money on the Milano team. We'll have an extra round of drinks when they win."

The arena was festively loud, with a colorfully mixed crowd of Egyptians and Europeans. It only took a half hour for Milan to pull off a win, after which they headed out to a series of charming cafes along Emad El-Din Street. Sally and Lucienne drank red aperitifs, enhanced by their flasks; Giacomo and Aldo alternated brandies and coffees. By the time they reached the theatre district, they were in peerlessly high spirits.

The Abbaye des Roses was French, from the chandeliers to the floor tiles, with blonde imported dancers and a soubrette chanteuse, presenting the latest (or, last year's latest at least) most popular songs from

Montmartre. Their beaux were enchanted, but Sally soon grew bored.

"You know, we lived in Paris for . . . a long time. Can't we please go somewhere more authentic?"

Giacomo and Aldo conferred with a brief shrug. "I've heard the Printanian is rather nice. Or the Moderne. Your wish, our command, Mademoiselle," Aldo said with a bow. They paid up and moved on.

The theatre district was thronged, Europeans in light-colored suits or occasionally evening dress mingling with locals wearing red tarboushes, paired either with tunics and loose trousers or with Western-style tailoring. Women were fewer, and Lucienne and Sally drew admiring or curious glances, but they saw occasional female figures in enveloping black robes or, more rarely, short coats with a glimmer of something glamourous beneath. They were approaching the Printanian, when Sally nudged Lucienne, rolling her eyes toward someone turning the corner up ahead.

"Let's go where *she's* going!"

The "she" in question was wearing a man's tweed suit, which hugged her hourglass curves so closely as to leave no doubt about her gender, just as her tarboush emphasized the allure of her delicate facial structure and gorgeously painted eyes. Her shoes were high-heeled pumps, and she nonchalantly swung a riding crop as she walked, causing passers-by to keep a careful distance.

Sally grabbed Giacomo's arm and steered him around the corner; Lucienne and Aldo caught up a moment later.

Seemingly oblivious to the heat and crowd, the woman kept up a brisk pace. Her followers were relieved when, before long, she slowed and stopped at a door whose sign proclaimed 'Sala Mounira.'

Sally skipped ahead of her friends to catch up and was fascinated to see, at the door, the woman handing her tarboush and jacket to a man who greeted her deferentially as Mme Mounira. She was loosening her tie and starting to unbutton her shirt as she hurried inside.

"Come in, come in, sirs and madams," the doorman urged, turning to them. "Only a small cover charge, the finest entertainment, all deluxe, first-class. This way, please."

Giacomo paid, grumbling good-naturedly about spending his pelota winnings, and they entered a dimly lit, lavishly decorated theatre, glittering with gold-leaf embellishments and sparkling ornaments.

They were seated at a good table; drinks were served, and they settled in to watch the show—a sort of potpourri, with chorus girls, a comedian juggler, a halfway-excellent jazz band. The woman they had followed, Mounira, appeared eventually, in a brilliantly spangled costume, to immense applause. Bowing profoundly, extending her arms and blowing kisses to her audience, she finally cued the band and began a long, evidently deeply emotional ballad. Sally listened, bemused, trying to see the relationship of the impassioned, almost maudlin performance and the jaunty figure who had caught her eye on the street. Clearly, whatever she did was deeply fulfilling to her fans—the response when she finished was deafening. Sally excused herself, to ponder and to powder her nose. Lucienne was playing a little game with matchsticks with their beaux, the three of them perceiving the music mostly as background to their amusing time.

In the ladies' lounge, Sally sat at a mirror, opened her bag and produced her Cartier enamel compact. A woman in the next seat looked over appreciatively.

"Ah," she said in French. "You have beautiful accessories. As do I." She smiled and placed a gold necessaire, machined with modernist geometric motifs, on the marble shelf below the mirror. "Are you enjoying the show?"

"Yes . . . but it's not quite what I expected. We saw Mounira on her way here, and I expected something . . . I don't know . . . more pointed?"

The other woman laughed lightly. "Well, Mounira is a great talent, with a lot of strings to her bow, so to speak. But she likes to please the crowd. All these Emad-al-Din clubs—you know, they call it Cairo's Broadway—have become so commercial, so international. You might think you were in Paris or New York. If you want to see the real old Cairene style, you have to go to the other side of Ezbekkiyah Gardens, the little streets that don't even have names . . . And you have to go after midnight."

"That sounds fascinating." Sally's eyes were shining. "I love music that has authenticity, the soul of the place."

"Here, take this." The woman had brought out a tiny leather-bound notebook and a gold pen. She jotted a few lines, tore out the small page and handed it to Sally.

They were laughing as Lucienne unlocked their room, but abruptly they both stopped, staring.

"The trunk. What's happened?" Sally gasped.

Six feet long, brass-bound and sturdy, Natalie's trunk had been placed carefully, at their direction, upright in the corner farthest from the windows. Now it lay on its side, as if it had fallen—or been knocked—over.

Sally clutched Lucienne's arm. "It isn't . . . she couldn't . . . Natalie didn't . . ."

"Natalie cannot have awakened; it's not possible. Either there was an earthquake—just in this room, hmm—or someone must have tried to open it. Come on, we have to make sure she's all right."

For years, Lucienne had worn a jade amulet around her neck, until she'd had to part with it as part of the price for arranging the ritual of the Long Sleep. Now, the key to the trunk had taken its place, worn at all times on a gold chain next to her skin. She fished it out, lifting the chain over her head.

Sally hung back, scanning the room for other things out of order. The windows were shuttered and securely closed. The personal effects they'd left strewn across the bureau—hairbrush, earrings, gloves, scent bottles—seemed undisturbed. The night table between the two beds had a lockable drawer, but she'd left the key in it. With a sick feeling, she went over and opened it; flooded with relief, she saw their stoneware bottles of blood, untouched.

"Help me, Sally." The trunk lay with its lock against the floor; it took both of them to turn it over.

"She always did have trouble keeping her weight down," Sally joked grimly.

Lucienne gave her a sharp look. "It's all your notebooks and sundries making it so heavy. Honestly, don't you have enough room in your own cases?"

"It's just a few things I want to keep safe: my journals, and my best Delman shoes and Cartier keepsakes. So I'm not tempted to sell them when times are tough. Oof, there—now she's right side up."

Lucienne fitted the key into the lock, pressing down and jiggling it a bit as she'd learned to do, and then raised the lid. As they'd intended, the trunk appeared, upon opening, to be full of clothes and accessories—luscious layers of silk lingerie and glittering lamé shawls. Sally's leather-bound books and collection of shoe boxes, stored at the foot, provided helpful verisimilitude, appearing to explain the trunk's weight.

"We should check," Lucienne said quietly, and began to carefully lift out the folded textiles. "Oh . . . here she is."

Natalie's body was wrapped in a length of gauzy, silvery-green silk. Lucienne ran a gentle hand over the smooth narrow shape. Their friend had stood almost as tall as Sally, but with a small-boned ballerina's build. She seemed now even smaller and more delicate; it was hard to believe the shroud contained a full-grown vamp.

Sally stared hard at the cloth, which just barely hinted at what was beneath it. Lucienne, with a little shake of her head, loosened the silk and folded it back.

Eyes closed, russet hair loose, Natalie appeared to be sleeping peacefully—except that her skin tone was several shades paler than extreme pallor, with a faint greenish cast. But there was no hint of decay below the waxy smooth surface.

Sally reached out a forefinger and stroked Natalie's cool cheek, once. Then she slumped against Lucienne with a sob of relief. "How long until she wakes?"

Lucienne considered briefly. "At least thirty years. 1962, perhaps?"

"We *have* to find a more permanent home."

"I know. This will become unbearable, eventually." Lucienne leaned over the trunk and, ever so gently, kissed their friend's lips. There was, of course, not the slightest tremor of response. She covered Natalie's face again, replaced the layers of decoy contents and finally lowered the lid, snapping the lock shut. "I really feel we should think about America."

Sally's eyes flashed. "Any place but there. I don't want to set foot in that land of intolerance and ignorance. You never heard all of Claude's stories—his life there was a living hell."

"Yes, but that was . . . some time ago. and Claude is—was—different from us."

"You mean Black. I don't think they'd necessarily welcome you either, Miss Indochine. Maybe not even me. They're provincials; they don't like foreigners. Any place where they could treat humans the way Claude was treated . . . is no place for a vamp. Not me, anyway."

"I'm just saying we might want to consider it. It's a big, rich, stable country. We could find a place to be safe there."

"No," Sally said flatly. "Not until we've exhausted all our other options."

On a late afternoon in early September, stepping out for a stroll from Shepheard's, they found themselves in a street of fashionable shops. Striped awnings and gilt-lettered signs—with a row of slender palms to remind them they weren't in Europe—tastefully announced jewelers, parfumiers, leather goods, an antiquarian bookshop.

"House of Wadjet?" Sally read the English sign with a laugh. "Doesn't that mean a . . . thing you don't know the name of? 'Whatsit,' they usually say."

"No, I've seen that word; I think it's some ancient Egyptian thing. A hieroglyph, perhaps? It's a dress shop; shall we go in and look?"

The interior was cool, incense-scented and extremely elegant, in the most modern manner. Silver-leaf walls curved sinuously to create a series of alcoves, with low simple armchairs and ottomans grouped around small sleek drinks tables. Only a few dresses, gowns and cloaks were on display, draped on stainless-steel mannequins, but they were exquisite.

Nodding at the vendeuse, who gave them a frosty look, Sally and Lucienne were immediately drawn to a dazzling evening gown which glittered with three colors of metal, apparently woven onto a dark green ground. A coat, trimmed with the same sumptuous textile, was thrown casually over the mannequin's shoulder.

"I've never seen anything like this," Sally marveled.

Lucienne gently lifted a skirt panel. "The weight of it, the way it drapes—incredible."

"Like a fabulous scarab's carapace. I bet it feels marvelous on."

"Would you like to try it? It would suit either of you, beautifully." The young woman who had appeared beside them had a low musical voice, huge dark eyes and a welcoming smile. Her dress was geometrically simple, with a sense of complete authority; it was evident she was the couturiere.

"Oh, you are too kind!" Lucienne said, turning to her. Wont you tell us about this remarkable textile, Miss . . . ?"

"Mrs. Sebastian. Do you not know our Egyptian assuit cloth? You can see many examples in the bazaar, though not so fine as mine, I admit. I have it specially made for me—no one else uses the mixed metals: brass, silver and copper. It is a pretty effect, I think, and can suit clients with different coloring. Though, of course, I think dark hair sets it off best." She smiled, clearly amused that all three of them had sleek black bobbed hair. "Truly, I would love to see this on you," she said to Lucienne. "And for your friend . . ." She gestured to her assistant and gave her some murmured instructions.

A moment later, they were in a dressing room with two gowns, the second a similar but differently-styled model, with the metalwork done on a lapis blue ground. The vendeuse had followed them, but withdrew when she saw the practiced way they stepped out of their frocks and assisted each other into the sleek gowns.

"You have to positively *slither* into it," Sally said, wriggling to settle the gown on her hips.

"Mm, more like a snakeskin than a carapace—delicious!"

Mrs. Sebastian clapped her hands at their emergence. "Oh, I knew you would wear them perfectly. You are professional models, are you not?"

"We haven't worked for a while, but we were at the House of Mlle in Paris." Sally ignored her friend's slight warning frown as she spoke.

The couturiere seemed to open her large eyes wider. "Ah, Mlle, of the rue Cambon—that shocking show at the end of 1929! Of course we heard all about it, even here.

The world of *la mode* is small, n'est-çe pas?" Imperceptibly, she had switched into French. "Come and sit down; let's have some tea, and please, leave the gowns on for a while. I love seeing them worn. Anouk, bring some of my special tea, please," she called to her assistant, adding some instructions in Egyptian.

As they settled on a gray velvet settee, the Egyptian woman gazed at them—or rather, gazed in their direction while she seemed to stare deeply into the past.

"So, you were there, that astonishing night on the rue Cambon," Mrs. Sebastian began. It was not a question. "Of course. You are rather famous, in certain circles. Lucienne Leung, Sally Lafayette. And a third, the Russian girl, Natalie . . . where is she?"

"Natalie is . . . taking a different route at present," Lucienne said quickly. "But how do you know about us— what do you mean, we're famous?"

"Only among certain of the cognoscenti, my dears. Please, let me give you some refreshments."

The tea set on the tray before them was of deep red porcelain with ornate gold detailing—an unusual touch in the impeccable modernism of the salon. Although a scent of mint hung in the air, neither Sally nor Lucienne was entirely surprised to taste rich, warm blood rather than tea.

Mrs. Sebastian took a long sip and then reached for a second small tray, which held smoking requisites: an alabaster box of Fatimas and a selection of amber holders.

Exhaling, she sat back and smiled broadly, the tips of her fangs just showing.

"Help yourselves, please. I can't tell you, again, what a pleasure it is to meet you. Tell me all about your travels—when did you arrive in Cairo?"

They briefly sketched their recent sojourns in London, Barcelona and Rome, and their delight in exploring the Queen of the Nile.

The couturiere nodded thoughtfully. "You are wise to stick to metropolises. Isn't the modern world marvelous—the ease of travel, it still amazes me! I am glad you are enjoying our city, but be careful where you wander, and whom you consort with. I should stick to the English, if I were you—much cleaner." She lifted her teacup and sipped. "And I can refer you to my source, for extra supplies." She jotted an address on a card and handed it to Sally.

"Oh yes, I think that's the place we found; I remember that funny street name."

"Clever girls. Come, I want to show you more of my work." She rose gracefully and led them through a curtained doorway to an inner studio, pleasantly lit by fixtures placed behind sheets of translucent glass, with the effect of faux windows.

Her worktable held several thick volumes, and she began paging through them. "Here is this season."

Dashing but finely detailed drawings showed the very gowns they were wearing, as well as others they'd seen in the showroom, and a profusion of yet other designs.

"Many of these are just ideas, not executed. My work is all couture; the pieces here are only samples. Although, you wear them as if they were made for you." She eyed Sally and Lucienne approvingly.

"It is a privilege, madame, to wear something so beautiful," Sally murmured.

Mrs. Sebastian turned more pages. "Here is what I was doing in 1929. Not too different from Mlle's work, although she gets the credit as revolutionary . . . . Oh, and you will like these, I think—After the opening of Tutankhamun's tomb, everyone was mad for Egyptian designs. I did several themed collections. In 1925, I was obsessed with sand-colored silk pongee and hieroglyphic appliqué. Of course, most people saw the short skirts as shockingly new, but for me, they were very traditional— what I grew up with."

"You mean, like children's frocks?" Lucienne asked.

The couturiere laughed. "I mean, like the clothes of the Old Kingdom. Here, let me show you what I was doing back in '98; the avant-garde aesthetes loved this. and in '82 . . . ." She turned more pages. "I did this for a very well-known Parisian *grande horizontale*. Once they saw it, any number of perfectly respectable ladies wanted the same thing."

"Gorgeous," Sally breathed. "Each piece is perfectly of its time, yet unique."

"How far back to your albums go?" Lucienne wondered.

Their hostess laughed. "Oh, I've got tons of them stored away—not even counting the papyrus scrolls. Of course, I can't show them to most people; even some of these older ones I have to say are my mother's or grandmother's work. But that's the beauty of *la mode*—most people don't want to look back. They only want what is *au courant.*"

Unexpectedly, a sleek gray, green-eyed cat emerged from a shadowy corner of the room, rubbed briefly against its mistress's legs and jumped onto the table. Mrs. Sebastian closed the album firmly.

"No you don't, Mau." She stroked the animal's silky flank. "He doesn't like me to share our history. But, my dears, this has been an absolute pleasure."

"We had better change and let you carry on with your work. You have been so kind, Madame."

"Come back any time at all. And, I must insist on loaning you the gowns. I will have them delivered to your hotel. I want you to wear them while you are here; I'm sure you will be invited to the very best parties."

As they were leaving the studio, Sally stopped with a little gasp before a framed montage of recent society-page clippings.

"Ah yes, my collection of boasts. These are all clients —Daisy Fellowes, Mona Von Bismarck. Gloria Swanson wrote to me from Hollywood."

"Isn't this . . . Cerise Massey? The American heiress?" Sally stared at the familiar face.

"American? Oh no, that is a lovely French lady, Mme. de Boiessiere; her husband is from a very old, aristocratic Belgian family. Madame is very chic, very correct, typically French."

Sally peered again at the photo, still struck by the resemblance, but the grainy print made it impossible to be certain. Recollecting her manners, she echoed Lucienne's profuse thanks and followed her to the dressing room.

Sally dealt with a knock at the door of their suite and returned with a large box. "The Wadjet frocks have arrived. Shall we wear them tonight?"

Lucienne frowned. "She wants them to be seen at important gatherings. Aren't we just dining with Aldo and Giacomo? I suppose they might take us to a nightclub later, but . . ."

There was another knock at the door. Lucienne went this time and returned, reading a note with a puzzled expression.

"It's from Aldo—he wonders if we'd like to attend an exclusive reception with them at the Italian embassy. Well, then."

"What's this part?" Sally asked, reading the Italian script over her shoulder.

"He says, 'I'm sorry it's such short notice, but I'm sure you have something fabulous to wear.'"

The embassy was a brilliantly lit expanse of golden marble, lavishly furnished, filled with massive floral arrangements and peopled with a formal yet convivial crowd of diplomats, businessmen and fashionable wives.

"Excuse us, please, just for a moment." Lucienne grabbed Sally's wrist, extricating her from a circle of admirers, and hustled her down an alabaster hallway to a powder room.

"I've never felt more magnetic," Sally said wonderingly. "I think it's the dress."

"I'm sure it is. With all due respect to your magnetic personality, darling. I don't know about you, but I need a break." Lucienne stretched out on a velvet sofa, patting the space next to her. Sally sprawled gratefully.

They compared notes about how many necks they'd nibbled and what extravagant compliments they'd collected—impressive numbers, in both cases.

"Did you meet the Italian ambassador? He bowed so low I thought he was going to lick my shoes." Sally regarded her gold t-straps with amusement.

"Of course, darling; I was just behind you. What a fellow—his nose grazed my knee on the way up! Probably not completely by accident. But I think Aldo and Giacomo were pleased; we've probably cemented their reputations as the most glamorous playboys of the expat set."

The door opened and several chattering ladies came in, a mixed group of Cairene locals and Europeans.

"There you are!" one exclaimed. "We've been looking all over—we *have* to get a closer look at that bimetallic assuit."

"No, it has *three* metals, just as I said." A dark, elegant woman had lifted one of the skirt panels of Lucienne's gown. "It's from House of Wadjet, isn't it? I'm Fatima Abaza, by the way."

They all exchanged names, some of which Sally recognized from a casual perusal of the society pages. The Italian woman, olive-skinned and sleekly blonde, was a contessa. Tall, bosomy Lady Arbuthnot was the wife of a vastly wealthy British businessman; willowy Fatima Abaza was her Egyptian counterpart. A powerful widow and her stunningly beautiful daughter rounded out the elegant group, all of them dressed in couture and spectacularly bejeweled. The ladies' lounge was large and accommodating, and soon they were all comfortably disposed, smoking scented cigarettes or nibbling rose-flavored candies.

With their gowns acting an an unquestioned passport into the highest social echelon, Lucienne and Sally were privy to exclusive jokes and gossip, the histories of all the major personages present and generous helpings of advice.

"You must see my seamstress; she's a whiz with nighties and lingerie."

"Don't let them send your laundry out of the hotel; you'll never get the Nile sand out of it."

"Come and see me when you need your hair trimmed; my maid does a perfect job."

"I've got the best pills for that time of the month—I get them in Rome and I can let you have some."

Finally, the impromptu private party broke up, as social duty to the larger gathering called. Fatima Abaza stayed behind when the others left and then, startlingly, leaned close to Lucienne, gently touching her chin just beside her lower lip. "You've got a tiny bit of blood, just there. I thought it was a lipstick smear at first—don't worry, that's what anyone else would have thought."

Lucienne peered into the mirror, widening her eyes at the woman behind her, who slightly bared her fangs. "Oh, so I have. Thanks."

"So you're . . ." Sally trailed off; it was clearly unnecessary to say more. "Are there many of us here? And how did you know we were?"

"There are not many of us; we're a small, select set. Mostly female, for some reason, except for a couple of ancients who hang around the tombs scaring tourists. And of course I knew you, even before I smelled you . . ." She paused to take a deep, appreciative sniff. "Lovely perfumes, are they French? I knew you because Bastet wouldn't let just anyone wear those gowns." She looked from one to the other with frank admiration. "I didn't even know she'd made a second one. Come, I want to show you something."

They followed Fatima past the fringes of the reception and out through French doors to a moonlit garden.

"Look!" Lucienne reached out a hand toward Sally's dress. The metallic bits were glimmering and glinting, light dancing over the surface like a live creature. She looked down and saw the same effect on her own gown.

"Not just beautiful and intricate, but magically powerful. Like the wearers, I might add." Fatima smiled. "Bastet has honored you indeed."

"Bastet—you said that before. Do you mean Mrs. Sebastian?" Sally wondered.

"Oh, yes, that is what she calls herself now. She . . . wait, what's that?" Fatima peered into the darkness where low shrubs edged the stone terrace.

"A cat!" Lucienne just caught the stealthy movement of the dusk-colored creature. "It looks very much like the one at . . ."

"Shh. We'd better go in."

Sally and Lucienne exchanged a baffled look and followed their guide.

The reception was clearly winding down, with distinguished and decorative guests taking verbose leave of each other.

"Your Italian beaux are looking bereft without you," Mme. Abaza smiled, inclining her head toward Aldo and Giacomo.

"I suppose we should go, but . . . I feel we're just getting to know each other," Sally said.

"Exactly! Do please come and have tea with me next Tuesday. Five o'clock?" Fatima slid a card from her purse.

"Oh, we'd love to, thank you so much." Lucienne tucked the card away before turning with a bright smile to Aldo.

"Signora Abaza." He gracefully greeted and took leave of their companion with a bow.

"Well, that was delightful. Thank you so much for inviting us," Sally said as they walked toward Giacomo's car. "I feel we've quite arrived in Cairo society."

"Arrived? No, I would say 'conquered.' You two made the most stunning impression, on everyone."

"Come, we cannot let the evening end," Aldo said eagerly. "Ladies, where can we take you next?"

Giacomo answered for them: "The Grand Casino! All the crème de la crème will be heading there. We can dine, have some champagne, and surely Lady Luck will help us to buy you diamond bracelets to go with your gorgeous gowns."

Lucienne stiffened. "A casino? Absolutely not. I'm sorry, I have personal reasons." Sally reached over and squeezed her hand.

"Beautiful girls, you have nothing to fear," Aldo insisted. "This is not a sordid place; it is the height of elegance, where all the best people go. And Giacomo is so right." He raised Lucienne's hand and brushed his lips over her wrist. "You need some diamonds, beautiful as your eyes, right here."

They had reached Giacomo's Fiat, near the end of the long drive. Sally, tall as he was, moved to pin him against the car and leaned in to his throat for a brief taste, ending in a kiss beside his ear.

"Darling boys, you are too sweet, but really, I think we've had enough of high society for one night. What we'd really love is seeing some more of the real Cairo. I met a woman at that club we went to, Mounira's, who said we should go to the little places on the other side of Ezbekkiya Gardens. She gave me a name, but I don't quite remember . . ."

Giacomo gazed at Sally for a long moment of utter adoration, then seemed to shake himself and shrugged. "I suppose we could go to Darwish . . ." He raised an eyebrow at Aldo, who shrugged in reply. "Kebabs and raki, hookahs and some quite good musicians."

"Oh yes, please—that's my idea of heaven!" Sally said fervently. "I'm mad for the local music. Sounds perfect, doesn't it, Loulou?"

Lucienne, still disturbed by the mention of the casino, composed herself and smiled. "Yes, that would be lovely. Come sit in the back with me, Aldo; we'll leave the front seats to the long-legs."

Giacomo took a minute to pull himself together, but then drove them skillfully through the city, turning from broad palm-lined avenues into narrow byways. He pulled up presently in front of a blue door set in a stone wall, where a dark-cloaked man stood in the light of a large lantern. As the man stepped forward to open their doors, Giacomo greeted him in rudimentary Egyptian and allowed him to take charge of the car. The blue door led to a courtyard and a lamplit structure beyond.

"*I signori italiani!*" The stout jovial host greeted them. "*E due signorine belle! Deux belles mademoiselles!* Two beautiful young ladies!" he added with a bow.

"*Grazie, merci*, thank you," Lucienne replied with a smile.

"Ah, polyglot citizens of the world, I see. Welcome to my establishment. Follow me, please."

The inner room he led them to was simpler than the elaborate, ceremonious entry would suggest. A dozen or so low tables, each with a candle, were surrounded with floor cushions. Most were occupied, mostly by Egyptian men; some had plates of food, most had jugs and glasses of water and raki, with hookah pipes at hand. A few of them smiled or called out greetings to Aldo and Giacomo as they passed; others ignored them or silently stared.

Sally nudged Lucienne, commenting wordlessly that they were almost the only women in the room. Two middle-aged women sat with a man at one of the tables, eating soup with downcast eyes. One of the four musicians, on a small stage in the corner, was female, playing a stringed instrument, which she occasionally put down to sing. And occupying the central space, moving with fascinating, graceful undulations, was the dancer.

"La danse du ventre—oh, I have always wanted to see it. Thank you, Giacomo!" Sally breathed, with shining eyes.

Tiny cups of anise-scented spirit had appeared before them, along with a tray of water glasses and a rather beautiful modern hookah of chromium and blue glass. Sally and Lucienne settled into the cushions with pleasure, drinking in the dim, fragrant atmosphere and the hypnotic music.

The dancer's arms were raised above her head, twining sinuously while her fingers crisply chimed tiny cymbals together. Her bare feet kissed the floor rhythmically; her torso swayed and curved. Her eyes were half-closed and yet her gaze seemed as riveted upon her vampire audience as they were on her. She moved closer to their table, then spun away, her eyes returning to them again and again. The music built to a crescendo, then subsided and came to a quiet stop, received with applause and ululation.

The dancer came straight to their table, sinking gracefully onto her haunches and helping herself to a glass of water, staring from Sally to Lucienne.

"*Shukran, kwayyis*," Aldo employed some of his few words of Egyptian with a small bow. Giacomo beamed his most dazzling smile and bowed as well.

Ignoring the men, the dancer reached out and touched Sally's dress. Her coat had fallen open, and the assuit gleamed in the candlelight. "Bast," she whispered. She looked questioningly at Lucienne, who also let her coat fall open and nodded.

The dancer recoiled with a snarl. "*Ghaddar*," she said in a low voice, almost a growl. "*Ghaddar*." She spat and made an odd gesture. Instantly, the musicians were on their feet, surrounding the table with menacing glares. Aldo and Giacomo sprang up, exchanging alarmed looks and attempting to shield their companions. Lucienne and Sally stood as well and summoned their most intense stares, directed at the musicians blocking their egress, as well as the men at other tables who were now moving restively.

After a few moments' tense stand-off, Giacomo carefully reached into his pocket, keeping his movements broadly obvious, and withdrew a large handful of money. He fanned the bills out and laid them on the table, then took Sally's arm and squeezed past the men hemming them in, while Aldo and Lucienne slipped out from the other side of the table. With all four of them keeping their eyes on the hostile crowd, they backed toward the door, where the host suddenly materialized and ushered them quickly out through the courtyard. Clearly, he had informed the valet, and the car was waiting at the street entrance. They jumped in, and Giacomo sped away. Sally turned to look out the rear window and saw a crowd emerging from the building, shouting and waving their arms.

"And . . . what was that about, may I ask?" Aldo muttered, leaning against Lucienne as the car cornered.

"Um . . . I think she didn't like our dresses?"

"She kept saying, '*Ghaddar,*'" Sally told Fatima. "'*Ghaddar.*' I'm not sure I'm pronouncing it right; it was very gutteral. I'm not good with languages, but I'm sure that was the word. Didn't you think, Loulou?"

Lucienne nodded and helped herself to a perfumed cigarette from a box on the table. Fatima Abaza's sitting room was large and gracious, with soft afternoon light filtered through pierced screens, and worn but handsome furniture. As at the House of Wadjet, there was a mixture of Egyptian and European styles, but Fatima's taste was more traditional, with comfort taking precedence over avant-garde elegance.

"Ghaddar . . . it means vampire. They also say 'ghul.' She recognized you. Most people probably wouldn't, but artists are sensitive, especially that sort. I don't know what you were doing in a place like that." Mme. Abaza's voice was brittle with irritation. "The lower classes . . . it's unwise. Dangerous for your young men, too."

"But it was their idea," Sally protested. "They've been there before."

"Sure, but I imagine it's different if it's just two fellows," Lucienne said thoughtfully. "Not as conspicuous as showing up, clearly slumming, with a couple of over-dressed socialites."

"My point exactly. Promise you'll be more careful. The common people can be hostile in any case, even if they don't sense your true nature." Fatima sighed, but then brightened as she topped up their cups and her own. The iron tang of warm blood hung in the air. "I want to invite you to a soiree, here. Next Thursday. It will be a mixed party, vamps and sympathetic mortals. I think you'll find it . . . refreshing." She smiled, her carefully painted, dark-red lips stretched wide, no trace of fangs showing.

"That sounds lovely," Lucienne responded. Sally had gone quiet, like a chastised child. "Will Mrs. Sebastian be there?"

Fatima seemed startled. "Bastet? I don't know. I will ask her." She folded back the loose sleeves of her tea gown and leaned down to stroke her fat white Persian cat.

"Pretty." Sally held out her hand, and the fluffy creature approached and nosed it gently. "What's her name?"

"Miau Miau. She's comfortable with us, as you can see."

"I know some animals can be—Mrs. Sebastian's cat was very nonchalant. But I once had a . . . friend, a mortal lady, with a pair of little lapdogs who went insane when they met me."

"Oh yes?" Fatima replied politely, and Sally wondered how she could explain the contessa—actually not so much a friend as a benefactress and ultimately lover, whom she'd met while dressed as a man and fleeing for her life.

But her hostess was distracted, not expecting an answer, as she examined her pet's ears. "Mau is a bad cat," she exclaimed abruptly. "Look what he has done; I shall have to speak to Bast." Her eyes went to the French doors, through which lush foliage shone. "Her house is over that way; our gardens adjoin. Mau comes over the wall, that bad boy, and bites my pretty one's ears. But, I will invite her for Thursday, if you like. I know she thinks highly of you." She placed a cigarette in her filigree holder and after a few moments grew calmer. "Let me refill your cups."

They drank warm blood, mint tea and spiced liqueurs, and Fatima discoursed on which gardens, palaces, museums and tombs they should be sure to see, with frequent confusing digressions about Cairo's social elite, both vampire and human.

"So many opinions—my brain is full," Sally murmured to Lucienne as they left.

"I know; we should have taken notes."

More tea was waiting for them back at Shepheard's, on the palm-shaded sidewalk-facing terrace, where Aldo and Giacomo sprang up from their wicker chairs with fervent cries: *"Carissime! Bellissime!"*

The sedate, mostly British tourists around them raised eyebrows at their Italian exuberance, but most of them smiled at the spectacle of decorative youth in the flower of courtship. Suppressing a faint sigh, Lucienne smiled too, and made her way between the tiny tables, followed by Sally. They had naturally dressed with special care for their visit to Mme. Abaza, in similar crisp frocks, cream and pale pink, with subtle edging in dark red which matched their oxblood shoes and handbags, as well as their deep red lipstick. Dark glasses, precise make-up and manicures, fine straw hats dipping just so over the right eyebrow—as always, their flawless glamour made staff and guests stare admiringly and conclude that they must be incognito movie stars.

After the doffing of panama hats and kissing of cheeks, tea was poured, and Lucienne gave a discreet account of their visit to Mme. Abaza's villa, omitting the blood. Sally, meanwhile, slouched in her chair, stretching her long legs, tapping a distracted rhythm against her teacup.

Giacomo turned to her with an inquiring smile. "What troubles *la bella ragazza*?"

"Oh . . . I can't get that music out of my head, the native players. I'm mad to hear it again."

Lucienne lowered her dark glasses to give Sally a stern look. "Bad idea, darling."

Sally pouted, thoughtful. "I know—what if I dress as a boy! You'd lend me some clothes, wouldn't you Giacomo?"

"*Che ragazza brava!* I will love to lend you my trousers. We can go tonight," he replied with shining eyes, clearly excited by the idea.

Lucienne grew firmer in her disapproval, enlisting Aldo to agree that another visit to the native quarter was far from prudent. Sally sank back in her chair in an attitude of defeat, but a subtle wink passed between her and Giacomo.

She tapped on his door very quietly, a little past midnight, as they'd agreed. It opened quickly, and Sally had just a whiff of the room's masculine musk before Giacomo shut the door behind himself and hustled them both down the corridor. He was smiling widely and carrying a bundle of clothes.

"*Ragazza salvaggia*, you wild girl, how I love you! Where can we go for you to dress—the ladies' lounge downstairs?"

"No need, this is fine." She pulled him into an alcove where the housekeepers stored their supplies during the day. "I can change in two seconds—professional experience, after all." She was, in fact, already stepping into the dark wool trousers, pulling them over her silk pyjama pants. Before fastening the waist, she buttoned a white shirt over her camisole and tucked it firmly into the trousers, smoothing the suspenders into place, and then made quick and expert work of a bow tie. Finally the jacket, double-breasted and peak-lapeled, fitting as nicely as she'd hoped across her slender but broad shoulders. She was just checking her reflection in a dark window, wondering if her hair was short enough, when he produced a motoring cap from his pocket. "Perfect!" she said as she kissed him.

Once again, Sally was impressed by Giacomo's skill as he navigated the narrow streets in his Fiat. This time he parked in an alley, paying a young boy a handful of coins to look after the car. The establishment nearby was small and unpretentious. They were welcomed graciously and soon were comfortably seated, with a hookah, glasses of raki and tea at hand. The musicians had just returned from a break, and once again the pulsing rhythm, haunting drone and minor key melody had Sally entranced. Though she tried to slouch inconspicuously under her cap, she couldn't keep from clapping along when the tune grew especially brilliant, and her eyes shone with delight.

Gradually, Sally became aware that one of the musicians, an oud player, was staring at her. When the song came to an end, he rose and walked past their table. Pausing, he glared at Sally, seeming to look right through her clothing, and spat on the ground. "Ghaddar," he hissed and then walked on.

"How can someone who plays so divinely be so . . . intolerant?" Sally looked around, feeling the start of panic. "I suppose we'd better go."

"Are you sure?" Giacomo asked with concern. "I will speak to the manager; this man should not insult you."

"No, I don't want to make another scene."

They emptied their glasses of raki; Giacomo paid and they headed for the door. Wrapped in a black shawl, a woman with huge dark eyes was just coming in. She drew back with a slight gasp.

"Mlle. Lafayette? What on earth are you doing here? It's really not the place for you."

"So I have discovered. A pity, because I adore the music. Good evening, Mrs. Sebastian."

Outside, Sally took Giacomo's arm and wrapped it around herself. She was trembling. "I wish I understood more."

"Gentlemens, your car!" The boy they'd dealt with was running toward them. "Come quick, they are stealing her!"

Giacomo held her hand tightly as they raced around the corner. Two rough-looking characters had the Fiat's doors open, and Giacomo let go of Sally and flung himself at the nearer one, who was fiddling with the gearshift. Sally dashed around to the other side and slammed the heavy car door against the other thief's mid-section, knocking him to the ground, where she gave him as hard a kick as she could, happy to be wearing sturdy brogues.

Grappling with his opponent, Giacomo was an agile and scrappy fighter, but the Egyptian was a heavy, muscular thug who soon had him in a dangerous-looking headlock.

"Giacomo!" Sally yelled in alarm, coming up behind them. The attacker turned to her, and instinctively she went for his throat, draining blood until he dropped to the pavement. She kicked him away. Looking up, she saw Giacomo bent over, vomiting. When he was done, he stood clutching the car door, pale and shivering.

"Come on, let's get out of here," Sally urged, but Giacomo didn't move, clearly in shock.

"Get in, get in!" She pushed him into the driver's seat. "You have to drive, I don't know how." She got in beside him, putting his hands on the steering wheel, patting his shoulder. "You can do it. Please! Hurry, before they get up."

Giacomo turned to stare at her. Her shirt front was spattered with blood. Self-consciously, she wiped her mouth with a handkerchief.

"What did you . . . how . . . ?"

"Ssh." She smoothed her hand over his forehead. "I'll explain later. Just drive, okay?"

Still dazed and operating by rote, he started the car and backed out of the alley. In the shadows, the boy crouched, wide-eyed.

Back at Shepheard's, Sally dashed to her room to change. It wasn't until the next afternoon, as she drifted through the lobby to the hotel hairdresser, that Giacomo caught up with her. Ensconced in a deep wing-chair, he appeared to be waiting for her.

"Sally, *mi amor*, come here." He patted the chair beside his. In their crisp, impeccable daywear, respectively ladylike and gentlemanly, they seemed miles away from the sordid adventure of the previous night. However, as she sat down and leaned toward him, Sally saw a bruise on Giacomo's cheek.

"Giacomo darling, I'm so sorry. I never meant to put you in danger. I just thought it would be a bit of a lark."

He stared at her. "But it is not your fault some *malvoli* tried to steal my car."

"No, I suppose not. But if we hadn't come out just then . . ."

Giacomo had not stopped staring. He reached out a hand to cup her jawline; then he brushed her lips, parting them with his fingers. "I saw what you did. Your mouth was covered with his blood. You must be . . ."

"Ssh." Sally reached her hand to Giacomo's lips. "It's nothing to be concerned about. I just know a few tricks—a girl has to be able to protect herself."

"No." Giacomo drew back. "Don't touch me. You are— my God, I can't believe this can be—you are a vampire."

Sally leaned back and began to laugh. "Oh, darling boy —no one has said that since 1923. Do I look like Theda Bara?" She unpinned her small straw hat and smoothed her hair, before checking her wristwatch. "Listen, I have to go and see the coiffeuse now. Meet me for a cocktail later at the bar round the corner. Just the two of us. I'll explain everything."

She spotted him from the doorway, at the bar with a glass of beer, and smiled. He was so attractive—tall and lanky, the way she liked, with a lock of dark hair falling onto his forehead. If she hadn't already known him, she would have seen him and immediately thought, 'That one.'

"Giacomo, caro." She touched his shoulder.

He stood up quickly, almost knocking over the stool. "Sally. Perhaps this is a bad idea. I think I should go."

"Don't be silly. Let's get a table. Gin and It, please," she called to the bartender. "And another beer for my friend."

She led the way to a corner table. Giacomo seemed reluctant even to sit at first, but finally leaned close to her, his brown eyes troubled.

"So, you must explain to me what I saw. What I think I saw."

"Which was . . .?" she asked cautiously.

"It seems to me that I saw you drinking blood from that man's neck. There was blood all over your mouth. That adorable mouth I have kissed. Holy Mary, mother of God . . ." He crossed himself. "*Una vampira.*"

Sally sat back as their drinks arrived and took a considering sip. "What if I told you I nicked his neck with the knife I always carry? Not fatally, just enough—as I said, a girl needs a few tricks. And then, I cut my lip when he struggled. Do you trust me?" She gazed at him, her eyes very wide, her look very level and open in a way she'd learned from her friend, the actress Louise Brooks.

Giacomo gazed back. "I . . . I want to."

Sally lowered her lids, which were dusted with silvery gray powder. Her eyes were enormous, blue and so beautifully shaped, the brows so elegant, Giacomo thought, entranced.

She took a long, silver and amber cigarette holder from her purse, and Giacomo hastened to light her violet-scented cigarette. She angled it toward him, creating the maximum distance between them, and exhaled fragrant smoke to the side, holding his eyes the entire time.

"Giacomo. You are such a beautiful man. I could very easily fall helplessly . . ." her lashes fluttered, "in love with you. But you must trust me."

"Yes." He barely breathed. "Of course I do. But . . . may I see it?"

"What?"

"The little knife you carry."

Sally's eyes flashed and continued to hold his. "No," she said. "It's in another purse."

"Then how can I . . ." He trailed off, lost in her eyes. "I . . . I trust you, Sally."

"Should we wear the Wadjet frocks again?" Lucienne asked. "I expect almost everyone there will have seen them."

"Yes, but I think we have to—they're like our calling card. Anyway, I love wearing them." Sally had, in fact, already slithered into her assuit gown and was at the dressing table, screwing on earrings.

Lucienne was still in her slip, fastening stockings to her garters. "Silver shoes or gold, do you think?"

"Silver. We wore gold to the embassy. Help me with this bracelet clasp, darling." Sally held her arm out, and Lucienne gasped.

"What's *that*? Is it real? Sapphires and diamonds, almost an inch wide—Giacomo?"

Sally nodded. "Isn't he sweet?"

"Sally! What have you been getting up to with that boy?"

Sally batted her eyelashes. "Just my innocent charm, darling."

"But he can't afford this kind of thing."

"Can't he? Maybe he's got rich parents and a lavish allowance."

Are you mad, Giacomo? You can't afford this sort of thing." Aldo turned away from the jeweler's window, where his friend was ogling diamond and sapphire earrings.

"For Sally, of course I can. I must! You should get something for Lucienne, too. Buy her emeralds! They are special girls; we cannot afford to lose them."

"I don't know what your new source of income is, my friend, but I know I am still a relatively starving architect. You say you bought her a bracelet already? Were they foolish enough to extend you credit?"

"I paid them . . . to some extent. I will have the balance shortly, without doubt. And enough for the earrings. I have a plan."

Mme. Abaza greeted them herself at the door and welcomed them into the foyer. In the salon beyond the open doorway, they could see about two dozen guests —men and women, standing and sitting, chatting and nibbling—while two maids circulated among them with trays. A young man in a white jacket was seated at the piano, playing a bright, sophisticated-sounding tune, while a woman in a red dress looked on admiringly.

"Darlings," Fatima said now, enveloping them in her complex, musky scent as they embraced. "I'm so glad you wore your assuits. I forgot to mention that it's semi-formal—but of course, you always dress perfectly. Anyone in red, by the way, is one of our special, mortal friends. A few you will recognize from the embassy, and the others—I am sure you will enjoy making their acquaintance. Let's see . . ." Their hostess led them into the room. "First you should meet Dr. El-Masri."

"Ah, our foreign guests. I hear you have been quite the sensation everywhere you've been. *Enchanté, mesdemoiselles.*" The tall gentleman, impeccably tailored, had a hawk's profile and piercing eyes. Beside him was a short, stout, round-faced man in a blue suit with a red bow tie and a red fez. He smiled and bowed, wordlessly.

"I didn't realize we'd acquired any sort of local reputation," Lucienne said, aiming a brief sharp glace at Sally. "We are pleased merely to be appreciative guests in your beautiful city."

"Creatures of such extravagant beauty cannot hope to escape notice," he replied. "And I have heard you are interested in Egyptian music. You must allow me to arrange a musicale for you at my home. It is considered somewhat . . . inappropriate to visit the native quarter."

A woman had appeared by his side, following their conversation intently. "Yes," she broke in, "you must allow us to guide you. You simply arrive in our city and set about making your own way—it isn't done, among our kind." Like Dr. El-Masri, she had a sharp profile and a commanding presence. She wore a simple black gown of indeterminate style. "Come and sit with me," she urged with a brusque gesture. "I want to know about your lineage."

"Nailah, you are being extremely rude." Mrs. Sebastian was there, suddenly. "Mlle. Leung and Mlle. Lafayette came to my shop, quite properly, and introduced themselves over tea. Their background is well-known and very illustrious. We are honored by their visit. Sally, Lucienne, come with me, I want to show you something."

She led them to a tall window overlooking the gardens. "My home is just over there, through those trees." In a lower voice, she added, "Forgive them. Some of the locals can be quite . . . old-fashioned. Still, I should have prepared you better for our social milieu. And the warnings about avoiding the native quarter are not completely wrong."

"Yes, that point seems to have been made very clearly," Sally said. "I won't make that mistake again. Forgive me for taking an interest in local culture."

Lucienne gave her a sharp look, but Mrs. Sebastian was unperturbed. "Not at all. In fact, we will have some Egyptian music here, later. I think you will enjoy it."

At Mrs. Sebastian's request, they visited House of Wadjet the next day. This time the vendeuse, so supercilious on their first visit, greeted them deferentially and showed them to the cushioned alcove where tea was served, again in gilt-embellished dark-red porcelain, and again enhanced with warm blood. Mrs. Sebastian was preceded by her cloud-soft gray cat, who now greeted them by winding delicately around their ankles and purring.

Their hostess, in black with an interesting Nile green collar, seated herself, filled their cups and lit a cigarette. She gazed at Sally (in pale gray) and Lucienne (in sand beige), her large eyes luminous and thoughtful.

"I think you will be leaving Cairo soon," she said finally.

Startled, Sally coughed and set her cup down. "Will we? Why do you say that?"

"The cards have foretold it. The Egyptian tarot—I will show you." She withdrew a deck of large cards from a side pocket of her dress. "But also, I just know it is time. Even if you had not upset the elders. Even if you hadn't put the local musicians in a frenzy. Even if you weren't driving those Italian boys mad—it is time."

While she spoke, she had been softly shuffling the cards. She moved the tea tray to make space and laid out three of the ornately figured rectangles.

"The Two Ways. People sometimes say they are the paths of virtue and vice. We know it is not so simple." A line drawing, in antique style, showed a man between two goddess-like women, one robed in linen, one bare-breasted. A celestial archer in a cloud above their heads aimed his arrow at the latter. Beside this card, she placed two more: the Moon and the World.

"You see, it is not necessary to know the ancient mystical arts—the message is perfectly plain. You must follow the moon and see the world."

Sally laughed lightly and helped herself to a cigarette, fitting it into a silver and amber holder. "Ridiculous. I don't believe in magical mumbo jumbo."

"Don't you?" Lucienne's eyes flashed. "Then I suppose we may as well leave Natalie's corpse to rot somewhere. Easier than carting it along with us." With a gasp, she covered her mouth with her hands, as if willing the words to go back and be unsaid. Her eyes went wide, welling with un-sheddable tears.

"There now. Come here, darling one." Mrs. Sebastian—Bastet—put her arms around Lucienne and hugged her close. "I knew there was something. Tell me."

Sally looked on, mournful and abashed, as Lucienne, after a brief spasm, told her about Natalie and her despair, the ritual of the Long Sleep, the difficulties of bringing her coffin along on their travels.

Bastet sat back, eyes closed, nodding slowly in profound understanding. "Yes," she breathed. "So that's where Natalie has been. You have done very well. You have learned how to wield power. And you too have played an important part," she said to Sally, turning to her, laying a hand on her arm. "The bond between the three of you is strong, not easily broken. But you must be careful. Have you . . . looked at her?"

Lucienne nodded. "The trunk had fallen over one day, in our hotel room. We had to check."

"She was pale and cold, but beautiful. Not decayed," Sally added.

"No decay? Good, good. But . . . fallen over? How?"

"We don't know. The wind, perhaps. No one seemed to have tampered."

Mrs. Sebastian clucked her tongue. "Seemed. Dangers. This is not a safe place for you. I will do what I can to help, but you must make plans to leave."

Back in their hotel room, Lucienne drained a flask and lay down for a nap. "We don't have anything on for tonight, do we? I'm exhausted."

"Hmm?" Sally was at the dressing table, playing with a sparkly new bracelet. "I'm meeting Giacomo down in the bar at eight. You should come; I'm sure Aldo will be there too."

"No, thank you—please give them my regrets. They're nice boys, and tasty, but I don't want to see them *every* night. We've quite run out of conversation."

Sally laughed. "Conversation? Giacomo and I hardly have more than a dozen phrases in common, but we manage." She clasped her sapphires about her wrist and crossed the room to sit on the bed. "Come on, Loulou— you should play along. Don't you want emeralds?"

"No, I do not." Her hand went to her breastbone where, for decades, she had worn an exquisite jade pendant, before she'd traded it away to acquire an artifact needed for the ritual of the Long Sleep. "I don't want jewelry, especially not given to me by men. I used to hang out sometimes with a group of tarts on Rue Saint-Denis, and it was all they ever talked about. No. I don't even miss my jade anymore."

"Liar," Sally said with a fond smile, smoothing her friend's hair. "I miss it—it was so much a part of you. I wonder where it will end up."

"Sally, carissima!" Giacomo stood up at her arrival. His hair was a bit disheveled and his eyes glowed with a wild intensity. He was still in his tan linen day suit, rumpled, tie undone, and he spoke loudly enough that other bar patrons turned around to look at him with annoyance.

"Giacomo darling, sit down," Sally spoke extra quietly, hoping to lower his volume. "What's wrong with you, are you drunk?"

"Drunk on your beauty, now that you are here." He took her hand and planted a sloppy kiss on her palm, continuing up her arm as he noticed her bracelet. "You are wearing my gift—cara mia!"

"Please darling, calm down. This isn't the place."

"No, of course not, not here. You should be in a palace, my queen. You will see; I will build you a palazzo. I'll hire Aldo to design it. You shall have all the finest things. Signorina Sally Lafayette, *la bellissima, reina delle tutte donne . . .*" He was shouting now, mostly in Italian. "*La vampira squisita . . .!*"

"Steady on, man," a nearby British voice warned, just as the barman and two waiters tackled the raving Italian. Giacomo was lightly built, and they soon had a hold on him, but he continued to struggle and momentarily broke free.

"Sally, carissima, they are going to take me away," he panted, close to her face, "but here, take this, you must have the sapphire earrings." He pulled a bundle of banknotes from his trouser pocket and pushed it into her hands. "And I will have more soon, you must have a palazzo and all the most beautiful . . . all right, I will come with you, no need to twist the arms . . .Sally don't worry, they cannot hold me long, we will be together, I will build your palazzo, just tell me where you wish to reside. Take your time; if they lock me up, I will have time to plan . . ." His voice faded as the staff were finally able to lead him from the room.

Sally stared after him, stunned, until a gentle cough made her turn to the man beside her. "Beg pardon, miss. Are you quite all right?" It was the English gentleman who had spoken before, rather stout and well-tailored, with a kind ruddy face.

"Oh, merci . . . thank you, sir. You are kind to enquire. I have just had a bit of a shock; my friend has never been like this before."

"Naturellement, mademoiselle," he said, in courteous but badly accented French. "Quite to be expected. Forgive me, but—this money . . ." He held out his hand so confidently that Sally felt she had no choice but to give him the banknotes, but she hesitated, clutching the roll of bills. "You see, I am employed by your young man's company, Fiat Motors, to keep an eye on things, and in fact, rather a large sum went missing from their safe just yesterday. I'm afraid your admirer has developed a case of sticky fingers."

Sally gave him a blank, wide-eyed look. "Sticky . . .?"

"What I mean, what I suspect is, he is no professional thief, just a young fellow head-over-heels in love, who'd do anything for a certain young lady, losing sight of all better judgment . . ." He was gazing into Sally's beautiful, long-lashed eyes. "Quite understandable, given the charm of the young lady in question."

Sally lowered her gaze demurely. "Monsieur is too kind."

"May I buy you a drink, my dear? You must have had quite a shock."

"Why, thank you. A Blood and Sand, please."

Sally had stopped by the kitchen for a couple of bottles of blood before returning to their room (they'd made a friend there, who kept it on hand for the young ladies' 'health tonic'); now she and Lucienne were having a cozy pick-me-up.

"So, they've got Giacomo in custody, but I don't think they'll keep him. Once Arthur wakes up, he'll find all the money in his own pocket, and he won't remember why they are holding Giacomo. He'll conclude it was all a misunderstanding."

Lucienne sighed. "I supposed Mrs. Sebastian is right; we should be moving on. I hate the thought, I have to say; it's been so comfortable here." She looked around the elegant room, her eyes coming to rest on the large trunk.

Sally ran her hands through her hair. "Oh Loulou, I'm so sorry, all the messy situations have been my fault. Why can't I be graceful and tactful like you? If both of us were like that—unobtrusively charming—we could probably stay here forever. They might even forget to charge us for the room."

Lucienne smiled. "I think they may have already done that—or they just like us here, being decorative. Anyway, you did a good job vamping that detective fellow; it could have been much worse. I should have gone to the bar with you; maybe Giacomo wouldn't have gotten so carried away."

Sally emptied her bottle with a thoughtful grunt. "I don't think it would have made any difference—he's truly gone off the deep end, for the moment. Why are men like that? I had another beau who did the same thing. When was that . . . 1760 or so. He bought me a chateau, not realizing I didn't want it. As if I could live in the country! But I must say, I don't mind the sapphires," she added, studying her wrist admiringly. "Anyway, when we do leave here, where shall we go?"

"Bombay," Lucienne said without hesitation. "It's cosmopolitan and glamorous, with a low cost of living."

"Oh yes, cost of living . . ." Sally sighed. "Why is it so difficult to get by these days? It used to be that one just moved in the right circles and everything was taken care of. Not that we're doing too badly here: generous beaux, society parties . . . Do you really think they'd let us stay on here in the hotel?" She leaned back against the pillows, musing, and then sat up. "I know, we can visit the Maharani. She *did* invite us, when we parted ways."

"Silly, that didn't actually mean anything—it's just the 'hospitality of the East,' only a gesture. She would be shocked if we actually showed up. Anyway, I'm sure she never wants to see *me* again, after what happened with my uncle."

Sally was bewildered. "But none of that was your fault! Can we at least send her a wire?"

"Sally, come out with me again tonight, *carissima*," Giacomo implored, as she crossed the lobby a few days later. Released from only the briefest custody, as she'd expected, he appeared much improved in his grooming and state of mind.

"Oh, darling boy. After our last date, I should think you'd had enough of my company," she laughed.

"Never! Anyway, tonight you must dress as *una bella ragazza*, and we will go someplace perfectly respectable —the Royal Automobile Club. No need for your little knife."

"But why should I go to an automobile club? I don't know a thing about cars."

"Why should you go? For the cocktails and dancing, of course! And, there is a very important card game, with Prince Farouk. I intend to win all his money, and you will bring me luck."

"Ah, I see. We mustn't invite Lucienne then—she hates anything to do with gambling."

"Yes, I remember that. Aldo too is not keen. But *we* are the adventurous ones, no?"

Sally felt herself tingle with pleasure; adventure always appealed to her. "Oh, all right then."

Sally was having a perfectly nice time, not minding the respectability of the venue at all. True, the palm-court-type trio playing in the corner was uninspired, but adequate to the task, as she allowed a succession of pleasantly bland gentlemen to steer her about in foxtrot-like movements. Giacomo had disappeared, but Sally used the time to practice her tact and social graces (when in doubt, she wondered, 'What would Lucienne do?' and found her course of action). The crowd was mortal and not particularly nibble-able, but she'd had a bottle before leaving the hotel, as well as a nice long drink of Giacomo out in the car park, so she was quite content. Dressed in a simple dark blue satin frock, she made no attempt to emphasize her glamour, and found herself having rather interesting, earnest conversations with both men and women: What antiquities had she seen? Wasn't there a natural affinity between France and Egypt? How vulgar Americans could be! Was the economic situation bound to get worse before it got better?

Presently, however, she needed a break, and she drifted through a doorway, wondering where the gaming room might be. Hadn't Giacomo wanted her there, as his lucky talisman—and wasn't this meant to be an adventure?

She came to a closed door, with a sound of voices beyond it; opening it, she was immediately stopped by a very large man in Egyptian dress.

"I am sorry, you cannot come in here; this is a private room." He held up a halting hand.

"Oh . . . I was just looking for my . . ." She scanned the room which was entirely populated by dark-haired men in dinner jackets. Luckily, the one she sought raised his head and stood up, with a huge smile.

"Carissima!" Giacomo exchanged words with the door-man in a mixture of Italian and Egyptian. With a sigh, he lowered the barrier of his arm, indicating with a nod that she should join her friend.

There were no extra chairs, so Sally draped herself over Giacomo's shoulders. She had no idea what the game was, but he seemed intensely focused on the dark, dapper man across the table, whom she guessed must be Prince Farouk.

Overcome with boredom—she had never been able to take an interest in card games—she began to nibble Giacomo's neck, casting a glamour to ensure no one no-ticed. The other gentlemen at the table were so focused on their cards that it was almost unnecessary. Giacomo was, apparently, bidding boldly and succeeding, so that a pile of chips grew in front of his place.

"Whatever you are doing, keep doing it," he whispered, patting her hand.

The man across the table narrowed his eyes at them. "Who is this? I wasn't aware that we were allowing guests —or should I say, mascots—at this game."

"Your highness, please allow me to present my fiancée, Mlle Sally Lafayette. Sally, his highness Prince Farouk."

Sally lowered her head. "A great honor, sir."

The prince gave her a long look. "The honor is all mine. *Enchanté, mademoiselle. Vous êtes française?*"

"Oui, bien sur."

The prince proceeded to converse, inconsequentially but with a flirtatious edge, in French, to the annoyance of Giacomo, whose French was rudimentary at best.

Presently, an emphatic cough from one of the other players recalled them both to their cards. Sally nuzzled Giacomo's ear reassuringly as he resumed play. At first she thought he had misplaced his rhythm, as he lost bets for a few rounds, but soon he regained ground and effected a gratifying transfer of chips from the prince's pile to his own.

The game came to an end—Sally hadn't been sure that it ever would—and the gentlemen stood and exchanged handshakes. Most of them ignored Sally, but Prince Farouk took her hand and gave it a courtly kiss, before handing Giacomo a slip of paper.

"My marker. You may come to my home tomorrow and collect your winnings. I hope your charming friend will be able to accompany you."

They had their first quarrel in the car going back to the hotel.

"Of course I should go with you—he invited me! One doesn't refuse a prince."

"Oh, one doesn't, eh? What's that they say in French, 'the right of the monsieur'? I'm damned if I'll let him do that. My 'charming friend!' He did not even recognize you as my fiancée."

"Maybe because I'm not . . .unless there's something you've neglected to ask me? Oh, don't be silly, Giacomo;

he just has nice manners. I expect he'll be pleased to see us together, to know that you plan to use your winnings to buy me a present. He might even throw in a little something extra."

Giacomo turned to her, furious. "What a mercenary little bitch you have become!"

"Have I?" Sally seemed genuinely shocked. "I didn't think I . . . watch the road!"

The brakes squealed and the Fiat swerved. Giacomo just managed to avoid hitting a large dog that had dashed into their path. He refused to speak for the rest of the trip, and would not let Sally have her customary nightcap at his neck. Frustrated and hungry, she went to her room.

Cairo - Bombay,
RMS Strathaird,
April 1933

The Strathaird, a British P&O liner, was brand-new, modern and brilliantly white, and it had the right itinerary, to Bombay via Aden. Aldo and Giacomo drove them to Port Said, parked the car and came aboard to help see to their luggage and say goodbye.

"Mind the large trunk," Lucienne cautioned the porters. "It's 'Wanted on Voyage,' in our stateroom, not the hold. Carefully please!"

Once that was settled, Aldo and Lucienne strolled the deck, perfectly *comme il faut*, chatting fondly and promising to stay in touch—knowing it would be impossible.

Giacomo, however, went a bit mad, clinging to Sally's hands, weeping, wrapping her in extravagant embraces against the forward bulkhead.

If I cared what people thought, I'd be embarrassed, Sally mused. But of course, she didn't care.

Finally, the horn blew, and Aldo dragged his friend away. The young men waved from the quay as the ship gradually widened its distance from the land. Lucienne turned to go to their stateroom; Sally was about to follow when she felt a hand on her wrist. It was Arthur Evans, the detective from Cairo.

"Hello Miss Lafayette. Pleasure to see you again."

"Bonjour, Monsieur Evans. Are you taking this boat too?"

"Only as far as Aden. My department is sending a launch for me. Quite frankly, I came in search of you." He was fingering her sapphire bracelet, turning it until he found the clasp.

"What do you think you're doing?"

"I'm afraid this is stolen property, miss. I'm sure you wouldn't want to be prosecuted for its return."

"I beg your pardon!" She glared at the pink-faced Englishman. "My bracelet was a gift from a friend . . . Er, I mean . . . an old family heirloom. How dare you!"

Mr. Evans smiled and undid the clasp. "Gift from a friend, indeed—a well-meaning but larcenous friend. We'll be picking him up shortly. I would advise you to have nothing to do with this, and no harm will come to you." He pocketed the bracelet with maddening rapidity.

Sally stared at him, eyes very wide. "I see that I am not allowed to have nice things. I think you have acted detestably. Good day to you, sir."

She turned away and fled toward her stateroom, comforted only by the delicate weight of the brilliants in her pocket—the diamond and sapphire earrings Giacomo had slipped her during their last embrace.

"I wonder who *that* is." Lucienne inclined her head toward the strikingly handsome man seated at the captain's table. Instead of conventional evening dress, he wore a high-collared silk jacket of peacock blue and a small, neat black turban, accentuating his flashing eyes.

A chic blonde woman passing behind their table overheard her. "Don't you know? He's some sort of royalty, traveling to Bombay with his harem—all seven of them."

Sally turned. "Really? There are really still sheikhs with harems? I had no idea."

"Believe it! I saw them coming on board in all their exotic finery," the woman said with a knowing smile. Although apparently on her way somewhere, she had paused.

"Would you like to join us?" Lucienne offered politely.

"Oh god, yes. I was sitting with some people over there, but they're hideously boring. I'd much rather meet you.

Don't you think there's something marvelously special about a group of three gorgeous women?"

Sally and Lucienne exchanged a look. "Well, yes," Sally said. "We've had some delightful times as a trio, with a friend of ours. How do you do? I'm Sally Lafayette, and this is Lucienne Leung."

"Nancy. Nancy Lawrence. How funny—we all have the same monogram. We could share accessories." She took out a gold case, engraved with a stylish L, and a matching lighter, and offered her strong American cigarettes around. "So, what's your story, dears? Wait, more important—what are you drinking? Double whiskey sour," she said to the waiter she'd flagged.

"Oh, what about two Negronis, please. That all right, Loulou?"

Lucienne nodded. "Perfect. So, Nancy, what brings you to this part of the world? You're American, aren't you?"

Their companion answered eagerly, not caring that her own question had been deflected. "Cleveland, born and bred. For the last ten years or so, I've traveled as much as possible, anywhere I can get a civilized drink. You know about my country's insanity, right?" She drummed her fingers, impatient for the cocktails to appear. "I married a jazz musician, Harry Greene, and went on tour with him, until that got old. Then I met the darlingest banker, Jasper Harrington Lawrence. Divorcing him was the best thing I ever did—I'm pretty much set for life. As long as I don't keep going *too* long. But who wants to be an old broad anyway?" She let out an unexpectedly raucous laugh. "But what about you young things? I *did* ask first. Are you both *French*?" She said the word as if 'French' might be code for something.

"Sally's a native Parisienne; I came there from Indochine. We met when we were both mannequins at the House of Mlle. We shared a flat and had a lot of fun. But, as you say, the scene got old—so we decided to take our savings and see a bit of the world."

"Modeling in Paris—how glamorous! I could see doing that, at your age." Nancy glanced down and adjusted the low neckline of her green crepe dress, complacently acknowledging her own forty-year-old attractiveness.

"It can be glamorous—and you'd be fantastic, Nancy, with your long legs—but sometimes, it's just a job. Our employer went a bit crazy . . ." Sally changed the subject at Lucienne's warning cough. "And then, I had a beau who got a bit too intense," she went on, actually thinking of recent times with Giacomo. "It was time for a change of scene."

The drinks arrived, and they clinked glasses festively. Nancy's was already half-empty as Sally and Lucienne savored their first sips; they saw her catch the waiter's eye and point to her glass for a refill.

"*He* really is easy on the eyes, isn't he?" Nancy was gazing once more toward the captain's table, where the handsome, turbaned man appeared to be telling a story. The captain let out a loud but forced-sounding laugh; their other table-mates, a distinguished-looking elderly couple, looked bored or perhaps uncomprehending. "Pity he's stuck with that bunch; it doesn't look like much fun. I suppose they're the ranking titles on board. Hmm . . . rich and gorgeous, what a waste!"

"Doesn't he . . . I mean, where do his . . . ladies dine?" Sally wondered.

"In their suite, I'm told. They're not supposed to be seen in public."

"Isn't that dull for them?"

"I imagine they're used to it; they're probably more comfortable that way. It's *him* I'm concerned about. He ought to be able to have a good time and meet people —like *us*." She swallowed the last of her drink just as the waiter arrived with a fresh one, along with the first course, shrimps in tomato aspic.

"Sorry, I can't eat this—I'm allergic." Sally pushed her plate away. In truth, she despised any form of tomato, finding it too suggestive of blood while devoid of its satisfaction.

The next few minutes were quiet as Nancy devoured her starter and Sally's, while Lucienne took a few dainty bites and slid the uneaten remnant under a lettuce leaf.

Nancy returned to her whiskey sour and her subject. "Pity he can't at least join us for a drink."

"He probably doesn't, though. Drink, I mean. His religion." Sally nodded toward the captain's table, where glasses of claret sat at three of the four places.

"Coffee is the wine of Islam, they say," Lucienne murmured.

"Yes—you're brilliant! Excuse me a moment, girls." Taking one more swig, Nancy slid out of her seat and crossed the room.

The captain and the other gentleman got courteously to their feet, but Nancy already had a hand on the turbaned man's shoulder, keeping him firmly in place. Her cleavage was at his eye level.

"Please, sit. I'm American; we're informal people. I was just wondering if His Majesty might possibly join my friends and I for coffee and dessert. If you could spare him, just for a bit, after the main course. I'm Mrs. Jasper Harrington Lawrence, by the way." She swayed slightly, interrupting the polite noise of introductions to add, "Formerly Mrs. Harry Greene, of the Greene Light Serenaders. But you really should meet my charming young Parisian friends, they're adorable!" She waved gaily toward their table, but Lucienne and Sally were preoccupied by the arrival of the roast beef cart (selecting the bloodiest slices possible). "Ah, I see the beef has arrived; I'd better get back—but do come and say hello!" She gave his shoulder a final pat and wove her way back to her place.

"There, that's taken care of," she said, seating herself. "Ooh, nice-looking roast—may I have that big slice, please? and would you ask the darling barman for another double, and two more Negronis. What's this, darlings? You've hardly touched your drinks."

"Oh, really, I don't need another; this is fine," Lucienne said, echoed by Sally.

"Bring them anyway," Nancy told the waiter firmly. "I'll drink them myself, if necessary."

The prince (as his title turned out to be) arrived along with the peche melba and the pot of coffee. Nancy, squinting just a bit, had just fitted a cigarette into her fluted gold holder, and he gave her a light along with a gallant half-bow.

"Mrs. Lawrence, here I am, as promised. You must introduce me to your exquisite companions."

"Uh . . . Lulu Looie, Sally DeParee, meet . . . the Sheik of Araby. I'm sorry, darlings; I've completely forgotten everyone's names."

With impeccable nonchalance, Prince Ahmed introduced himself and, over coffee, made charming small talk, skillfully maneuvering the conversation around Nancy's increasing incoherence. He was Indian, it turned out—a member of the royal family of a Muslim princely state. His uncle, the Nizam, was one of the richest men in the world, he admitted sheepishly. He was delighted that Sally and Lucienne were traveling to Bombay and clearly impressed at their invitation from the Maharani.

"I have met her highness—a remarkable personality, very free-thinking. Of course, my uncle would disapprove, but then, he disapproves of most things. Including modern music—one of the reasons I find it essential to spend time in Europe. I'd love to go to America, too; I'm an absolute jazz maniac."

"Oh, so am I!" Sally exclaimed, and they started down the path of comparing their favorite artists, tunes and arrangements, until Nancy interrupted.

"That's all very well—you know, don't you, I was married to a jazz musician for ten years; the things I could tell you—but what we really want to know about is your harem! All those exotic wives! Do they wear those gauzy trousers? Do they squabble amongst themselves and nibble Turkish delight? Do you have a favorite?"

Lucienne looked away, discomfited by their companion's rudeness, and Ahmed seemed momentarily startled, but then he laughed. "Actually, I don't think you'd find them particularly exotic. They are lovely and talented women, and you are welcome to meet them, if you'd like. Pamela is English and has a degree in art history; she's brilliant at decorating our homes. I met Mireille when she was singing in a jazz club; she turned out to be a marquise and a poet. And of course, being French, she's a phenomenal cook." He winked at Sally. "And Navid is, actually, a distant cousin of some sort; we've known each other forever. She's massively clever and does all my accounts; I'd be lost without her. Or all of them, really."

"*Only* three?" Nancy raised an eyebrow at him. "I thought you sheiks went in for dozens of cuties. But maybe this is just the compact travel harem." Nancy was having some difficulty putting a new cigarette into her holder.

"May I?" Ahmed offered. He took the objects from her, filled her holder and handed it back to her, immediately offering a light. "No, it's just the four of us. We all get along very happily together, and we're able to live quite well, half the year in Europe, on my income. Of course, I *could* support another bride or two (*Was that another wink?* Sally wondered) if the right person came along— but we would all have to agree."

The coffeepot was empty, the ice cream melted and the ashtray full. Lucienne was starting to wonder what to do about Nancy, who was leaning forward on her elbows, eyes half-closed.

The question was answered by a suave dinner-jacketed gentleman who appeared at her side. "Señora Lawrence, we have an engagement to dance a rhumba, I believe. Please come, the band is just starting."

Nancy was instantly wide awake and sparkling. "Of course we do, Alejandro! Darlings, it's been tremendous. See you all later." With unexpected composure, she gathered her things, stood up and took her escort's arm. He appeared to have a tight hold on her, but there was no trace of unsteadiness as they headed for the Grand Salon.

"It was *so* kind of you to invite us," Lucienne told Navid, who had sent the note the next morning asking them to lunch. "I'm afraid our friend Nancy is indisp . . ."

"Massively hungover, I would imagine!" Ahmed laughed. "I *would* like to know more about Harry Greene, but not enough . . . . No, we only invited you two." He had spoken in French—all of the ladies were fluent—and soon they were talking of their favorite Parisian places, pleasures and mutual acquaintances. Mireille knew, and had sung with, the Chocolate Dandies, although it was a completely different line-up from the group Sally and Lucienne had known just a few years before.

Sally sighed. "So many things must be different. We haven't been back since the end of '29."

"Well, that was the peak, really. Things aren't quite as much fun these days," Pamela said thoughtfully.

"So many Americans left—and they gave the best parties," Navid added.

"Hmm, yes . . ." Sally fell silent, thinking of her fateful encounter with a certain American couple. "Sorry!" she brightened. "I was just remembering some of those parties!" Everyone laughed.

"In a way, I don't mind so much. It feels more normal now, more *vrai* Paris." Mireille gave Sally a complicit look. "*You* know what I mean. In what *arrondissement* did you grow up?"

As the lunch arrived, brought in by the steward and two waiters, with a good deal of chair-scraping and table arranging, Mireille pulled Sally aside for an in-depth *parisienne* questionnaire about favorite patisseries, flower shops, shoemakers and so forth. Despite her genuine, impeccable pedigree, Sally had to fake a great deal, since she'd gone to school in the 1710s, not the 1910s, and the parks she'd played in as a child were now altered beyond recognition. But as she steered the topic to the shops and craftspeople associated with recent fashion, she was on firmer ground. Mireille had great respect for the house of Mlle, their erstwhile employer.

"I have to say, though, I like the turn styles have taken recently. I'm sure *you* were stunning *à la garçonne*, but the boyish look is not so flattering to all of us." Mireille gestured unselfconsciously to her ample bosom, attractively showcased by the draped neckline of her violet crepe dress. "But Mlle was brilliant; she foresaw the changes ahead. Oh—were you in that scandalous show in the fall of 1929? What happened—there were so many wild stories! And afterward, didn't she have some sort of breakdown?"

"I don't really know," Sally said cautiously, of the fashion show that had ended in bloodshed. "Things were a bit chaotic that season, and we had to leave immediately afterward for an engagement in London. But you're right," she quickly changed the subject; "the current styles are awfully pretty. I love your frock—Patou?"

"Vionnet."

On safer ground, they chatted for a few more minutes and then joined the others at the table. Sally was dismayed to see the same tomato aspic starter from the previous evening, and again had to plead allergies, but the rest of the meal was pleasant enough. There were individual small meat pies, whose crust conveniently concealed how much one ate (or didn't), and there was copious champagne. Ahmed, who only had a single glass, observed that he didn't abstain from alcohol completely, but preferred to indulge in private. After the main course they enjoyed an array of petits fours, glacé fruits, chocolates, liqueurs and multi-colored scented cigarettes.

The suite had been brightened with wall-hangings, silk throws and small pillows. "I always bring some of our things along when we travel, so we can feel at home," Pamela noted. "And Navid chooses the incense."

"It's lovely, I've been enjoying it. Sandalwood, frankincense and . . . what else?"

"Just some other resins and spices. It's not a secret, but I never remember what's in it. I have it blended for me by a clever old man. Now—would you like to play a card game, or mah-jongg, or chess?"

"Oh! I haven't played chess in—I can't remember how long. But I'd love to give it a try," Lucienne said. She actually remembered quite clearly that she had last played with her lover, Luc, in Indochine more than fifty years ago.

Navid set up the game on a table below the porthole. Sally, meanwhile, lounged at the luncheon table with Pamela and Mireille, sipping eau de vie, smoking pink and pale green cigarettes and telling increasingly risqué and hilarious stories. Ahmed had retired to a divan for a post-prandial lie-down, with a handkerchief over his eyes, but he removed it now and then to beam beneficently at the room full of lively women.

"Remember that time, Pam, when we went to that lingerie shop on rue de la Chaussée d'Antin, and we all wanted to get matching brassieres and slips?"

"Oh Atelier Cadolle! They have the loveliest things; do you know them, Sally?"

"*Bien sûr*, I love them! They have colors no one else has."

"Yes, but . . ." Mireille pouted prettily. "The vendeuse took one look at my hips and my *jeaunes filles*" (cupping her breasts and jiggling them) "and said, 'We are deeply sorry, Madame, but there is not enough lilac silk for you. It will have to be wisteria.'"

Pamela let out a hoot of laughter. "Oh, I'm sorry, Mimi, but it was too funny—wisteria! It's a perfectly sweet color, though."

"I know, I love it. I'm wearing that set now. But she hurt my feelings! I'm *not* that big. Look, Sally." She leaned toward Sally, pulling down the neckline of her dress.

"Of course, you're a perfect size! How rude—why wouldn't she just say the lilac was out of stock? Anyway, the wisteria is *très jolie*." Sally's lips grazed Mireille's throat as she took in the invited view. Batting her eyelashes and smiling hypnotically to project a glamour, she took a few butterfly sips at the velvety skin below Mireille's ear.

Pamela, tipsy and enchanted, leaned on Sally's other shoulder and nuzzled her hair. "How lucky that you're on this boat—it's wonderful to meet new friends!"

Sally turned and took a few sips of Pamela. "Lucky indeed! This would have been a very boring trip if we hadn't met."

"And it's all because of that wildly uninhibited American woman," Mireille laughed. "Ahmed told us all about her."

"Yes, Loulou and I would have been far too reticent to push ourselves forward and meet you, much as we might have wanted to. Here's to Nancy Lawrence!" Sally raised her tiny liqueur glass, but instead of toasting, she tasted her companions again, and they lounged against each other in perfect contentment.

"What's going on over there?" Ahmed said sleepily, smiling, before turning away with a snore.

Lucienne looked over at them, wide-eyed. "Someone come and help me, please! I wasn't warned that Navid is a championship chess master."

"Here, darlings—you need more drinks, clearly." Pamela got to her feet and brought the decanter over to the chess table. After filling their glasses, she draped herself over Lucienne's shoulders. "I don't even remember how chess works, but I'll help. I always love the horses."

Lucienne fluttered her lashes and bared her tiny fangs, turning her head to Pamela's throat. "Mmm, your perfume is delicious, Pamela. But I'm afraid my horse is immobilized. Navid is just too good."

"May I kibitz?" Sally asked. She leaned over Navid, enjoying a discreet taste while she studied the board. "Oh, I see what you're doing."

After a few more moves were exchanged, Navid employed the lorgnette she wore on a ribbon to peer at the board. "And . . . mate," she smiled, moving her queen, and downed her glass. "Mireille, bring the chocolates over here, will you? Lucienne, will you accept a chocolate marron glacé as a consolation prize? You played beautifully."

"Gladly. Marrons are my favorite, and at least now the suspense is over. I'm pleased that I was able to hold you off for a little while, at least."

"Let's have some tunes, now that the chess masters are done." Mireille opened the portable gramophone, which was another part of their travel accoutrements.

"Won't it wake him?" Sally looked over at the prince.

"Already awake." Smiling, he stretched luxuriantly. "I've been having the loveliest dreams—all about chess and chestnuts and wisteria hysteria and lilac lingerie, in a sort of paradise surrounded by beautiful women."

Mireille handed him a glass of eau de vie and the plate of Turkish delight. "Naughty man, I believe you've been awake and spying on us, the whole time. Or not," she added, as Ahmed yawned in oblivious innocence.

"What? Did I miss something?"

"*Pas du tout.*" Mireille gave him an affectionate kiss on the cheek. He stood up to hug her back, and was joined by Navid and Pamela.

As they exchanged embraces, Navid said, "And you must kiss Lucienne and Sally. They are our sisters now."

Ahmed extended a genial arm to his guests, who accepted formal but warm kisses on each cheek, in the French manner Both managed to enjoy a few discreet sips in the process. Then Mireille wound the gramophone and put on "Clarinet Marmelade." Soon they were all dancing, in changeable pairings.

Sally flipped through the record collection. "Oh, we have to hear this next—'Mood Indigo'!"

"We've got tons of Ellington at home; I love their sound. You *have* to come and visit us in Hyderabad—don't they, Ahmed?"

"We would be delighted to entertain you, whenever you can come," the prince agreed.

"That would be fantastic!" Sally exclaimed. "But we'll have to see how long Indira wants us to stay. How long do you expect to be in residence, before you head back to Europe?"

"Don't worry, we're in no rush. Will you be in Cooch Behar?"

"No, the maharani's asked us to join her at her winter home in Poonah. We're to take a train called the Deccan Queen from Bombay."

"Oh, that's a gorgeous train, very new and super-fast," Pamela said. "And you'll love Poonah; it's got horse races and smart clubs and it's full of handsome young university men—or so I'm told. *What*, why are you looking at me like that, Ahmed? It's called the Oxford of the East, you know."

Ahmed gave Pamela a mock-severe look before they both laughed. "Indeed. I am sure you will enjoy yourselves. And when you have exhausted the charms of the town—or the patience of the maharani—just ring us up, and we'll send the Rolls for you."

"The Rolls-Royce, ooh, lavish!" Navid teased. "You must really like them. Shall we start planning weddings four and five?"

"I hope you'll join us again for luncheon, or dinner," Mireille said warmly, as Sally and Lucienne started collecting their things. "But we'd better wait a day or two; you should probably keep making regular appearances in the dining room, or people will talk."

"Talk about what? Why should they?" Sally wondered.

"Oh my dears, this is a British ship," Pamela said. "You spent some time in London; didn't you notice how rule-bound we are, and how obsessed with class and reputation?"

"Reputation?"

"Oh, you've already got one, trust me. 'The two French girls traveling alone . . .' Everyone saw you saying good-bye to boyfriends at Port Said, so they know you're not lesbians. Now the great minds of shipboard gossip just have to figure out which box to put you in. If you were English, they'd assume you were part of the 'fishing fleet,' headed out to land an army officer husband. But young Frenchwomen en route to the Orient could be gold-diggers, entertainers, who knows! Any number of less than perfectly respectable possibilities."

"On the other hand, since you have such nice clothes, perhaps you're frivolous aristocrats," Mireille winked. "Why do you think we keep to ourselves here? We're not required to be in purdah, at least not when we travel in the west. But to be subject to scrutiny, everyone speculating about our relationships—ugh, it's just not worth it."

"I don't blame you," said Lucienne. "But I guess we're used to a bit of scrutiny and speculation, aren't we, Sally? Keeps things interesting. Well, do let us know when we can come again—until then, we'll try to stay out of trouble."

"Oh, one other thing," Navid added. "Could we ask you not to mention to Nancy that you visited us? We wouldn't want her to feel she could invite herself in here. She seems a bit . . . predatory."

Back in their stateroom, slipping out of her frock, Sally paused and ran a hand over the large trunk—Natalie's trunk—stowed in the corner. "You know," she sighed, "I miss Natalie horribly, all the time. But . . . I don't think what just happened could never have happened with three of us."

Nancy joined them for dinner again, two nights later.

"How are my favorite mademoiselles?" Before they could answer, she'd flagged a waiter and ordered a round of negronis. "I didn't see you yesterday, but I tried your drink; I like it! So, what have you been up to?"

"Oh, not much—a touch of *mal de mer*, actually. We lay low all day yesterday," Sally improvised.

"Really? A friend of mine said she saw you at the door of the harem suite." She gave the word a prurient emphasis. "I thought you'd been *abducted*!"

Lucienne laughed and answered smoothly, "Oh, we were just passing by there when a steward was delivering tea. We exchanged some brief, formal greetings." Without looking, she knew that Sally intuited the wink in what she'd said and was daydreaming about their delicious idyll, which had been far from formal.

"I see." Nancy sounded somewhat unconvinced. "Well, did you at least get a look in? Were they all lounging about in gauzy trousers?"

"Hmm, I didn't really notice—just something colorful."

"And what about *himself*—what I wouldn't give to see *him* lazing about in some magnificent brocade caftan, with that turban, those eyes . . . Oh, here are the drinks. Cheers, darlings."

To Nancy's disappointment, Prince Ahmed did not appear at the captain's table that night, his place being taken by two bald gentlemen in ornate military uniforms. When they'd gotten through the interminable meal (cream of asparagus soup and turbot meunière with new potatoes—none of it to a vamp's taste, and calling for extra efforts in concealment), Lucienne and Sally acquiesced in following Nancy to the Crystal Ballroom where Alejandro waited, eager to teach them the rhumba.

A huge golden full moon polished the promenade deck, and a slight breeze ruffled Lucienne's hair. She walked fast, relishing the freedom of the open space after the crowded dance floor, her bias cut silk gown floating gracefully about her ankles. Being on a ship stirred memories of her first voyages—always of escape from untenable situations—and at the same time, made her feel trapped. A ship was such a closed world, bounded by waters, finite in its possibilities. She preferred to travel overland; one could always leave a train, simply get off at the next station, even if it was short of one's official destination. Better still, she preferred not to travel—to have a safe, cozy home, in a large beautiful city full of parks, cafes and byways, places to disappear. Oh, Paris . . . would she ever be able to return?

A sailor, coiling lines beside the railing, turned to watch her. Feeling his gaze, Lucienne slowed her pace and smiled. He stared at the moonlit gleam of her eyes and teeth as she approached; then, unbelievably, the lithe beautiful girl was beside him.

"Salut, matelôt," she purred, not really expecting or needing him to speak French. Her wide smile did the rest of the talking, as she nestled into his strong arms, dazed him with a kiss and fed at his neck. He was so warm and deliciously salty; she took a bit more than her usual fleeting sips, and he began to sway a bit. She eased him down to lean against a cleat, and as an extra precaution wrapped a rope around his waist and through the device. She didn't need a drowning on her conscience.

"Sally, are you still awake?" Lucienne whispered, slipping into their stateroom. She had walked for hours, drinking in the moonlight—and another sailor. The night was beautiful, but instead of contentment, she felt increasingly anxious.

Sally yawned. "Not really . . . but, what is is, Loulou?" Registering her friend's tone, she shook off her sleepiness.

"I've been walking and walking, round and round this thing—I don't know if I can go on."

"What? I don't understand, dearest; come and rest. It's bedtime, you don't need to walk any more. Have you fed? I've got a flask right here."

"No, no," Lucienne gestured distractedly. "I had two nice sailors. But I mean, I don't think I can go on traveling. I want *so much* to be back in Paris. It hurts me not to be there. Can't we just go back?"

"Darling, you know we can't. Even for the two of us, it would be dangerous, and for Natalie—unthinkable."

Lucienne pressed her hands over her own eyes with a deep groan. "Sally—I *need* to go. Even if you don't."

"But I can't manage that on my own." Sally's eyes inevitably turned to the trunk in the corner.

Lucienne sighed. "Honestly, sometimes I think we should just let her go. It's what she wanted, until I tried to talk her out of it with the Long Sleep nonsense. Who knows if it even works?"

"You're the one talking nonsense. Stop it!" Sally's voice rose.

"Ssh. Just think about it for one minute. Over the side. Splash. Rest in peace, in the cool deep. *Fini*. And get on with the rest of our lives, someplace nice. Preferably Paris. Or America."

"Lou, I am either rigid with shock or too damn tired to listen to this. Please, go to sleep. We'll talk tomorrow."

The next day, they slept til late afternoon. Barring breakfast (unthinkably early), they'd been making some effort to conform with the shipboard schedule, with its relentless round of meals and social occasions, but for once they followed their natural inclinations—awakening slowly in their darkened stateroom, sipping from the flasks they kept bedside, yawning and chatting gently until it was time to bathe and dress. Lucienne was calm and cheerful, to Sally's relief.

"Do you think I should go blonde again? And perhaps get a permanent wave? Curls seem to be quite the thing these days." Sally studied herself idly in the mirror.

Lucienne gave her a wide-eyed look. "Do you know how hard it is to get my hair to curl? I can't believe you'd say that—*I'm* to be quite omitted from fashion because of my *cheveux chinois*?"

Sally gasped. "Darling, I'm so sorry, how utterly stupid of me; I wasn't thinking . . ."

Lucienne laughed. "I'm just being silly. I have no desire to be Jean Harlow; I'm quite happy to emulate Miss Anna Mae Wong. But no, I don't think you should go blonde at the moment. We're going to appear obviously foreign in the part of the world we're heading to; no need to look like complete freaks of nature. And it's not at all certain we'll find a decent hairdresser."

"Thanks, love, I knew I could count on your sage advice." Sally gave her smooth dark coiffure a pat and blotted her lipstick, before turning to her friend. "Lucienne, I have to ask—about last night. I can't bear it if you're really suffering. If you *have* to go back to Paris . . . we'll find a way."

"Oh, Sally . . ." Lucienne wiped a tiny bit of moisture from the corner of her eye, sniffed and dabbed her nose with a handkerchief. "I'm all right, really. I just get tired, sometimes, of not having a home. But I'll be fine; I don't know what got into me last night. We'll be fine, all of us." Her smile included the trunk in the corner. "It's cocktail time, isn't it?"

"So, where do you find these tasty sailors? Can I come tonight?" Sally asked as they headed for the prom deck.

Prince Ahmed was standing near the bar in the Grand Saloon, looking particularly gorgeous in a white high-collared jacket, with a princely necklace of large pearls and a midnight-blue turban. He held a goblet of mango juice. Spotting Sally and Lucienne, he smiled warmly and seemed about to ask them to join him, but instead gave them a wink before turning away to chat with someone nearby.

It was a particularly warm evening, and it was one of those occasions when, by unspoken agreement, virtually all the women were wearing the same color—in this case, white. Sally looked around the room, then at Lucienne (in tomato crepe) and down at her own gown (cherry satin), and could hardly keep from laughing aloud.

"Hmm, not very subtle, are we?"

"I'm sure no one will notice," Lucienne deadpanned.

"I have just the thing for you beautiful ladies!" The bartender, with a flourish, produced two 'Chinese' cocktails, sticky with too much grenadine.

"Sorry darling, I wasn't paying attention," Sally said, handing one to Lucienne. "This might be undrinkable."

They clinked, sipped and grimaced simultaneously. Lucienne led the way out on deck. Leaning on the rail, she emptied most of her drink into the brownish-green water and refilled her glass from the flask she'd brought in her purse. Sally did likewise.

"Ah, that's better." They lingered for a little while, watching the setting sun melt into the sea in shades of muddy orange; then they returned to the party.

The talk was of how soon the ship would reach Bombay. There were four days left, and three nights, so tomorrow night was the traditional fancy-dress ball, to be followed by the most formal night, the captain's gala, and finally the quiet, informal last night at sea.

"I suppose we'll have to dine with Nancy again," Sally sighed.

"Well, poor dear, it can't be easy being on her own. Still . . . if I have to hear one more story about being on tour with Al Greene . . . Don't you wish we could slip away and spend the evening with Navid and Mireille and Pamela? What do you suppose they're up to?"

"I think we should find out."

No one seemed to notice as they—again—slipped out of the Grand Saloon. Reaching the door of the Royal Suite, Lucienne tapped gently.

"Hello? It's Lucienne and Sally."

There was a rustling, a moment's delay, and then the door opened a few inches. Navid, smiling widely, motioned them in.

Pamela, in a silvery brocade dressing gown, was shaking a cocktail. Mireille lounged on the chaise in a diaphanous negligée and Navid, in a simple salwar kameez, led them to the table she'd risen from, spread with a feast of tasty small nibbles. A record was playing on the gramophone.

"Who *is* that?" Sally had to know immediately.

"Cab Calloway—isn't he the best!" Mireille gestured enthusiastically with a rose-scented cigarette.

"We're playing truant from dinner; it all seemed a bit much tonight. Please may we visit with you instead?" Lucienne appealed.

"Of course. I'll just ring the steward for some more food." Navid picked up the telephone.

"Oh please, there's no need. We don't really eat . . . much," Sally began.

Lucienne hastened to add, without a grain of truth, "We had a big lunch."

Pamela laughed. "Was it . . . liquid? Here, let me mix you a cocktail. Don't worry, darlings, we know you don't go in for much *solid* food."

They exchanged banter about slimming and the virtues of delicious cocktails and spicy snacks over dull, European-style meals, Lucienne and Sally wondering all the while if there was a coded subtext about their vamp nature.

Mireille moved to one of the sofas and patted the seat. "Anyone want to come and share a bite with me? Sally?" There was a cheese plate on the table in front of her, but her meaning was still open to interpretation.

"Mm, camembert," Sally murmured, while looking at Mireille's alluring profile. Mireille moved her chestnut hair off her shoulder and smiled. Sally took a nibble. "Ah, *le vrai fromage francais.*"

"I've always been an exceptionally good sailor." Nancy complacently patted her flat stomach. "From the very first trip with Al Greene—never a moment's *mal de mer.* You poor things." She gave them sympathetic shoulder pats. "Oh well, whatever keeps us svelte, right?"

"It's not my favorite mode of appetite control, but at least that's a positive way to look at it," Lucienne smiled ruefully.

Sally did her best to look as if she too had been ill. They'd decided it would be wise to rejoin Nancy and the rest of the crowd for after-dinner drinks and dancing, after reluctantly taking leave of their friends.

"What are you drinking, girls—those Chinese cocktails?" Nancy, as usual, had quickly flagged a waiter.

"Oh, no thanks. I think that's what made me sick," Sally said quickly.

"I don't doubt it—best to stick to something simple. Three whiskey-sodas, Frank." She winked at the waiter and tucked a bill into his vest pocket. "Come on, let's snag a table by the dance floor; he'll find us. So . . . what are you doing for the fancy-dress ball? And more important, *why* doesn't his majesty dance?" Her eyes traced the prince. "Look at him—hurrying back to his harem. If he's going to be polygamous anyway, you'd think he'd want to expand his horizons, meet some *new* women. He'll have plenty of time with his frumpy brides once they get home."

Sally and Lucienne exchanged the faintest look, thinking of luscious Mireille, stylish Pamela, elegant Navid.

After an hour or so of dancing, with an assortment of young and old, skillful and indifferent partners, they said goodnight to Nancy. Lucienne let the way to the boat deck, where they found a convenient pair of sailors, thrilled to be approached by a couple of attractive, adventurous passengers. After a healthy serving of fresh warm blood ("Is it my imagination, or are they extra salty?" Sally wondered), they returned to their cabin to finish a flask as dessert.

"How's our supply?" Lucienne asked. Sally had been in charge of packing the bottles in their insulated case when they left Cairo. Stored in the large trunk with Natalie, they seemed to stay perfectly cooled.

"Three each, and we're on board for three more days. We should be all right if we're careful—especially if we keep finding nice sailors, and visiting Ahmed's wives. Does it seem as if they've consciously invited us to partake of them? Or are they just . . . friendly? I can't really tell."

"I'm not sure either, but I'm really becoming quite fond of them. It will be lovely to visit their home. I almost wish we didn't have to spend time with the maharani."

"Oh, Loulou! She's expecting us, and she's so much fun; it will be wonderful."

"I hope so," Lucienne sighed. "So . . . what *are* we going to wear for fancy-dress night?"

"Well, we have the couture pieces we kept from Mlle's '28 collection. There's that stunning one with the ombré beaded fringe and . . ."

"No one is going to think an out-of-date evening frock is a costume. Fancy dress is always people dressed as Napoleon, or the spirit of electricity."

"We should wear the assuit," Sally said decisively.

His evening clothes were elegant and unremarkable, but the man's face was paper-pale, his eyes like two black holes. And his mouth, sharp-toothed and apparently smeared with blood, sent a frisson of horror through the more impressionable guests.

Nancy, an exotic vision in diaphanous layers of purple and gold, actually shrieked behind her half-veil as he walked by: "Nosferatu!" She seemed truly terrified, and reached out to clutch the nearest arm, Sally's.

"Oh, I just hate vampire stories; I can't bear anything frightening. I'm sure if I ever met one in life—if they were real—I'd just die!"

Sally patted her shoulder reassuringly. "Nonsense, dear. It's only in fun. Who *is* that, anyway? I can't recognize him under all that make-up."

Nancy squinted, trying to avoid the alarming face and focus on the man's figure. "I *should* know, I've flirted with everyone in trousers for the past week. Too tall to be Alejandro; slimmer than most of the Brits or Americans . . . It's not Prince Ahmed—have you seen him yet? *Too* funny, you won't believe it; I won't say more. The captain's got that sort of build, but he *wouldn't* surely, would he? It's his job to keep us safe, not scare the day-lights out of us."

"I'm surprised at you, Nancy. You strike me as the most fearless of women. I think you should go and dance with him; you'll soon figure him out."

Nancy shuddered. "Oh, I really couldn't, not quite yet anyway. Why don't you go?"

Sally laughed. "All right, then, I will. But if they play a rhumba, he'll be the one in danger—I still can't get the footwork straight and I'm sure I'll step all over him."

She took her time crossing the room, admiring the costumes her fellow passengers had put together. There was indeed a Napoleon. (*Why is everyone still so fascinated by our dreadful, destructive megalomaniac emperor?* Sally mused.) She admired the clever way the man had fashioned epaulets out of two hairbrushes. Several women had made daring use of their peignoirs or night-gowns, embellished with flowers and gauzy wings, for a fetching nymph or fairy look. One couple had clearly planned ahead, with professionally-made matching harlequin costumes.

She caught up with her quarry near the punchbowl, though he was ignoring it in favor of his own flask.

"Good evening, Count . . . Dracula, is it?"

He turned quickly toward her with a hiss, followed by an attempt at an evil smile. Up close, his make-up was obvious, heavily and somewhat crudely applied, but there was something undeniably sinister about his presence. He was not quite as tall as he had appeared; coming close, Sally realized that she had an inch or two over him, but his extreme slenderness gave him an illusion of height.

"Yes, I am the Count." He attempted Bela Lugosi's accent. "And you are . . .?"

"Nesret, handmaiden of the Sphinx." Sally quickly produced the persona she'd devised to go with her assuit gown, and arranged her arms in a hieroglyphic gesture. There was something odd about the man's voice—creaky, as if he hadn't spoken in a long time, as if he'd emerged from a crypt. She knew he wasn't a real vampire—this close, she could pick up his mortal scent, and yet . . .

"So, you are Egyptian. The Egyptians knew of vampires." He paused, staring ominously. "We could dance . . . if you are not too frightened of me?"

"I would like to dance, very much." Sally smiled. As soon as she was in his arms, the mystery was solved. He was an adolescent, sixteen perhaps, some awkward unnoticed son of a tourist family, now come into his own through the magic of costuming, and trembling with fear and excitement at embracing her.

Sally was enchanted. She wanted to drink him in, eat him up, teach him the ways of vamp pleasure—but she held back. He was so young; he had all of human love before him, all in good time. She danced in a way that let him lead more masterfully than he'd known he could, and when they were in a dim corner, she leaned back and looked up at him, arching her throat.

"Would you like," she murmured, "to do the thing vampires do? To bite my neck? Just gently, mind you; we don't want to get blood all over the dance floor."

"The deck. All the floors on a ship are called decks, even here in the ballroom. Yes, I would like that." He put his mouth to her throat and kissed her, fiercely but harmlessly, for a long time. "Thank you," he whispered. "My first victim. Oh, there's red on you. I think I have a handkerchief somewhere . . ."

"That's all right; I will wear it with pride." She fluttered her eyelashes and knew she could have had anything she wanted from the boy, but she only gave his hand a squeeze. "Good evening, Count Dracula. I hope we will meet again."

Still smiling, Sally glided back across the room, passing a sheik, a ballerina, a couple of bedsheet Romans and Sherlock Holmes—*wait, that wasn't . . . it was . . . Prince Ahmed!* She winked at him and hurried back to find Nancy, who had just finished a foxtrot with a pirate.

"What did you find out? *Is* he the captain?"

"No, definitely not. I don't know who he is—probably one of those colorless commercial travelers—but I'd steer clear if I were you. He seemed really rather creepy, and yet dull at the same time. And he had an odd smell." (*There, that should do it*, Sally thought. The last thing she wanted was for Nancy to get an innocent young lad in her clutches.)

Lucienne was dancing with a tiger—or perhaps an out-sized tabby cat. The costume was a bit moth-eaten and musty, a veteran, no doubt, of many fancy-dress balls. As was the man underneath, she suspected. Muffled a bit by his furry head-covering, his voice was British and apparently elderly, with the occasional dash of outdated slang.

"I must say, you look a right treat in that Cleopaterer get-up. I used to think it was a silly business, fancy dress, but now I quite enjoy it. All that nonsense I *used* to be occupied with—politics, trade relations, tariffs—*that's* what seems like a waste of time."

"So, you've retired from your job? What do you occupy yourself with?" It was a question Lucienne had often pondered in her own life; she had come to realize that, even with their so-much-shorter spans, it was a concern to mortals too.

"Oh yes, I'm well out of the daily grind, but there's no end of things to be carrying on with. I am meant to be writing my memoirs, for the edification of those who care about that sort of thing . . . Lessons learned in the Great War and so on . . . but does anyone ever learn? I'd rather be in my rose garden, or more to the point, danc-ing with an exceptionally pretty young woman. If you don't mind my asking, how old are you, my dear?"

"Hm, let's see . . . I'll be seventy-three, come August." Lucienne answered with unguarded candor, then flut-tered her eyelashes to ensure he mis-heard. But the old gent's blue eyes peered at her keenly through the holes in his striped mask.

"Indeed. I must bore you to tears if you feel so old. Or else you're some sort of immortal being—remarkably well-preserved, eh?"

Three women wearing movie-star masks (Greta Garbo, Claudette Colbert and Myrna Loy) and draped gowns in shades of blue (royal, hyacinth and peacock) were clearly recognizable, to those who knew them, as Pamela, Mireille and Navid.

"Everyone's trying to figure out who you are," Sally told them, greeting them with air-kisses.

"Yes, that's the idea," Pamela said. Though her face was hidden, her voice suggested a wink.

"I don't know how long I'll be able to endure this mask," Navid complained. "My face is so hot, I'm sure my make-up is completely melted."

"It's just as well we don't want any of the refreshments—it wouldn't be possible. Not without revealing ourselves, anyway," Mireille added. "We won't stay long; we just wanted to see the costumes. I'm so glad we've run into you—what an exquisite gown. What kind of fabric is that?"

"It's an Egyptian technique called assuit. Tiny pieces of metal are wrapped onto net."

"What a shimmer—it's magical!"

"Yes, I believe it is." Sally spun about to swing out the floating panel of her dress, then took advantage of the dazzle to glide behind the three women, taking a brief sip at each smooth neck. Navid's was pleasingly tangy with sweat.

"See you later darlings!"

"Come tomorrow for lunch, if you can."

"Love to—thanks!"

Scanning the passageway to ensure no one was around, Lucienne tapped gently at the door of the Royal Suite. Sally was right behind her, and they slipped in quickly as soon as it opened. They were immediately enveloped in French-perfumed hugs.

"It's just us, for a while at least." Mireille sounded gleeful. "Ahmed was invited to the captain's table and didn't feel he could refuse."

"Just as well, really. We've got a lot to settle before we reach Bombay," Navid said. Pamela, as usual, was shaking cocktails and poured out a round of tiny drinks.

"Ooh, blue ones!"

"Yes, it's a floral tincture. I've been saving it for a special occasion. But what do you mean, 'a lot to settle,' Navee? All we need to do is send the Rolls to Poonah as soon as they wire. Or, I imagine Indira's on the telephone; I'll give you our number. You probably won't need more than a week or two to pay your respects, will you?"

"If that," Lucienne said, a touch fretfully. "There was a bit of bad blood between us, a few years back. A family situation . . ."

"Oh, nonsense, Loulou, I know she'll be happy to see us. Anyway, they don't want to hear all that. The point is, we've got all the time in the world . . ."

He was taller than her, much taller, with thin, elongated arms and grasping fingers, reaching to capture her. He smelled strong and strange. Foreign soil, Sally found herself thinking. She knew somehow that he smelled of his own grave. He opened his mouth to speak, and at first nothing came out, but then there was that creaking sound of a voice long unused.

"My first victim . . . in a long, long time . . ."

His mouth was full of pointed teeth, and his eyes were empty, black holes. He came closer, closer . . . She screamed and woke up.

Sitting up against the satinwood headboard, Sally lit a cigarette and pondered her nightmare. Why should she dream about "Count Dracula?" The boy she'd danced with was harmless and endearing. He might have inspired the image, but not the visceral fear she felt. She and Lucienne had gone to see the movie, with Bela Lugosi, when it came out, and found it a bit of a giggle. But those black, empty eyes . . . she'd seen them somewhere.

She put out her cigarette and sank back into slumber, but when she woke hours later, it was with a clear image in her mind: Lucienne's Uncle Yu and the Maharani Indira, facing each other across a card table at Yu's Casino Impériale in Cannes. Indira's eyes were wide and dark as windows on a moonless starry sky. Liu Yu's eyes held no stars; they were fathomless as deep wells.

She waited, thoughtfully, until Lucienne was not just stirring awake, but sitting up and taking a morning nip from her flask.

"Loulou?"

"Morning, darling. What is it?"

"Where is your uncle these days; do you know?"

"Uncle Yu? I expect he's still in Cannes. Why?"

"I think . . . I just dreamed about him. A nightmare."

"Oh!" Lucienne registered her usually unflappable friend's expression. "Oh Sally, I wish you didn't know me. Then you'd never have met . . . *him*."

Sally looked at her with shock. "How can you say that? I can deal with an occasional nightmare, but if *we'd* never met . . . I don't even want to think about it!" She got out of bed and gave Lucienne a fierce hug. They held each other for a few moments, and then Sally settled at the end of Lucienne's bed.

"I wish you still had your jade amulet, Loulou. I can't help feeling as if it kept you—and all of us—safe."

"And yet Uncle Yu is the one who gave it to me. But at the same time, maybe it protected me *from* him."

"I wonder what's happened to it."

"Probably still on a shelf at C.T. Loo's showrooms. Hmm . . ."

Disembarkation was unexpectedly chaotic, when they reached Bombay in mid-afternoon. Nancy, who had lunched with them, had promised to see them off properly and to impart some final words of wisdom, but she was nowhere to be seen. Prince Ahmed and his wives were surrounded by a army of retainers who had swarmed on board to handle their vast amounts of luggage, and to safeguard the ladies' modesty. On the quay, they tried to wave and call farewells to their friends, but it was impossible as they were trying to keep track of their own luggage.

With a surprising sense of loss, Sally watched as fellow passengers, who had been their temporary community for the past two weeks, dispersed in different directions. Among them were a British family—quietly dressed couple, neat little daughter with her hair in braids, and gawky teenaged son. He suddenly turned, looked her way and blushed, and Sally waved at her vampire dance partner.

Bombay, April, 1933

"What do you mean, you've lost our trunk!" White-faced, icy with anger, Sally stared at the shipping clerk.

He inclined his head gently, staring pleadingly past Sally at Lucienne, who was marginally less tall, Western and intimidating. "Please not to worry, memsahibs; the trunk will most certainly be found."

"Not acceptable," Sally insisted. "We require our trunk *immediately*." She gave the word her crispest, most British pronunciation.

Visibly intimidated, the clerk retreated through a door and returned a few moments later with his superior: a tall, portly, self-assured man, wearing a tailored wool suit despite the intense, humid heat.

"Ladies, allow me to say how much we appreciate your patronage. The P and O Line has always taken the utmost good care of our passengers, and I assure you, there is absolutely no cause for alarm about this very minor delay in unloading and, er, locating your property.

I promise you, I shall care for your trunk as if it were my own."

Sally coughed to interrupt him. "Sir, it is absolutely imperative . . ."

"Dear lady, please do not distress yourself. As you can see, I am writing out your confirmation of ownership. We will convey a message to your hotel the *very* minute your trunk is found."

Sally glowered. "We will wait here. It is absolutely . . ."

"I implore you, madam, please be reasonable. Surely you have sufficient changes of clothing for the present time." He gestured toward their impressive array of luggage. Lucienne was perched on one of their larger suitcases, and two porters were standing by, waiting to load everything into a taxi.

Lucienne fanned herself with a folded newspaper and sighed. "We may as well go to our hotel, Sally. I don't think there's any way to speed things up."

Sally turned to her friend with dismay. "But what if . . . I mean, it's essential to take care . . ."

Lucienne stood up and joined Sally at the counter. "I'm sure these good people will take the very best care of our trunk." Discreetly, she placed several folded rupee notes beside the clerk's open ledger. "Of course, the contents are valuable only to us—our books and special mementos—we have all the clothes and jewels we need, here. But we will be *very* grateful to have our trunk located and delivered to us, promptly." She managed to subtly flash an indication of the reward that might be expected. "We will be at the Majestic Hotel for one night only, before we go on to visit our friend the Maharani of Cooch Behar. We trust you will deliver our trunk tonight, or tomorrow morning at the latest."

Porters, tips, taxi, hotel, more porters, more tips. One final tip, to the waiter who delivered a tea tray to their room, and then they were alone.

Their hotel room was comically enormous, with two of everything: immense beds, plush sofas, tall velvet-draped windows, lazily rotating ceiling fans. There were even two bathrooms.

Lucienne drank half a cup of tea, slid out of her travel suit and flung herself onto one of the beds.

"Ow, what is this mattress made of? I've slept in crypts that were more comfy."

"How can you sleep?'

"Not very well, perhaps, but I intend to try. It's after two already; I need some beauty rest before nightfall."

"But, with Natalie's trunk missing . . ." Sally said anxiously. But Lucienne's eyes were closed, and she had begun to (rather adorably) snore.

Despite her distress, Sally eventually slept too. They awoke after dark, put on evening frocks with gauzy wraps and left their room, hot and hungry. It was just as hot outside, where they turned away from hopeful taxi drivers and rickshaw pullers to stroll the odorous streets.

Lucienne inhaled deeply, as the humid air awakened long-forgotten memories.

Sally sniffed, coughed, frowned. "How can it be so hot at night? It's wrong."

Lucienne put a hand on her arm. "Relax. Slow down. Breathe gently. Do you smell it? Jasmine, spices, mangos, excrement: the smells of life. And death . . ." She looked down along the sidewalk, where several whole poor families were sleeping, parents curved like parentheses around small rows of children. One fretful baby was clearly ill.

"Oh dear, poor things. Should we . . .?" Sally was almost dizzy with hunger.

Lucienne shook her head. "Not them; they're probably too weak to spare a drop. Come on."

She led the way toward a brightly lit corner, where well-dressed, overfed tourists were emerging from a festive-looking establishment.

"Say, another of those 'Balloons' and I'd never come down from the ceiling," a tall American was saying to a friend.

Sally salivated at his scent of meat and whiskey. She nodded to Lucienne and they stepped forward. "Might one of you gentlemen have a light?" She gestured gracefully with a Mourad in her amber holder.

"Well! Good evening, ladies." While he patted his pockets, one of his companions stepped forward, silver Dunhill lighter already aflame.

"Here you go, Miss." He had a London accent. "Or is it Mademoiselle?"

Sally batted her eyelashes. "Ah, Monsieur, I am hurt zat you would say zat. My English, she is flawless, *n'est-çe pas?*"

There was good-natured laughter at her comically exaggerated accent, and soon they were all chatting agreeably.

"And what brings you lovely young ladies to Bombay?"

"This is just a stopover," Lucienne explained. "We're traveling on tomorrow to Poonah, to visit our friend, the Maharani of Cooch Behar."

"Oh, I say. She's supposed to be quite modern and a marvelous person. Why don't we all go back inside and have another round of Firpo's Balloons. Ladies, we'd be honored if you'd be our guests and tell us how you met the fabulous Maharani."

Sally and Lucienne exchanged looks and faint shrugs; the gents were clearly in favor of this idea and were already at the restaurant door. The party was greeted with genial welcome as they made their way to a large round table which had not yet been cleared.

"Yes, I know we just left, but we can't stay away!" the tall American told the maitre d'. "We've just met these lovely ladies, and we want to hear their stories. They're friends of the Maharani of . . . Whatsit. Tell your splendid barman we'd like another round of his Balloons."

The cocktails (a powerful concoction of rye, vermouth and absinthe) arrived and were indeed stimulating, especially on an empty stomach. Unbidden, the waiter brought plates of kebabs and bowls of spaghetti in tomato sauce (an exotic specialty of the house), but the food disgusted Sally, particularly the thick tomato sauce —so superficially like, but so far from, what she craved.

Lucienne was regaling their hosts with a hilarious version of their stay with the Maharani at Lucienne's uncle's casino in Cannes (which had actually been deadly serious and far from fun at the time). As she sipped her second Firpo's Balloon, Sally suddenly couldn't stand it anymore.

"The thing is, dear gentlemen—we're vampires, and we're frightfully hungry, and we need to suck some of your blood right now. It won't hurt, and you won't remember a thing. It helps that you are extremely drunk— as am I, or I wouldn't be saying this aloud."

Without further ado, she turned to the man on her left, a quiet Russian diplomat, and bit his neck so carefully that not a drop of blood reached his collar.

"I say, that looks rather exciting. Would you like to do me?" The Englishman loosened his tie slightly and offered his throat to Lucienne.

Their companions roared with laughter, and each took a turn, with Sally drinking from three of them and Lucienne two. Some degree of glamour was in effect, but the vamps were also skillful and discreet enough that the other people in the restaurant only saw the two young women bestowing affectionate but respectable embraces, as if they were taking leave of old friends.

"Thank you so much for the lovely drinks, gentlemen—it has been delightful!" A chorus of jolly farewells followed them as they stepped back out into the warm, fragrant night.

There was no message from the shipping office that night, or the next morning. Lucienne had made the supreme sacrifice of rising before noon in the hope of news, but she reported back to Sally that she could learn nothing from the hotel concierge.

Sally, still in bed in their velvet-curtained room, groaned. "Bless you for trying, Loulou darling. I don't know how you can be so . . . so dressed and . . . functional. Are you not as hung-over as I am? Those chaps —their blood must have been half alcohol!" She pulled herself laboriously upright and rubbed her eyes, smearing last night's mascara.

Lucienne kicked her shoes off and sank into an armchair., smoothing the skirt of her smart day dress. "Good old wrinkle-free pebble crepe. I don't feel nearly as crisp as I look. But I recommend a cool shower-bath. You're right, that was an excessively *rich* meal." There was a knock at the door. "Put on a peignoir darling; I've ordered coffee. When you're up to it, we can go back to that ridiculous office."

The clerks—there were two of them now—and their manager were, by turns, faultlessly courteous, deferential, sympathetic, avuncular, occasionally patronizing. It was suggested that the superbly skillful local tailors could surely replace the young ladies' entire wardrobe, in almost no time and for very little money. The office manager would be happy to make the arrangements; his cousin, in fact, owned a first-class tailoring establishment. Undoubtedly, they could reproduce the latest European modes—or perhaps, the lovely ladies would enjoy dressing in the Indian manner for a change.

"You don't understand," Sally burst out in exasperation. "We have all the clothes we need, but our trunk is of vital importance. Personal importance. Importance only to us, but . . . so important."

The portly manager frowned and adjusted his glasses. "Perhaps if you could give us a description of the contents. Just in case there has been any opening or tampering . . . although we are most strictly on guard against any sort of theft or interference."

Lucienne directed her most severe look at him, one she had learned from her uncle. "As I said yesterday, our trunk contains personal effects—books, papers and mementos of value only to ourselves." She leaned closer and continued softly. "I know I can rely on your discretion if I mention that matters of national security are involved . . . top secret intelligence . . . the French consulate could be severely embarrassed . . . Any mishandling

of this affair could have the most unfortunate conse-
quences. Please take another look now. We will wait."

Hushed and anxious words were exchanged, and the
two clerk disappeared through two different doors; the
manager picked up a telephone and was soon speaking
rapidly and scribbling notes. Lucienne sat on a hard
chair, her eyes closed, while Sally paced.

"We are doing our very utmost to resolve this unfortunate situation." Lucienne's mimicry was dead-on, her
tone utterly weary, as the taxi took them back to their
hotel.

"We'll have to wire the Maharani. And, if we have to
stay much longer, we may have to move to a cheaper
hotel."

Lucienne nodded. "Indira would wire us money in a
heartbeat, but we can't let her do that. Oh, I'm too exhausted to think. Naps first." She closed her eyes.

"Loulou, wake up darling, it's almost midnight." Lucienne struggled up from sleep, blinking, composing her
face.

One soft-shaded lamp was lit, and Sally sat beside
her, fully dressed in a dark blouse and a pair of billowy,
black silk trousers she'd had made in Cairo. She held
out a flask.

"Here you go, love. Drink up."

Lucienne sniffed the fresh iron tang and took a long gulp. "You've been busy. Where'd you find this?"

"I went scouting round the kitchens. They were slaughtering a sheep and, er, some chickens. They told me it's 'halal'--something to do with Muslims—and they have to let the animal bleed out. They were happy not to have it go to waste. Have as much as you want; I filled both our flasks."

Lucienne drank some more. "I'm not a big fan of chicken usually, but it's not bad."

"Good. I wanted us to be well-nourished and not have to spend time hunting. As soon as you've had enough, get dressed and let's go."

"Go where?"

"That damned shipping office, of course. We're going to break into that go-down."

There were several impressive-looking locks on the door, but Lucienne was good with locks.

"Just think, I almost told you to take that brooch off," Sally said, as Lucienne used the pin on the last of the tumblers and returned the diamanté arrow to her lapel.

Lucienne said nothing, listening intently and feeling for additional hidden catches or an alarm of some kind. Finally satisfied, she eased the door gently inward into absolute darkness. The air was cool and slightly musty, but dry.

They moved slowly inside, pulling the door almost shut, but with a piece of paper wedged into the latch so they wouldn't be trapped. A few feet in, they stopped, waiting for their eyes to adjust.

"Bloody hell, I can't see a thing," Sally whispered. "I thought we were supposed to have perfect night vision."

"Close your eyes for a moment. Breathe deep, smell and feel the air. If our trunk is here, we should be able to sense it, and feel Natalie."

Sally closed her eyes and took deep breaths. When she opened them again, she could see shapes, if not details. "You're amazing, Loulou—how do you . . .?"

"Shh. Let's go this way."

They followed a narrow walkway between stacks of stored, lost and abandoned goods: crates, bales, boxes, bundles. They smelled sandalwood and spices, and crossed a sticky river of treacle leaking from an ancient-looking barrel. Elderly valises had burst open where their straps had rotted. They sensed, rather than saw, the occasional scurry of rats in their peripheral vision.

"I don't know why they don't have a couple of cats in here," Lucienne said, and then stopped. "We're close; I can smell it."

They both began to feel the objects nearby, hands seeking the brass-bound corners of their trunk.

"What *is* all this, it's so slippery," Sally said. "I'm going to strike a light."

"All right, just for a moment. Be careful, we don't want to set the place on fire."

Sally pulled out her faithful, beautiful Cartier lighter and looked around, eyes widening as the flame rose.

They both memorized the scene in the few seconds before she shut it.

"Yes! Here's the edge. Here's the top. I can see the label from Shepheard's Hotel!"

"Did you see those doors? We're quite near to where the clerks came in from the office."

"Those idiots! How could they not see it? Or do you think they wanted more bribes out of us?"

"No, look—this enormous stack of movie posters collapsed all over it—that's what was so slippery—only a little bit of the trunk was showing."

"You're right. They were probably too distracted by this Bollywood starlet's heaving bosom to see what was behind it."

It took several minutes to uncover the trunk. Sally flung her arms around it and hugged the sturdy shape. Lucienne almost fell, skidding on one of the slick, glossy posters—which gave them an idea. Lucienne took a sheaf of the posters and laid a trail, which allowed the trunk, tipped up on one edge, to slide while Sally pushed. It was cumbersome and slow, but they were making gradual progress toward the door when Lucienne screamed—suddenly enveloped in leathery bat wings.

Sally dropped the trunk and rushed forward. She still could hardly see, but a figure as tall as she was had hold of Lucienne. Sally beat fiercely at its back, and it turned on her with a hideous snarl.

The creature's breath was rasping, hot and foul. It was immensely strong, pinning her arms behind her as it bent its mouth toward her neck.

"Hey! What the hell are you doing? I'm a vampire!" Sally yelled as her fangs came out. She managed a quick slash at her attacker's arm.

The creature jumped back with a surprised shriek, and Lucienne, now fanged as well, growled at it.

With her hands free, Sally took out her lighter, and the creature cowered away from the flame. In the illumination, they saw a rather fine-featured, human-like face, with a full beard. His fangs were retracting, and the large batlike wings that grew from his shoulders fell back and folded behind him. He was bare-chested and barefoot, slightly furry, and covered from waist to knees by a traditional Indian dhoti.

He now put his palms together in what they had learned was the 'namaste' gesture, and then gracefully sat down, cross-legged, patting the floor to indicate they should join him. His eyes, however, continued to stare at the lighter flame with a look of alarm, and he was clearly relieved when Sally put it away. She was not entirely convinced by the creature's show of harmlessness, nor was Lucienne.

"You! You stay there. We will go. Do not follow, or we will hurt you," Sally commanded, still fanged.

"But please, memsahibs—I would so much like to speak with you. Never do I have occasion to meet any-one, except the few *goondas* who try to steal goods here.

Never have I met any of our own kind. I entreat you, just stay and talk for a little while."

Sally considered. "Are you trying to trick us? You should know, we are not stealing. This trunk is our property; those idiots in the shipping office thought it was lost."

"Absolutely understood, memsahibs. I just ask for, oh, a quarter-hour of your company. And then I will help you carry your trunk."

Even in the dark, Sally felt she could see Lucienne's expression, and she knew what it would wordlessly convey: '*We can take him if we have to—isn't it worth it if he'll wrangle that monstrous trunk?*'

"All right, we'll stay and talk for a bit." Sally eased down into a crouch, ready to spring up and run if need be; Lucienne remained standing. "Tell us about yourself. How old are you? How long have you been here in this . . . ?"

"In this go-down, I have been for more than twenty years. Once, I used to roam free in the city, but a vampire-hunter trapped me and made me take this job, as the bargain for letting me live."

"What? Why can't you just leave, if you want to?"

"At every threshold, there is a subterranean rivulet of sacred water from Holy Mother Ganges, which I may not cross . . . or so he told me . . ." His voice trailed off, and they could almost hear his thoughts before he spoke. "Memsahibs, vampire sisters—how then can you be here? Nothing prevented you coming in?"

"Only some fairly flimsy locks. By the way, I'm Lucienne, and my friend is Sally. We ought to know your name if we're going to sit here sharing confidences in the dark."

"Of course, mem . . . Lucienne and Sally. My name is Ragesh Lal—Lal means, in English, 'red.' You are English?"

"Sally is French, although her English is very good; I am originally from Indochine, in east Asia, although I have lived in France for many years."

Ragesh courteously switched to French for a while—he was relatively fluent—and they traded life histories. He had grown up and been turned in the early days of the East India Company, so he had never known a time when the British were not a presence in India. He had, in fact, spent his youth targeting foreigners exclusively, as his small gesture toward an independent country free of imperial domination.

"The hunter who captured you—was he British?" Sally asked.

"No, but he might as well have been—he was a government office-wallah, a bureaucrat. One of those who *believes* the British crown actually civilized our country—Mother India, so much older, wiser and richer than the British Raj! But . . ." his shrug was somehow audible, "I cannot complain. I have job security, civil service ranking, all the rats I can eat. And the occasional *goonda*." Ragesh sighed.

Sally pulled out her flask and passed it to him. "Here, my friend, have some of this. We weren't meant for a steady diet of rats' blood. And I'm guessing it's been a while since your last goonda."

Ragesh took a deep drink and smacked his lips. "Oh goodness, how delicious! Is that chicken blood I taste?"

Lucienne laughed. "*Chacun à son gout.* Come on then, we should be going. Ragesh, can you help Sally slide the trunk?"

"No need, it is not heavy for me." As he lifted it easily to his shoulder, they heard a sniff. "But what is in this trunk—or rather, who?"

So they told him, as they made their way steadily toward the door, about Natalie: her long life, her depression and weariness, her wish to die, how dear she was to them, the ritual of the Long Sleep. And how they had been conveying her, in her trunk, on their journey as they searched for a new place to call home.

They reached the outer door, and Lucienne pulled it gently open.

Ragesh gasped. "The threshold—water running, underground . . ."

Lucienne stepped across it without hesitation. "Do you know what the city of Paris is like? Running water everywhere, a city of bridges. We've decided a lot of those old tales are just . . . tales."

"Like garlic," Sally said. "If it were really fatal to us, a French vamp wouldn't last an hour." She stepped out into the humid open air. "Do you want to try it? Or, you can just slide the trunk out. I'm sure we can get it to the corner and find a taxi."

"Garlic," Ragesh mused. "Garlic makes things delicious. Do they really say we can't abide it? Well, in for a penny, in for a pound," he quoted in English. "Anyway, what kind of life is it, stuck in this go-down? Of course, there is the security . . . still, I think I should find out." Hefting the trunk, he took a long step across the threshold and kept going. "Ha! I am not struck dead, am I, ladies? I suppose the man who told me that might well be dead himself by now. What a fool I've been. Still, it wasn't altogether a bad place, for a while. But now, meeting you, knowing how much is possible—I feel reborn! Which way are we going?" He was still taking long steps, holding the heavy trunk as easily as if it were an armful of twigs.

They directed him and headed toward the Majestic. Lucienne and Sally fell back, as Ragesh moved quickly ahead.

"Do you think we've done the right thing?" Sally said quietly. "Perhaps he was better off where he was."

"He can always go back there—but no, I don't think being trapped against his will is any sort of life for a vamp. I just hope it won't be awkward when we reach the hotel—what if he thinks he's going to be our traveling companion now?"

There were no difficulties, however. Despite it being four in the morning, a bellman met them at the hotel entrance and loaded the trunk onto a cart, nodding brusquely to their 'porter.'

"Ragesh, please take this," Sally handed him her flask. "And thank you so much for your help tonight."

"It is I who must thank you, dear ladies. You have truly opened my eyes. Knowing that we—our kind—can live free lives, travel, especially that we can have friendships with others of our kind—this is a revelation to me."

"It's been remarkable for us, too, meeting you," Lucienne said. "We will always remember you . . ."

"Forgive me, memsahibs, but I think I should go now." The bellman hovered a short distance away, waiting for their instructions. "I must go and discover my own new way of life, and perhaps a friend or two. And . . ." In the light spilling from the lobby, he regarded their clothes, and the bellman's smart uniform; "I think I need to find a tailor."

Poonah - Paris - Hyderabad - Pondicherry - Poonah, April 1933 - January 1935

"Darlings, I am so happy to see you!" the maharani exclaimed. "We will have a wonderful time together, isn't it?" Indira opened her arms wide and hugged Sally and Lucienne, in turn, to her amethyst-chiffon-clad bosom.

"Maharani—Indira—we can't thank you enough for inviting us," Sally said. "Here is a little present from Egypt." She held out a tiny alabaster sphinx.

"Oh yes, I love it." Indira closed her palm around the statuette with childlike greed. "You must stay as long as you like. Benevenuto will be so glad to see you," she added, referring to her pet miniature tortoise. Looking deep into Lucienne's eyes, she spoke directly to her mind, about their last meeting years ago: 'Benevenuto and I will never forgive you if you *ever* try tricking us again.' Her large, kohl-rimmed eyes stared implacably, with depths of cloudy amber. The *bindi* spot, marking her third eye, might have winked.

'Of course, maharani. I am absolutely in your debt,' Lucienne's eyes replied.

"Now," Indira went on gaily, aloud, "How about some delicious cocktails?"

It was not until the next day that they met the maharani's cousin and secretary, Princess Annie Mahendra, a pert young aviatrix who rarely wore anything but crisp shirts and jodhpurs.

"Indira's told me a bit about you—she said you are beautiful and clever. Do you want to learn to fly?"

"Yes, that would be terrific," Sally said, at the same moment that Lucienne was answering, "Absolutely not."

Annie laughed and nudged Sally. "I see your partner is not as adventurous as you."

Sally bristled. "Lucienne has had adventures you can't even imagine; she's also very sensible. And we're not 'partners,' just friends."

"Really? You seem extremely close. Aren't you Sapphists? I am. Cousin Indira warned me to watch out for you, so naturally I assumed . . ."

Lucienne was busy lighting a Russian cigarette in her jade holder; she fitted one into Sally's amber holder (she'd been carrying both in her bag) and handed it to her.

"Light, darling?" she asked mischievously.

Miss Mahendra eyed them quizzically, eyebrows arched below her gamine-cropped hair. "You could, at least, offer me one." She helped herself to Lucienne's case, pulled a lighter from her own pocket and lit up, holding the flame out for Sally.

"Would you like a holder?" Lucienne asked, producing a choice of ivory or silver from her bag.

"No, thanks." Annie exhaled. "A rather old-fashioned affectation, if you ask me. I mean, it's something I associate with cousin Indira, women her age."

Lucienne blew a languid smoke ring. "Oh dear. We've become the older generation."

The princess had the good grace to look abashed. "Forgive me, I've had a sheltered upbringing, and my manners aren't all that they should be. I'm only eighteen, so I'm used to everyone being older than me. But you're not old at all, are you? Perhaps 21 or 22?"

Lucienne smiled. "Close enough. Anyway, tell us more about flying, and whatever else you do for fun around here."

"Fun . . . well, there are movies, and the race track—I don't go in for that much—and there are always dances. But the young men are a sad lot, and I don't dare dance with my girlfriend here. I mean, we might bounce around to a hot tune for a bit, but nothing serious. Oh, I can't wait til I can move to England and lead a free, bohemian life. But only for a few years, while I'm young; I know my real work is here."

"And what is your real work?" Sally tried hard not to sound patronizing, but the princess was so very young and so earnest.

"Oh, nothing I'd expect you silk-frocked sybarites to understand."

"Is it the advancement of your people? Are you a socialist?" Lucienne asked.

"Yes, in fact, I am. And proud of it. Women in this country, in particular . . ." Annie trailed off, seeming close to tears. "I intend to go into politics," she finished, with a defiant lift of her chin.

"Good for you. I'm sure you'll do heaps of good things," Sally said. "Would you like another cigarette? And tell me more about flying; I really would love to go up."

Annie accepted a cigarette and a light and looked her guests over carefully. "You must be thirsty, I'll ring for some tea. And forgive me if I've been abrasive; as I said, my manners aren't all they could be. I must say, you're not nearly as bourgeoise as you look."

"Well, thank you," Sally said. "Personally, I try not to judge people by their appearance—although it can be hard not to. For instance, I adore jodhpurs—such a smart look—and that makes me inclined to like you a great deal. Do you know," she confided, "I once spent most of a month wearing men's clothes all the time. In Berlin. It was most interesting." She winked.

Far from being charmed and intrigued, Annie frowned. "Berlin? Isn't it rather horrible there?"

"Oh, but this was . . ." Sally was about to say 'years ago, before Hitler was on the scene,' but realized she couldn't. She coughed and Lucienne came to her rescue.

"Sally darling, you're impossible with names! It wasn't Berlin, it was Brussels."

Leafy, dark-green squares of mango orchards, and the lighter green of rice fields made an irregular checkerboard below, broken by the occasional irruptions of brown and white villages. Above (Sally hardly dared look), the sky was blazingly clear, while the horizon was rimmed with a fringe of brownish dust.

"Better now?" Annie looked over with a sly smile and passed Sally a thermos of tepid tea. Sally nodded, abashed. Two hundred years of life and varied experience had not prepared her for the phenomenon of aeronautic lift-off, and she had screamed uncontrollably as the Belanca monoplane angled up—impossibly!—into the air.

Annie grinned again as Sally handed the thermos back. "I don't usually get screams until I'm landing. I'll try to bring us down gently, I promise. But anyway, what do you think? Isn't it amazing? Would you like a turn at the controls?"

As if to emphasize what she meant, she executed a slight dip and waggled the wings. Sally went pale.

"Thank you, no. I mean yes, it's amazing. You . . . keep on doing what you do. A gentle landing would be most appreciated."

"Smart, sophisticated and worldly—and a big baby about flying," Annie scoffed. "Come on, I want you to try it. You can drive, can't you?"

"Actually . . . no." In a flash of memory, Sally reviewed her life as a passenger: horse carriages, trains, ships, taxis. She hadn't been an equestrienne before turning, and knew that horses wouldn't take to her now. The thought of being in the driver's seat had really never occurred to her. "I suppose I'm not such a modern woman after all."

"I find that hard to believe. You *do* think we should have the vote, don't you? Oh no, really??" she reacted to Sally's silence. "You're not anti-suffrage?"

"No, of course not," Sally said, a bit bemused. "I've just never thought about it a great deal. I mean . . . politics doesn't seem all that important when you've lived . . ." About to say, 'as long as I have,' she finished lamely, "in a lot of different places."

Annie looked at her curiously. "I thought you lived in France, until you took this trip here. I must say, for a so-called enlightened country, they're remarkably backward in women's rights."

Before Sally could reply, the plane jolted, buffeted by a strong gust. "Hang on, we're in a rough patch. Don't worry, this happens all the time." Annie turned her attention to the controls, and the fuselage soon stabilized. Below them, a green-brown river divided one field from another. Tiny toy bullock carts followed a track alongside.

"Okay, we're absolutely fine now. I want you to look in front of you, and put both hands on the yoke, like this."

"Oh no, I can't possibly," Sally demurred.

"I just want you to try it. We've got dual controls, and I'm right here. I won't let you do anything too bad."

"*Too* bad—how reassuring," Sally muttered, but she took hold of the control.

"Move it slowly toward you . . . gently. Not *that* gently, a little harder."

The nose of the plane rose, and Sally gasped.

"Keep going, keep going . . . okay, now let the stick go back to the center."

The plane climbed and then leveled out. Sally gripped the joystick tightly, her knuckles sharp in her thin kid glove.

"Relax. That was beautiful, wasn't it?"

Sally slowly loosened her grip and looked over at Annie, her eyes shining. "Amazing!" she breathed. "I can see why you love it."

"Isn't it! Go on for a while; I can use the break."

I'm flying!' Sally thought, fizzing inside. The sensation was completely new, completely thrilling. Surrounded by wide brilliant sky, she was aware of the earth below and of their comfortable distance from it. Sunlight glinted on the left-hand wing, beyond Annie's crisp profile.

"This is divine, I could go on forever—but I supposed the fuel isn't infinite."

"True. We should head back now, and then start our descent. Help me turn her around."

Following Annie's calm, simple instructions, Sally brought the plane around to the left until their heading was correct. Presently, the big white mansion, with its extensive lands and outbuildings, came into view. But when Annie told her to move the joystick forward to head down, she flatly refused.

"Silly. Are you afraid you'd do something like this?" Annie moved abruptly, and suddenly their nose was down, diving earthward.

Sally shrieked and pulled at her controls. Annie let go of hers, and laughed as they continued dropping, until finally the throttle took hold and they leveled out.

"Beautiful! I hoped you'd know enough to do that. You see, you're a natural pilot. But I'll take it from here." With a show of nonchalance, but with complete focus and skill, Annie flew them in a gradual descent to the landing field.

Sally, pale and shaking, did not scream this time—she kept her eyes tightly closed until she felt the bump of the wheels against the packed earth. As they stopped, just before the ground crew came running up, Annie clambered out of her seat, grabbed Sally and kissed her hard on the lips. "I knew you could do it!"

Sally pulled away and stared at her. "You are a madwoman! But thanks for not killing us." She kissed her back.

"Annie, why does your plane have dual controls?" Sally asked as they walked back to the palace.

"Some do, some don't. It's good for teaching, of course, and also valuable in emergencies, if the pilot should become incapacitated. But I have them for one main reason—so that, when I meet the love of my life, we can fly together."

"Off in that flying machine again? You know, you may be immortal, but you're not indestructible. I really don't want to have to collect little bits of you from some valley if you crash." Lucienne was carefully outlining her eyes with kohl while she spoke, turned completely away from Sally, as if she'd observed her jodhpurs, leather jacket and long scarf with eyes at the back of her head.

"I *am* off flying, and I have every confidence in Annie's skill. I'm even learning a bit myself—can you believe it? It's the most amazing feeling, Loulou. I wish you'd try it, at least once." She sighed. "No, I know—no. What do you have on for today—playing cards with the Maharani? Careful, I've heard she cheats."

Lucienne's chair scraped, and she turned to give Sally a ferocious glare.

"Sorry, darling, I'm joking!"

"Indira is a very fascinating woman, and I have much to learn from her," Lucienne said gravely. "And, I have to say, those jodhpurs look perfect on you."

"They have amazing tailors here, don't they?"

"Have a safe flight, darling. I'll see you at cocktail time."

Lunch began with Negronis and fish paste canapés, followed by a lamb and spinach curry served on Sevres porcelain. Lucienne had learned to eat with two dainty fingers of her right hand—it made it easier, actually, to ingest the tiny portion which was all she could manage.

Indira smiled at her across the table. "Don't you feel that food eaten with a fork has a metal taste? I use silverware in Europe, of course, but this is so much nicer, isn't it?"

"I quite agree. Forks are so . . . aggressive. I much prefer chopsticks or fingers. Thank you for inviting me to join you."

"Of course, my dear. But don't feel you need to eat, if it is not comfortable for you. I know you nourish yourself in other ways. I trust you've found suitable accommodations."

"Yes, thank you. Your cook has been so kind. Maharani, I would like to ask . . . please tell me if this is out of line, but . . . can you tell me more about the Old Magic?"

Indira took a long sip of her drink, gazing at Lucienne with widened eyes. She sighed. "What would you like to know?"

Lucienne looked down, twisting her pink linen napkin. "Well . . . can I tell you about my friend Natalie?"

The butler had brought another shaker of Negronis, and they'd each refilled their glasses at least twice before Lucienne finished her story.

Natalie had been a very old vampire, having lived over four centuries, with a troubled history, surviving wars, famines and a host of violent and desperate times. Toward the end of 1929, she'd grown unutterably weary and depressed, and had tried to end her life by starving herself. Sally and Lucienne had persuaded her to stay with them, at least until the end of the season, and Lucienne had come up with a plan. From researching in her Uncle Yu's papers, she'd come upon the concept of the Long Sleep. By performing a ritual, detailed in Yu's library, she had—she hoped—put Natalie into a deep sleep that would last at least thirty years, giving Natalie the chance to rest and recover enough strength and optimism to go on.

"But . . . I have no way of knowing if I did everything correctly, if it will really work. So far, we've checked a few times, and Natalie's body seems undecayed. But will she wake again, when the time comes? Will she . . . be herself? I can't tell Sally, but I'm so frightened that something could go wrong. Is there anything you've ever seen or heard of that's at all like that? Is the Long Sleep even a real thing?"

Bemused, Indira shook her head and placed a cigarette in her long silver holder.

"No!?" Lucienne went pale. "You shook your head, 'No.' You mean, there is no such thing?"

Indira lit her cigarette and gave Lucienne a long look, with a faint smile. "Oh my dear young friend. No, I do not mean to discourage you. Your Natalie will, most likely, be fine. I only meant . . . thirty years is nothing, really. Four hundred years, even, is not long. Not to some of us."

She picked up her glass, regarding its emptiness with surprise. With a blink of her huge eyes, it was again filled with ruddy, aromatic Campari and gin. "You see . . . in the beginning . . ."

And she began to tell a tale of gods and goddesses, the birth of the world, the clouds and the moon, millennia of memories. Lucienne, lost in her words, tossed in the sea of time, drifted in and out. Until the sharp herbal scent of her cocktail brought her back once more to this room, and this formidable woman, speaking of the magical card game she had won.

"So, you see, when it came down to it, Yu didn't stand a chance. And neither did *you*," she quipped with a wink at Lucienne. "But I'm glad I intervened on your behalf. Liu Yu isn't an evil entity, not really—but he is very rigid in his ways, something of a bore, actually. Whereas you are a bright spirit, adding sparkle to the world wherever you go. And I believe you will go far—around this world, and perhaps further yet."

Sally and Lucienne came downstairs to find the morning room in a quiet uproar. The maharani sat facing her housekeeper, who looked far from pleased.

"Always your highness's wish is my duty, but . . . so many persons? And at such short notice? How am I to get sufficient rooms ready?"

"Do you not understand the nature of *emergency*, Lakhshmi? This is a matter of life and death. Believe me, they will be grateful to be here; they will not fuss about their rooms. Put them all in the blue suite in the east corner."

"But . . . three men and four women . . . they cannot . . ."

"They are a family. They can share a room; their ways are not the same as ours. Nor are they British, so you can just put your anti-imperial feelings aside."

They met the new arrivals at dinner. Professor Benjamin Bloomstein was a philologist, who had gotten to know the maharani decades ago, in the course of his research. She had once invited him and his wife, Sophia, to visit her in Cooch Behar.

"But that was in our previous life, before the children. It must have been thirty years ago," Sophia said. She was a handsome woman, as round as her husband was angular. "I remember it like yesterday—a beautiful place."

The Bloomsteins spoke English fluently, though with a strong accent.

"I'm sure we will find it beautiful here, too." The professor patted his wife's hand. "And even if it were not beautiful, we would be grateful to be here with you, our kind friend. Away from the evil that is brewing in our country."

"Evil?" Sally raised her head from her soup bowl. "What do you mean, is it . . . politics?"

Professor Bloomstein stiffened a bit and, beside him, his elderly mother seemed to mutter something under her breath. "Politics, yes, you could say that. Like most of the world, you are not aware of the vile and stupid things that have been happening in our formerly intelligent and cultured Germany. Even in lovely Berlin itself."

"Berlin!" Sally couldn't help feeling excitement at the mention of the city, where she'd had some extraordinary adventures.

"You know Berlin?"

"Oh, yes." Sally's eyes shone. "A bit, anyway. I was there, hmm, about four years ago—I was quite young, of course—but it had the most wonderful feeling. So vibrant and tolerant, the *Berliner lüft*."

Across the table, the Bloomsteins' daughter, Lotte, looked at Sally sharply. She was about twenty; judging by appearances, Lucienne and Sally were her approximate contemporaries. She smiled now.

"You must have been quite precocious, or less strictly watched than I was, to be able to enjoy vibrancy and tolerance, and *Berliner lüft*, our famous, magical atmosphere. It's quite annoying—I'll never see those notorious cabarets, now that I'm finally old enough to go. But it's all changing, anyway."

"You must forgive us," Lucienne said now. "We've been traveling, and not really keeping up with the news. But what is this 'evil' you spoke of?"

"Ach, it is not a nice topic for the dinner table," the professor said. "We will talk of it another time."

"Of course, another time—so we don't all spoil our digestion. But you should at least know, for now, that my father was forced to leave his post at the University of Frankfurt, where he has worked with honor and distinction for over thirty years. And that I was expelled from the military academy, despite my exemplary record. For no other reason than because we are Jews. I call that evil." Aaron Bloomstein pushed back his chair, threw his napkin on the table and left the room. his mother's eyes followed him anxiously, while the professor turned to their hostess.

"My deepest apologies, Maharani. I have not raised my son to be so rude. It will not happen again."

"Oh, please do not distress yourself. He has every reason to be upset."

Over coffee, while Lucienne found herself deep in conversation with Professor Bloomstein about Oriental languages, Sally and Lotte stepped out into the gardens.

"Thank you," Lotte said, accepting a Mourad and a light from Sally. "Mama doesn't approve, so I don't indulge often."

The conversation was not restful for Sally, having to be constantly aware of the limits of a twenty-some-year existence. Skirting education ("No, I haven't been to university. But I had some rather good tutors when I was younger."), she tried to steer the talk to the easier topics of fashion and make-up trends.

"Oh, I've never been encouraged to think too much about clothes . . . but I do admire the French sense of chic. It's as if you're *born* sophisticated; you seem so much older. In a good way, I mean." She coughed to cover her sense of awkwardness. "Have you and your friend—Lucienne?—had many adventures on your trip?"

"Well, there was the Italian boy in Cairo who robbed a bank to buy me sapphires," Sally said, exaggerating only slightly. "So, you could say that."

As they both laughed, there was a crunch of gravel and Aaron came around the corner, glowering. "Surely nothing's *that* funny," he said with a scowl. "We're safe for the moment, but don't get too comfortable, Lottzl. It's just a matter of time."

"What is?" Sally asked.

He looked at her with annoyance. "Nothing to concern you. Worldwide persecution of Jews. And probably a worldwide war."

Sally started. "That's what my grandmother predicted, years ago."

"Your grandmother was a Jew?" Aaron looked at her with a flicker of interest.

"No—a very wise, very old French lady. She had the second sight."

He sniffed dismissively and turned to frown at Lotte's cigarette. "You should come in soon. Mama wants us to go up to our room."

"Wait." Sally put a hand on his arm. "I'm sorry if I've offended you in any way. And I'm sorry for what your family is going through. Believe it or not, I've known what it is to be persecuted, an outsider."

"Hmph. Come on Lotte, time to go."

Sharp features, intense dark eyes—so attractive, Sally thought, watching him walk away. *I wonder what he tastes like.*

"No flying today?" Lucienne asked, watching Sally put on a day dress rather than jodhpurs.

"Probably not for the rest of the month. Annie's busy with her classes. Let's see if we can go somewhere with Lotte—and her annoying but attractive brother. I think there's a tea dance at one of those clubs."

"You really like them? I mean, they're perfectly nice, but don't you find it difficult to talk to such young people? Annie's different somehow; she must be an old soul, as they say. But those two . . . I'd rather spend time with the professor. He's quite brilliant, and his wife is too."

"Oh, for heaven's sake, granny! All right, you stay home and drink tea with the old folks. I want to go dancing."

"Fine, I'll come. I wish we had another young man to bring."

"Don't worry, I'll share Aaron with you."

"That young man is altogether *too* attractive," Sally said glumly, as she sat between Lucienne and Lotte, a row of pretty wallflowers in their bright gauzy dresses.

"Yes, the English girls are all over him, aren't they? Even with his big nose and sticking-out ears—I'm amazed."

"You're his sister, so you don't see it," Lucienne noted. "But he's got those dark good looks, rather like the Indian men they're not allowed to even think about. A whiff of the exotic, but everyone knows he's European, so it's all right."

"That doesn't explain why we're being ignored. Aren't *we* exotic and European too? And guests of the ma-harani." Sally pouted. "Just too many girls here. Lotte, dance with me; I'm petrifying here."

"All right, let's."

Just as they moved into the flow of the dance floor, Aaron bee-lined for where they'd been sitting. "Oy, Gott . . ." he groaned, sitting heavily, hands over his eyes.

"Do you have a headache?" Lucienne asked in German.

"Splitting—from the inane chatter of these young idiots. Can we leave?"

"The car doesn't come for us for another hour; we'll have to tough it out." She gestured discreetly to where a cluster of young women were whispering, giggling and pointing in their direction. "They're going to keep coming after you. I think you'd better dance with me. We won't talk; it will be restful."

"All right—though I don't mind talking with you. How did you learn German?" They glided into a waltz.

"Oh, I just picked up a bit here and there; I don't know much, really. Here, I have an idea." She leaned on his shoulder, nuzzling comfortably into his neck. "There, now the English girls should stop bothering you."

"It was when that vampire nonsense started up again that I knew we had to leave."

Lucienne, passing the doorway to the drawing room, froze in her tracks, wondering what Professor Bloomstein could be talking about.

The maharani sighed in commiseration. "People can be so ignorant. It's truly disgusting. Ah, Lucienne, join us." Not surprisingly, Indira seemed aware of Lucienne's presence without even looking toward the doorway.

"Good afternoon, Maharani, Professor. Excuse me—*what* were you saying about vampires?" She'd already decided there was nothing suspicious in the question; anyone would have been intrigued.

"Ach, only the language of anti-semitism: the Jews are vampires, draining the life-blood of society. Vampires!

The age-old blood slander all over again—you know, what they say about our rituals. So, we drink wine! As if they cannot imagine such a thing, so they say it must be blood. It's as if someone were to see you drinking a cocktail, red with grenadine, and said, 'That young woman is a vampire.'" He smiled and patted her hand. "Begging your pardon, my dear. But when the words reach a certain level of viciousness, it is safest to assume that actions may follow. And once I was forbidden to hold my position . . . the country of my birth is no longer my home. I will find a new career here; I am making inquiries at the university."

"Excellent, my dear Benjamin. I shall use whatever influence I can." Indira gazed at him so fondly that Lucienne wondered if there was—or had ever been—a more than intellectual relationship between them. "Meanwhile," the maharani continued, "I am more than delighted to have your family stay here, as long as you like. And how nice for the young people to have each other for company, isn't it, Lucienne?"

"Absolutely," Lucienne nodded. "We all went to the tea dance at the Poonah Club today. Aaron and Lotte made quite a splash in local society."

"Ah yes, the young English people are starved for novelty. I'm sure they ate you all up." The maharani winked at Lucienne quite openly. "And speaking of you young people—Annie will be here tomorrow. She has a week's mid-term break. My grand-niece," she said to the professor. "She's a sapphic aviatrix, a very fine young woman.

So, your children will have plenty of congenial company. Now we just need an occupation for your Sophia, while you and I talk of philology and horrible politics."

"Sophy has her sketchpad out and has spent the morning in your beautiful gardens. Truly, Maharani, I cannot tell you how grateful we are to be here."

"Well," Indira considered, "everyone has to be somewhere. You are meant to be here, at the moment. Do not feel burdened by gratitude, my dear friend. I have no doubt that good things will come of this. Will you both excuse me now for a bit—I have to have a word with my housekeeper. Lucienne, my dear, help yourself to some tea or a cocktail. Perhaps with grenadine." She winked again.

When Indira had left, Lucienne turned to Professor Bloomstein. "May I ask you something, Professor?"

"Certainly, Miss Leung—if you will also let me ask you how many languages you speak, and how you come to know them so well? You seem to me quite unusually gifted."

"You are too kind. I don't really think I am so unusual. I was raised in a household where almost everyone, except the servants, spoke Vietnamese, Chinese and French. So I needed to sort out those sounds from an early age. After that, I traveled quite a bit, and picked up, really, just a smattering wherever I've gone."

"But it is remarkable, because you are so young, and yet your quality of thought . . .Lotte tells me that you and your friend worked as models in Paris, so . . . you've had no formal higher education? I suppose your family thought it unnecessary for a girl—such a waste! But tell me . . ."

Lucienne began blinking rapidly, looking intently into the professor's eyes. He was becoming dangerously inquisitive.

"Professor, listen to me. I'm going to tell you things you won't remember. I'm a vampire, and I'm almost a hundred years old, so I've learned a thing or two, including several languages. But that's not important. I need to ask you about the origin of some words I once used in a ritual. I want to know their meaning and pronunciation, whether I used them correctly. It's very important, a matter of life and death . . ."

The professor sat completely motionless, almost paralyzed. "*Leben und tod*. What . . . were the words?" he said slowly, his voice low and hollow.

"Benjamin? What are you doing? Miss Leung?" Sophia Bloomstein entered the room, staring.

"Frau Bloomstein!" Lucienne sprang up, aware that she and the professor had been leaning very close together. "How lovely to see you! Herr Professor was just helping me with my pronunciation of a word, *leben*. He was looking closely to see the position of my tongue . . ." She trailed off, realizing this explanation was unlikely to please the professor's wife, who was narrowing her eyes in suspicion.

"*Sleep now, both of you.*" Lucienne spoke directly to their minds, something she had only done rarely and never to mortals. They were both gazing at her, wide-eyed with incomprehension, and Lucienne felt a rising panic, but she kept her inner voice—a voice that transcended language—calm. "*Sleep for ten minutes, and forget. Sit, Sophia, here next to Benjamin.*" Obediently, the woman sat. "*Forget everything I said, forget I was here.*"

She hurried out of the room as the couple leaned comfortably into each other, as if suddenly taken by the need for a mid-afternoon doze.

Sally dressed carefully in jodhpurs and a crisp shirt and tie, unexpectedly excited to be seeing Annie again. Lucienne, she noticed, also seemed especially attentive to her toilette.

"Where did you get that, Loulou?" Lucienne was pinning a small silver brooch in the shape of an aeroplane to her lapel.

"I spotted it in the bazaar yesterday—isn't it sweet? I thought it would amuse Annie; I'll give it to her if she likes it. I admit, I've grown quite fond of her too. Ready? Let's go down."

As usual, they arrived in the dining room toward the very end of breakfast (even though the meal was served relatively late in the maharani's household), and they found Annie and Lotte draining the last of the coffee pot as they sat, heads close together over a notebook, at the mahogany table.

"Oh, hello!" Annie gave them a brief glance. "I'll ring for more coffee; we've just killed it. No worries, we'll be out of your way soon. Lotte's coming with me on one of my village women's welfare visits, and then we're going up in the Belanca."

"Oh! How . . . daring." Sally sat down, nonplussed. "Won't your parents mind?"

"What they don't know won't hurt them," Lotte answered with an astonishing wink. Her eyes were shining. "I've always been fascinated by aviation. And Lotte's work in the villages is just the sort of thing I want to devote myself to."

"Shall we?" Annie stood. "See you later, ladies."

"Well," Sally sniffed, pouring from a fresh coffee pot. "Don't you hate how people think they can arrange everything, just because they get up early?"

"Most unfair," Lucienne agreed.

"Loulou, have you seen my green patterned scarf? The one with . . . Oh! What *are* you doing?" A few feet into the room, Sally stopped short.

Lucienne stood before their trunk—Natalie's trunk—which was standing on end and was open. With a look of the deepest concentration, she was peering at Natalie, gently stroking her face, leaning in as if to whisper in her ear.

"Sally," she said, without turning around, "come here. Do you think she's cool enough? Or *too* cold? I wish I knew what was supposed to happen at this stage."

Sally approached and gingerly reached out a hand. "She seems cool, the same as the last time we looked. She looks . . . fine. Her hair has grown quite a bit, hasn't it? That's good; it will cushion her head when we move again."

"Indira thinks we should leave her here, not subject her to the jostling of travel, the temperature changes. I wonder."

Sally sat down. "You told her about Natalie? And everything?"

"She's met Natalie, remember; she knew how close we all were, so naturally she was curious. And then . . . I wanted her advice, her wisdom. So I told her about the ritual. But now, I don't know, I almost feel afraid . . ."

"Afraid?"

"She became quite insistent that Natalie should stay here, at least until we're permanently settled some-where; she kept saying that travel could be damaging her and we've been doing something very irresponsible. But I don't know what her motives really are; I'm not sure I trust her. What do you think?"

Sally stood, walked up to the trunk, kissed Natalie's cheek and smoothed her hair. Then she closed the trunk and locked it, and took Lucienne's hand. "Natalie trusted us to take care of her, and we have, and we will. Indira may be old and wise, but she's not one of us and she doesn't know what's best for us. I think we should pack up and wire Prince Ahmed."

"Hmm, yes, perhaps it is time for us to go. But not until Sunday."

"Three more days? Why?"

"I still have a few things to ask the professor. And we promised to go with Lotte and Aaron to another dance, at the University Club."

"Another dance." Sally sighed.

The letter was on a tray at the breakfast table next day.

'My most esteemed memsahibs, Mlle Sally and Mlle Lucienne,

I rejoice to address you and hope this finds you both well. I owe you the most tremendous debt of gratitude for my freedom and the life I am now able to enjoy. When I remember the long, dark and desolate years I spent—so dreadfully alone—in my godown prison, I could weep. But instead, I am filled with joy in reporting that I have found a new home in a most wonderful place, with a community of like-minded companions who provide the utmost in sympathetic consideration. Though I do not wish to overstate its charms, I must say that I find Pondicherry a veritable paradise. Among its other virtues, it is a French-speaking region (being under the administrative control of your native nation), with all the *bonhomie, joie de vivre, ésprit* and *elàn* that one might wish. Its architecture and amenities are, I am told, reminiscent of seaside towns such as Biarritz or Deauville. The inhabitants are, in the main, of a scholarly, spiritual and artistic bent, with gentle and tolerant habits.

Imagine (something I could never have done in my years of darkness) sitting in the deeply shaded but airy verandah of an elegant cafe, sipping a *vin rouge*, perhaps chatting amiably with friends who may stop by. (Yes, I have *friends*!!) When night falls, I take a pleasant stroll through the streets and along the seafront. I still catch the occasional rodent, out of habit, but have also learned some of the techniques you spoke of, dear ladies, my benefactresses. In the course of social interactions with humans, I am able to sample them in discreet ways that satisfy both of us.

There is a constant coming and going of visitors to this town—tourists, artists, seekers—providing a highly varied, frequently refreshed blood pool. It is, I must say, ideal for those of our persuasion, and there are at least a score of us here. I have been welcomed into this group, which is composed of cultured, sensitive and intelligent individuals. They have joined together to devise a simple form of governance, so that we may live in harmony with each other and with the human citizenry.

In short, I implore you, if it is at all possible, to visit me here. I think you will find it as congenial as do I. I have told some of my new vampire friends about you, and they are eager to welcome you to visit, for as long as you would like—along with your dear friend who occupies that fateful trunk which strayed into my godown and, as it were, introduced us.

As for me, I plan to stay here for the rest of my life, and who knows, perhaps you will too.

Yours, with the utmost gratitude and respect,
Ragesh Lal'

"So, Pondicherry. Yes, it is a nice enough place, I have heard. A bit . . . insipid, perhaps." Indira raised her pale blue enamel cigarette holder and inhaled thoughtfully.

"What you mean, insipid?" Sally asked.

"Well, you know . . ." The maharani trailed off as if she was not going to elaborate. "A lot of Europeans go there, not only the French. Gentle, spiritual bohemians who fancy themselves artistic but who haven't been able to make a go of it at home . . . I just don't think you'd find it very exciting. Would you plan to stay long?"

"Impossible to say. We might actually find it a comfortable place to settle for quite a while."

"I would implore you again—Lucienne and I have spoken of this—to leave your *friend* here, for safe-keeping.

The jostling and changeable conditions of travel cannot be good for her. Surely this is the best place to keep her."

"On the contrary, with all due respect, Maharani, for the very reasons you suggest—sparing Natalie the rigors of movement—Pondicherry may well be ideal. Not only is it, as you say, a tranquil place, but we have a trusted friend, deeply indebted to us, who would guard the trunk with his life, if necessary. His immortal life, that is."

"I see. Well, you must do as you think best. A trusted friend, indeed. Who lives in, what, a rooming house? Of course, far preferable. Excuse me, won't you, my dears. I have some letters to write." She turned away from them and crossed the room to a small secretary desk.

"Maharani, please—we've no wish to offend you. We truly appreciate your kind offer; it's just that . . . we cannot leave Natalie behind. We feel bound to her by our very blood, and where we go, we will bring her with us."

Indira, bending over her desk, merely waved a dismissive hand.

"Well, this is a conundrum. Pondicherry or Hyderabad? South or, er, east?" Sally mused.

"Are you going to Pondy? I could fly you there." Annie had come up behind them as they crossed the cool, polished floor of the foyer, heading for the stairs. "I'd go there first, if I were you. The weather's decent in the south at the moment; later, when it hots up, you can head to Hyderabad."

"Thank you, Annie. We'll take that into consideration. Could we really fly there? How long would it take?"

"Well, it's not exactly a short hop—probably seven or eight hours, plus a fueling stop. But it's at least two days by road or train."

"But your plane's only a two-seater, isn't it?" Lucienne pointed out. "And don't tell me you can squeeze me in. We've got quite a lot of luggage."

"Oh, well . . . if the ladies must bring all their luggage, all bets are off! Honestly, I've never seen anyone dress like you two, except for film stars. Even the poshest English memsahibs—I see them in the same few frocks at one dinner party after another, but every time *you* head out to the Poonah Club, you'd think it was a first night at the Opèra. The purple gloves with that hydrangea-patterned gown, by the way, Lucienne—I don't even like dressing up, but that was sensational, I have to say."

Lucienne accepted the compliment gracefully. "We can't unlearn our mannequin habits: the ensemble must be complete. And you can do a lot with accessories— we really don't have that many different gowns. Anyway, thank you for the offer of a ride."

They were dressing for dinner, in floral gowns with ribbon sashes—a traveler's trick, changing the look of a patterned fabric with different-colored accents.

"I'd wear those purple gloves again, to amuse Annie, but it's silly to wear gloves at home," Lucienne was saying, when there was a knock at the door. Sally answered.

"Excuse the interruption, memsahib," said the maid, "but you are called to the telephone. In the library, please."

"*I* am called to the telephone?"

"Yes." The maid subtly tilted her head side to side. "You—or she—or both of you. It is a call for the *farangi* memsahibs, from the royal household of Hyderabad." She straightened her sari and drew herself up taller, at the extraordinary dignity of this message.

"Hyderabad! Yes, of course, we are coming at once."

"Darlings! It's divine to hear your voices!" It was Mireille, speaking rapidly in French, on a slightly crackly line. They had the receiver pressed tightly between them.

"Cherie, it's so good to hear you too!" Lucienne shouted breathlessly into the 'phone. "We've just been talking about coming to visit. When is the best time for you?"

"We have been longing to show you our home here— the gardens will soon be at their peak—but now, *hèlas*, we must leave for France in a few days time. My *maman* is very ill, and I must be with her. I told the others they don't need to come along, but they want to—in case I need help. And because we are all very close, you know. So, I am calling to let you know we must postpone a visit in Hyderabad, but darlings—won't you come with us? I know how much you miss France. We are taking the car to Bombay, and then we are going to travel to Paris by aeroplane! We could all go together; it would be so lovely. Please say you'll come. We could have a beautiful summer in France, and then come back here with you."

Mireille had been talking faster and faster, but finally she paused. Lucienne and Sally stared at each other, agape and uncertain.

"Mireille, dearest," Sally said finally, "Your offer is so kind and so tempting. May we take a little time to think it over?"

'We would adore traveling with you, without questions," Lucienne added quickly, "but there are certain . . . considerations."

"Of course, of course, I completely understand. This comes out of the blue—for us, too. Do please think about it. Shall I call you again, the day after tomorrow, about this time?"

"Yes, that's perfect. Merci, cherie. Je t'embrace. À tout à l'heure." They signed off together, and put the receiver down.

"Well!" Sally exclaimed as they stared at each other.

Lucienne, trembling slightly, consulted her watch. "We'll have to talk later; it's dinner time."

With a table full of intelligent, passionate guests, conversation was lively and unceasing. Between the silver serving platters circulating—everyone exclaiming at the varied and beautifully made dishes—Professor Bloomstein expounded on the discoveries he'd made studying the local dialect; the maharani and Frau Bloomstein compared notes on the care of orchids; Annie and Lotte deplored the lack of educational opportunities, especially for girls, in the villages they'd visited.

"You're awfully quiet," Lucienne said to Aaron, sitting beside her. "What was your day like?"

"Actually . . . I have an announcement." His voice rose, and as attention turned toward him, he took a deep breath. "I'm leaving here, next week. I've booked passage for Tel Aviv, in Palestine. They're holding an event called the Levant Fair—all the latest in art and technology from that part of the world. I want to find opportunities, in a place where Jews can be more than victims, second-class citizens, refugees. I'm sorry, Mother," he replied to Frau Bloomstein's stricken gasp. "I didn't mean to shock you. You must think this is very sudden, but I've been thinking of it for some time, and now I can think of nothing else."

"But Aaron," his sister said, "don't you think we should all stick together? Why must you go off on your own?"

"You've found things, good things, to do here, Lotte. I'm proud of you. But I need to work, to develop a new life, and I cannot see it happening here—with all respect to this beautiful place and our hostess's kindness. On my own, I can travel rough; it won't cost much. And if Palestine is a land of milk and honey—or at least, a good enough place for a peaceful life—I'll write and urge you all to join me."

Amid a renewed spate of talk, punctuated by the occasional sob from Sophie or Lotte, Sally and Lucienne excused themselves and slipped away to their room, stepping out through the French windows to the wide, third-floor balcony outside. They lit cigarettes and settled into wicker armchairs.

"So?" Sally raised her eyebrows.

"So." Lucienne nodded, and they sat in wordless agreement for a while, in the mild mauve dusk.

"Perhaps everyone will be setting out in different directions soon," Sally mused. "Good for Aaron; he needs to do something like that. I wish him all the best."

"I want to go to Paris, you know. Desperately. The way I felt on the ship—it hasn't changed."

"I know, Loulou," Sally said, after a few silent smoke rings. "I think you should go."

"*I* should? What about you?"

"We don't have to be together every moment. In the long run, of course, we will be—at least I certainly hope so. But we can take different paths for a while and then meet up again."

"But Sally, wouldn't you love to come to Paris too? Especially with our friends—think how much fun it would be!"

"Honestly . . . no, darling. You have to realize that, up til now, I've spent my entire life in France, mostly in Paris. It will always be my home, of course, but *this . . .*" she swept an arm toward the lush gardens beyond the railing, "this journey is the adventure I've always craved. I don't want to turn back, even for a short detour. I want to stay here in Asia a good long time, and I'd love to go even further east, see the places you've lived. Shanghai, perhaps."

"Oh, Shanghai." Lucienne shook her head, with an unreadable expression.

"Anyway, if we were to both go to Europe, I don't know how we'd manage Natalie. What if there isn't enough room on this aeroplane? Did you think about that?"

"I did. I thought she could stay here, like Indira said."

"What?! But we didn't like that idea at all. We talked it over. Now you think we can trust her?"

"Oh, of course we can trust her. I think. I don't know." Lucienne sighed, stubbed out her cigarette, removed it and blew a last puff of smoke through her white jade holder. "I get so tired sometimes. Don't you find it strenuous, living with mortals—all the different cultures, the languages, the etiquette, the eating? I just need a rest, a month or two, that's all."

"You're tired of spending time with mortals, but you want to commit yourself to traveling with a pack of them? Why don't we visit Ragesh and meet the vampire society of Pondicherry?"

"I know, but Ahmed and the ladies are . . . so easy to spend time with. I feel at home with them, somehow. And maybe a little bit in love. Wouldn't they be wonderful vamps?"

"Loulou!"

"Don't worry, I won't do anything rash. But Paris . . ." The longing in her voice was undeniable. "I suppose, if you stay here, you can look after Natalie. That *would* be better."

"Fine," Sally said coldly. "That's what we'll do then."

"Sally! Don't be cross, please darling."

"I'm not cross. Everything will be fine. I just have things to think about."

There were more telephone calls, arrangements, packing. "Bring your lightest silks, darling; there's a weight restriction," Navid instructed.

The privately chartered flight to Paris was leaving from Bombay's Juhu Aerodrome. Annie offered to "buzz" Lucienne over, but Pamela insisted that Poonah was right on their way, and there was plenty of room in the Rolls, even for Sally to come along to see them off.

The day came, an unusually cool morning, which was fortunate since Lucienne wanted to wear a light wool suit for travel. They expected the car at noon . . . which came and went. Lucienne had already said farewell to Indira and the Bloomsteins, but they all came drifting out to the verandah after luncheon, to find Lucienne and Sally pacing, smoking and anxiously scanning the horizon for dust clouds. The day had grown hotter, and Lucienne had shed her jacket.

"You're sure it's today?" Sally asked, unnecessarily. There had been a final call just that morning.

"What time is it?" Lucienne snapped, equally pointlessly, consulting her own watch. "Almost half past two!"

Tea was brought, and after some desultory, anticlimactic conversation, the various household members wandered away, leaving two elegant but increasingly wilted young women waiting beside a small heap of luggage.

Over an hour later, they heard a rumble, a hum, and the cheerful tooting of an automobile horn. A long, gleaming, cream-colored car drew up, bedecked with gilded brightwork, including a custom-made modernistic grille and a unique version of the 'Spirit of Ecstasy' hood ornament which bore a strong resemblance to the goddess Durga.

"Sorry sorry sorry!" Navid, Pamela and Mireille spilled from the back seat, all talking at once, while Ahmed waved affably from his seat beside the driver.

"We're ridiculously late, you must think we're monsters!'

"We were already off to a late start, and then *someone* forgot her shoe trunk!"

"Oh, I suppose I should have gone barefoot in France then?"

"They do sell shoes in Paris, darling."

"But I like my own ones best. They already fit."

"And then, we hadn't gone twenty miles when the car started to make a peculiar noise . . ."

"We had to turn back and bring this one instead—isn't it gaudy?"

"I like it!"

"I much prefer the green and silver."

"Anyway, let's get your bags stowed. That's all you've got? Easy-peasy. Sally, you'll come see us off?"

"Is there really enough room?"

"Of course there is! We're all good friends; we'll snuggle."

Two hours in the car passed surprisingly fast. (*Loulou's right, they really are such good company*, Sally thought.) All five of them in the back seat wore different perfumes, which blended into a warm, delicious scented fog, remarkably harmonious: the gardenia sweetness of Pamela's Jicky, Sally's dark spicy carnation, Navid's jasmine and tuberose, Lucienne's dusky Tabac Blonde and Mireille's impeccable Chanel No. 5.

Then suddenly they were driving across an open area of tarmac, toward a beautifully shining, silver winged machine. The car stopped and was surrounded by men in coveralls who collected all the luggage from the boot and the roof rack. Another man, in a blue uniform, hurried up, shook hands with Prince Ahmed and spoke to him in an urgent undertone.

"Ladies." Ahmed turned to them. "Because we are so shockingly late, we must board at once." He quickly clasped Sally's hand, and leaned in to kiss her on each cheek. "Come along, ladies."

"You're sure you won't change your mind, Sally?" Mireille cajoled. "The plane seats eight."

"Yes, do, come with us!" Navid urged.

"No, no, I really can't—and you must hurry. Just take good care of each other. Loulou, I"ll miss you so much," Sally whispered in her friend's ear. "But have a wonderful time. We'll see each other soon."

In a flurry of color and bustle, they all ascended the steep ladder-like staircase and disappeared into the airplane. The noise became deafening. Sally stood beside the ornate car, watching as the large bright solid plane rose into the sky, higher and higher, dwindling until it was a large bird and then a smaller bird, far up in the pale blue. She felt empty and very alone.

Still staring at the sky, she gradually became aware of a buzzing sound, which grew louder, less insect- and more motor-like. A small plane, with a familiar shape silhouetted against the bright sky, tilted its wings in a jaunty salute and then began circling into a descent.

Annie, with a radiant smile and a new green leather flight suit, hopped out of her plane.

"I thought you might like a quicker ride home." She patted the Rolls's fender. "You can send this white elephant on its way."

Sally had a nightmare that night. *Natalie crouched over her in a feline, predatory pose—her eyes blazing, her skin cold, giving off a dark, bitter smell of decay. Shaking out her long russet hair so that it brushed Sally's face, she bared her fangs in a snarl.*

"You've let her go. She's the only one who knows how to wake me. Now she's gone forever, and I'm dead, dead, dead."

"Natalie, darling . . . don't worry," Sally said with diffi-culty, paralyzed by the dream weight on her chest. "I will always take care of you. And Loulou will be back soon, I'm sure."

"Dead. Dead. Dead," the apparition repeated. The tolling words, the cold and the putrid smell increased until Sally, with an effortful gasp, woke herself and sat up.

'Mlle Lucienne Leung

> c/o Prince Ahmed of Hyderabad
> Hotel Ritz, Paris, France
> June 2, 1933
> 'Darling Loulou ~
> You must tell me all the Paris news—what flowers are blooming, what new shops and bars have opened, what people are wearing, and of course, what music and dances are the rage in the nightclubs. I am so happy' (was the underscore a bit much? Sally wondered), 'so very happy that you are there, seeing those dear sights de notre ville. Oh, the weather must be enchanting—no matter what it's like —after these months of incessant heat.'

Sally laid down her pen and stretched. The heat suited her, actually; she felt lithe and physically content as a cat. Lucienne's absence, of course, was like a hole in her heart, but Loulou must never know. A vamp could not be needy.

'Lots going on here. Aaron has left for Palestine, but on his last night, we all went to the Poonah Club. To my surprise, Aaron danced with me, divinely, almost the entire time. I'm going to miss that boy, he's got a unique flavor, very vibrant. Lotte and Annie danced every dance together too. Not the way girls usually dance together—they quite scandalized the local set, especially their rhumbas and tangos! Annie led, and I'd no idea she was so good; I'd love to dance with her myself if she were taller.

'The Bloomsteins are going to Burma, Herr and Frau Professor, that is, and they want Lotte to go with them, but she's quite set on continuing her village development work. Not to mention her aviation lessons . . .

'You'll think I must be getting lonely with everyone dispersing in all directions, but not a bit. I've been really enjoying spending time with Indira. You won't believe it, but we've been playing chess! I'll be ready to challenge Navid when you get back. And I've made a lovely friend—one of the gardeners, an older gentleman, likes to walk with me in the grounds at night. We have an understanding —he shows me the most fragrant night-blooming flowers, and I drink just enough of him to put him into a delicious daze, so he can forget his aches and pains, and how much he misses his wife.

'But the very best thing is, I'm learning about Indian classical music. There's this brilliant man, Pandit Ghosh, whom Indira sponsors. He was away on a pilgrimage, apparently, but now that he's back, he comes every evening and plays the tabla— that's a kind of hand drum, incredibly expressive. Sometimes another musician plays with him, on a stringed instrument; sometimes he's alone. And then he sings—well, more like scatting really, like Li'l Red used to do with the Chocolate Dandies— these rhythmic patterns . . . Oh, I could listen all night; it's just amazing. What a shame those musi- cians in Cairo were so hateful to us. But Pandit-ji isn't a bit like that; he loves that I appreciate his art. I may even take some lessons!

'So, do go on enjoying yourself, darling, and be sure to store up lots of things to tell me. Oh no, I almost forgot to ask—how is Mireille's poor mother doing, and how is Mireille bearing up? I hope it's not too dreadful. Give them all my fondest love. I'd better go now. *Alor, je t'embrace, chère Loulou.*'

An ink blot fell to embellish her signature, so she turned it into a bizarre bird-like doodle, and then added an urgent postscript: 'Bring me perfume!'

"*Teental: Ka, ghe, kat, ta, na, ke . . .*" Pandit Ghosh's diction was as skilled as his astonishing hands, as he spoke the mnemonic syllables faster and faster. Sally was lost in the rhythm, dazzled. At the same time, it resonated in her core, making her feel she's found something she'd always been looking for. The whirlwind of beats accelerated until she was amazed she could still hear them; then, like an engine running down, the rhythm ebbed. He started the piece over, slow enough for her to follow and join in.

"*Tak, tikka tikka tak, tak, tak.* Here, place your hands like this, fingers and palms so, let yourself go into the tala. Close your eyes, let your head follow . . . yes, good."

The membrane taut and warm under her fingertips, the vibration spreading through her body, Sally swayed and gently nodded her head. '*I'm playing, I'm playing with Pandit Ghosh—this music, it's perfection, it's eternity.*' At the same time, another part of her mind was telling her, '*Loulou is gone, gone, gone, never coming back,*' and when the harmonium player joined in suddenly on a plaintive note, Sally broke off and let out a long, heartbroken wail.

"No my dear," Pandit Ghosh said gently. "Not that way. Put the feeling into your hands. Let the tabla speak it."

'Dear Sally,

'Thank you for your letter and all the news of the Bloomsteins and other doings. And how marvelous that you are able to indulge your passion for music again. I hope you will play for us when we are back in Hyderabad.

'Paris is . . . the same and yet different. To tell the truth, everything looks and feels different, now that I'm part of the Hydras, as we call ourselves. Instead of feeling as if I'm always on the prowl for handsome men, or delicious throats, or amusing company—I've got it all, already. We go about together, are accepted everywhere and form our own small private club within the most exclusive circles. People who know Ahmed just assume I'm a new wife, and we don't bother to tell them otherwise. In a way, it feels true: I sleep with Ahmed now and then, although more often I'm with one of the girls; I'm included in every-thing; and if he's buying clothes or jewels or treats for the others, I get them too. You'll like this—we're all having *taillures* and frocks made at Patou! Re-member how Mlle detested him and considered him her arch-rival, and we models were told to avoid him like the plague? It's most amusing and rather fun to go into the house as a client.

'Fashions are not too different from when we left London, and I'd say we've been keeping ourselves pretty well up-to-date, only waists are even more nipped in now. Hats usually have a bit of a brim and are worn very definitely tilted, always to the right. Some darker and also some brighter lipstick shades have come in—I'll bring you some—and nail varnish has become quite *de rigeur*, I'm afraid. I find it rather a bore—the stuff doesn't seem subject to normal vamp glamour, and I'm always getting chips. But it does look pretty when it's freshly done; I suppose I'll get used to it.

'I can't tell you much about the nightclubs. We either go to private parties—some are quite spectacular, like the Proust ball, or the all-white party— or we stay in and read and have a quiet evening on our own.

'Darling, I'm having the loveliest time and don't want it to end! I often think there would be nothing more wonderful than turning all four of them; we could be our own exquisite vamp tribe. I think they must not want to have children, or they already would, don't you think? They never talk about it; just sometimes they mention or write to some people they seem fond of back home, cousins perhaps. But I really feel the five of us are magical together, destined to be. We could be six, if you joined us . . . I don't know if you would feel the same.

'I wish you were here, to help me sort out my feelings. Be well, darling Sally, and write soon. I'll let you know when we have travel plans.

'Toujours, ta Loulou

'p.s. Mireille's mother is doing very poorly. I think she will die. M. is very sad, but I'm able to comfort her sometimes.'

Sally returned the letter to its thin blue envelope with a sigh, left the suite and wandered downstairs. On the terrace overlooking the rose garden, she found Annie, smoking and scribbling in a notebook.

"Salut, mademoiselle!" the jodhpur-clad princess greeted her. "Come, sit. How are you? Any news from Lucienne?"

"Oh, she's having a grand time, no idea when they'll be back. I think she's going to marry into the Hyderabad harem. But I'm all right," she finished with a rueful smile. "What about you? Any news from Lotte?"

"They've reached Burma; it's lush and beautiful. Her father's already made connections at the university, and they'll probably stay quite a while. She plans to try to start a village women's development program! Amazing girl, isn't she? Maybe I'll visit her there, sometime." They fell silent for a bit.

"Listen, Annie—I want to visit a friend in Pondicherry. Did you mean it when you said you could fly there?"

"Absolutely, if it's in the next week, while I'm still off from school. It'll be a lark—fly down, stay in a little seaside place a few days, fly back . . . I mean, if that suits you. You don't have to stay with me if you're visiting your friend, and of course, you might want to stay longer."

"No, that's perfect. It would be lovely to go with you. We can just see what it's like, and work things out from there."

"My wings are yours! Shall we say tomorrow? Or the day after?"

"The next day, please. I want to have one more tabla lesson with Pandit Ghosh before I go, and I should talk to Indira."

"All right then. But Sally, two things: I know you like to sleep late, but we really need an early start, to catch enough daylight. Ten a.m., at the latest. And just a *small* valise, please."

Sally made herself get up relatively early the next day, as practice, so she was able to have breakfast with the maharani.

"So, you are going to Pondicherry, after all. But you will leave your . . . effects here. Your trunk."

"Yes. I'll only be staying a few days. And Annie is flying me down, so I can't bring much."

Indira smiled. "Ah yes, of course. She likes to try new air routes. Well, you will be in good hands. And, I understand. You have to do something, get on with your life; you can't just sit here waiting, wishing to turn the clock back . . ."

Sally poured herself some fragrant spiced tea and considered. "I don't know what you mean."

"Lucienne, of course. She's moved on, chosen a new path. Your roads have diverged. You can't pretend otherwise."

Sally set her cup down abruptly and lit a cigarette with shaking hands. "I can't imagine where you got that idea, Maharani. Lucienne is just on a brief holiday with friends—friends of both of ours. She missed Paris so much, their invitation was irresistible. But they'll be back soon, and I'll join them in Hyderabad."

The maharani smiled and smoked serenely, one eyebrow slightly raised. A silver snake coiled around her ivory cigarette holder, and its sapphire eyes seemed to wink. "Yes, it is possible. And also possible you will not see her for a very long time. Life is unpredictable—even immortal life. Meanwhile, your Natalie will be safe here. You should know that at the end of June, we will close up this house and go to Cooch Behar, but there is a most trustworthy caretaker; do not worry."

"Thank you for telling me," Sally said coolly. "However, I will be back in less than a week."

Indira nodded absently, gazing out the window. "There are some rather good musicians in Pondy. Be sure to ask Pandit Ghosh for letters of introduction. He tells me you are a very promising student."

Pondicherry

"I see the sea!" Sally was amazed at how excited she felt. The water was a brilliant silver in the late afternoon sun; the glare would have hurt her eyes, but they were well-protected by dark glasses as well as flight goggles. "It's so beautiful. I've never spent much time by the seaside; I'm quite looking forward to it."

"Hmm," Annie said, staring straight ahead. "I used to go to Juhu Beach a lot, with Asha."

"Oh—your girl friend? How's she doing? I'd love to meet her—could we get together some time?"

"I can't see her any more. She had to get married."

"Oh no, how beastly. I'm so sorry. You must miss her."

Annie shrugged. "I do. And then, just when I was getting to be good friends with Lotte, her parents took her away to Burma. I must be cursed . . ."

Sally gasped. "You don't think Indira . . ."

Annie laughed. "Don't be silly, my aunt loves me. I was just speaking figuratively. It's hard sometimes, loving women. Loving anyone. *You* must be crushed that Lucienne has left."

"Indira said the same thing—have you been talking about me? I don't know why everyone thinks it's some dramatic separation; she's just on a short trip to Paris, and she'll be back any day now—with lovely new clothes and French scent."

"Ah well, don't mind me. I'm going to stop talking now; I need to concentrate. We're almost there."

Pondicherry had no official aerodrome, but Annie had learned from aviating acquaintances about a convenient field just outside the town, and Sally had wired Ragesh about their arrival, hoping he might be able to meet them with some sort of transport.

Hoping was all she could do, since there hadn't been time for him to send a reply. "I shouldn't worry, Annie had said breezily. "It's only a couple of miles; we'll take shank's mare."

Having no desire to walk, Sally was relieved to see a colorfully-painted charabanc parked at the edge of the field as they began circling in for landing.

The Belanca touched down with elegant lightness and ran along the field with a trailing wake of dust. At last it came to a stop, and they climbed out, stretching and shedding their warm leather flight coats, helmets and goggles.

"Ragesh!" Sally waved, as two figures ran toward them. "You look wonderful," she added as they got close. It was true—the hunched, emaciated creature of darkness (had it been only weeks ago?) was now a well-dressed, poised and rather handsome gentleman. He gave Sally a radiant smile, in which she caught just a glint of fang, and quickly turned to Annie with a low bow.

"You must be Princess Mahendra. It is an honor—and how kind and clever of you to fly Mlle Lafayette here."

"Please, call me Annie. Sally, you didn't tell me how charming your friend is. Thank you for coming to meet us."

"It is our pleasure," Ragesh said with another bow. "Ladies, may I present my friend Etienne DuPont, who has so helpfully provided his excellent vehicle."

'Darlingest Loulou,

'I am looking out the window of the most enchanting seaside cottage. Dusk light is shimmering on the Indian Ocean. The sea is so gentle, the water like blue satin—and now it's starting to change color every moment, like some magical color-shifting brocade. I could watch it for hours, even after night falls. And last night, under the moon, I went out in my silk cami-knickers (the nights are deliciously warm) and waded into the lapping waves up to my thighs. Why have I never spent time near the sea before?

'You would hardly recognize Ragesh! After all those years in a loin-cloth, he has become quite the dandy. Not quite a matinee idol, but very well turned-out and perfectly groomed. (He was overjoyed, he said, to discover—as we did-- that if one wants to have a mirror reflection, one does.) There's quite a vamp social scene here—I've met several of his friends, very pleasant types, and he's actually throwing a party for me tomorrow night. Annie has to head back, as her university term is starting, but I want to stay on for a little while, so I'll take the train back to Poonah. If you get back to the subcontinent in the next couple of weeks, come and join me here. . . .'

Sally put her pen down and let her eyes unfocus. *She'll never come here.* She didn't know the exact configuration of the complexity Lucienne was caught up in, but she could tell it would not end quickly or cleanly.

Paris

Ahmed, Mireille, Pamela, Lucienne and Navid stayed up most of the night, intertwined with each other in the largest room of their suite at the Ritz. Pamela mixed round after round of delicate, aromatic cocktails, while Ahmed swigged from his own personal bottle of Veuve Cliquot.

"We're a blur, a spectacular blur," Mireille proclaimed, a bit fuzzily. "I don't know where I end and where you begin. Thank you all for staying with me this whole time. *Ma mère est morte; vive ma mère.* She had a good life, now she's at peace. I'll weep again, sometime, but for now . . . we have life and love, my darlings."

"Hear, hear, we all drink to that!" Pamela raised her glass.

"We are, I think, rather drunk," Ahmed began, "but nevertheless, I wish to speak in all seriousness. Lucienne, chérie, we have all taken you into our hearts. I would like to propose . . . Here, this is how it is done in the West . . ." He slid gracefully off the chair where he was lounging and knelt before Lucienne. "I would like to *propose*, my dear. Marry me, and join our family."

Lucienne leaned forward and embraced him. "Oh, Ahmed, I'm overwhelmed. You must know I love you all dearly. But there are things we should establish, if we are going to truly join our lives. You should know . . ."

She had rehearsed in her mind a long, slow, carefully structured way to reveal her nature, but she now found herself just blurting it out. "I think you might suspect . . . I'm not quite a normal human. I live on blood, and I am, basically, immortal. I have the power to share that condition with you, all of you. We could all live forever, loving each other. Never having to mourn another death of our loved ones. I . . . I think I need a little time to think about marriage—no one has asked me in, well, a very long time. But will you also, all of you, think about letting me give you this gift?"

The room fell quiet. The record that had been play-ing had finished, unnoticed, and the needle scratched quietly along the inner grooves.

"Vampire life. Immortality," Navid said softly. "Yes, you are right; we have known this, in a way . . ."

"Not in so many words, but . . ."

"Certainly, I've never thought of it for myself . . ." Mireille mused.

"There is no hurry," Ahmed said. "We will all con-sider. And of course, you should see our home, chere Lucienne. Come, it's almost dawn. Let's all kiss and then get a couple of hours of sleep, before we go out to the airfield."

"You can sleep, Ahmed my love," Pamela said fondly, wrapping her arms around him. "*We* still have packing to do."

'Dearest Sally,

'I can only tell you—no one else would begin to understand: They all have children. Beautiful little persons—Navid's three brown as toast, Mireille's two a little lighter, and Pamela's one bizarrely blonde but with Ahmed's features. How was I to know? They never spoke of them. Or perhaps they did, and I wasn't paying attention. Now that we are back here in Hyderabad, it is quite clear that these small creatures are the apples of their parents' eyes. The centers of their worlds. If the children were only, occasionally, decoratively, peripherally present . . . it might be manageable. But they demand so much attention! They have minds and personalities that are not at all as small as their little round faces, and their parents find them end-lessly interesting.

I think that may be one of the reasons they travel so often—when they are away, they can take a break and be their own adult selves, but when they are home with the children, they give them-selves over entirely to being parental.

Oh, Sally, I don't know what to do. Here's what happened: Ahmed proposed I marry him and become part of their family; I, at the same time (in Paris, in love, in an intoxicated dream) suggested they let me turn them so we could all live in immortal bliss. Then we came back here, and everything is so different—all maman, mummy, amma and papa, papa, appa. I feel . . . ridiculous, embarrassed and confused. And I can see that turning them (four of them! What was I thinking?) would be quite impossible. It's not accidental, I'm sure, that we vamps are rarely parents. Because either you turn your own children, and ugh, that's just too peculiar, isn't it? Or else you watch them grow old, while you don't. Utterly horrible.

I've telephoned the house at Poonah, and the housekeeper tells me you have not returned yet, so you must still be in your seaside cottage—unless you have left. When you receive this—I hope you do—if there is a telephone in that pathetic town, please call me so we can figure out where to meet. If you want to come here, to Hydra, they'd all love to see you . . . though not the way I would. I miss you so much. Things have become ever so subtly awkward here, as it has become clear to all of us that our intoxicated Paris enthusiasm was quite unrealistic.

I really think I should leave here soon. I will go to Poonah, and you can 'phone me there. Soon, please!

Your Lucienne'

Sally was learning the Karnataka style, an entirely different set of *talas*. The teacher was kind enough to compliment her on the technique she'd learned from Pandit Ghosh, but she felt as if she was starting over, learning the rudiments like a child. She thought back through the many many years, to when she actually was a child, learning her letters and numbers. It was a good feeling, fresh and innocent, simple—not like the endless complexities that had made up her life among mortals.

Here, she could study music, bathe in the moonlit seas and enjoy the undemanding company of the local vampires. She'd met a half-dozen of Ragesh's friends, and they were cultured, courteous ad accepting. They tended to gather late in the day on fragrant cafe terraces, to chat about the news and make plans. The evening might hold a concert or an art exhibition, and then later at night, they'd go their separate ways to hunt.

She could imagine living a quiet, peaceful life here for quite a long time. Of course, there was no jazz, little dancing or glamour or romance . . . but perhaps she needed a break from all that. She thought about Cairo, her madcap adventures with mad Giacomo, the intensely structured vamp social circles, the fascinating but hostile musicians. And back further: the bright young people of London, the confusingly politics-obsessed Catalan vamps of Barcelona . . .

Thinking of it all made her so tired, sometimes. Just as she imagined Natalie must have felt. Natalie! Sally was startled to realize she had not thought at all about her dear, sleeping friend in several days, even though it had been her custom to at least touch the surface of the trunk, Natalie's sepulchre, every night when she retired. But, Sally reassured herself, she's safe, in the large cool room in the maharani's well-kept house.

When Lucienne's letter arrived, she read it once and set it down. She wasn't ready yet to think about the intense, hectic, emotional scenes her friend described. Her friend . . . were they still friends? Had they gone too far in different directions? Sally put the letter in a drawer; she would sort it out later.

Poonah

There were lights on in the maharani's house, as Lucienne approached along the dusk-dark, gleaming wet garden path. Although it was what would normally be the dinner hour, the long windows opening from the dining room to the verandah showed an empty table. Lucienne rang the front door bell and waited; the only sound was heavy drops, from the afternoon's rain, dripping from the mango trees.

After what seemed a very long time, the door was opened by a blond, powerfully-built man in some sort of dark uniform. Lucienne stared, with a sense of complete dislocation, before recovering her manners and introducing herself.

"I'm so very sorry to intrude. I've been a recent guest of the Maharani, and I realize she has departed for her summer residence . . ."

"Of course, Miss Leung; we spoke on the telephone. And her majesty told me I might expect to see you. I am Major Hjalvarsen, the off-season caretaker. Do come in. Are you here to collect some of your things, or do you with to stay the night?"

"Thank you, how kind of you. I would like to stay in my old room for a night or two, if I may." She heard a faint sigh. "I don't want to put you to any trouble at all."

"Certainly, miss." Hjalvarsen sounded weary, but perhaps it was only his accent. "Do you have luggage?"

"Just this." She hefted her train-case with a smile, emphasizing its lightness. She had left her two large valises checked in Left Luggage at the train station (with some trepidation, after the misadventure of the Bombay shipping office.) But her cases were only full of clothes —very nice clothes, newly brought back from Paris—not like the irreplaceable trunk upstairs. "I'll see myself up."

"Very well. I'll send the boy with fresh linens."

She reached the top of the wide, hardwood staircase and turned left, opening the familiar door, switching on the light—and stopped. Was this the right room? There were the two beds with their elaborate carved headboards, the green brocade curtains, the chaise longue. Where was the trunk? Her eyes had gone immediately to the corner where it had stood—a corner which was now empty. She set down her case and began opening the drawers of the desk, the bureau—all very much as they'd left them. Nightgowns, underthings, letter paper, ribbons. The wardrobe had a lot of empty hangers, but a few frocks, both hers and Sally's, still lingered. She was turning wildly around, trying to see something that wasn't there, wide-eyed with a mix of fear and fury, when a young boy with an armload of towels appeared in the doorway.

"Where is the trunk, the big trunk?" she demanded.

The boy froze, looking terror-stricken.

Lucienne forced herself to calm down and smile reassuringly. Putting a hand on his shoulder, she guided him into the room and pointed to the empty corner. "Do you know the big trunk that was here?" She sketched the size and shape of it with her hands. "Big, big box? Maybe someone has put it in the box room?"

Still holding the towels, the boy was nodding, but in a glassy-eyed and uncomprehending way.

"Never mind," she sighed. "I suppose I'll have to bother Major Hjalvarsen after all. Please, can you call him for me?"

The boy looked worried at the thought of disturbing the formidable major. Unexpectedly, he set the towels on the bed and went to the corner, sketching a shape just as Lucienne had done. "Big box?" he said, turning the x-sound into two syllables, *bokiss.* "Mali takes him." He gestured toward the window.

"Molly? Who on earth is that, and why would she take the box?"

"Friend Miss Sally. Out, garden."

"I don't understand." Lucienne tried to will more information out of the boy, staring into his eyes, but he had clearly had enough. "Out, garden," he said one more time, and fled.

"All right then," she whispered. "I suppose I'd better go out to the garden and try to find this Molly." It didn't seem a particularly promising plan—why would some flighty 'friend' of Sally's be here, outside in the rainy evening? Surely it would make more sense to question the major in the morning, or perhaps make inquiries at the Poonah Club. But she had to do something to distract herself from gnawing despair. She changed her shoes and went downstairs.

It was astonishingly lovely outside. The sky had cleared, revealing an almost-full moon, and the air was cool and soft, redolent of moist leaves and jasmine. She wandered the garden paths at random, soothed by the nocturnal beauty, reminded of the moonlit terraces and formal plantings at her uncle's casino in Cannes. She'd only visited the gardens once in the time she'd spent there, but the recollection was sweet; it was the moment when she'd begun to return to her senses, after months of her uncle's brainwashing.

Lost in memory, she startled at the approach of a tall, lean male figure, with the irrational sense that she'd conjured Uncle Yu by thinking about him. But Yu always wore black, and despite his centuries of age his hair was dark; this man was white-haired and dressed all in white.

"A good evening to you, memsahib." His greeting was courteous but not obsequious. *Of course,* Lucienne realized, *this must be the gardener Sally mentioned in her letter. This is his domain.*

"Good evening, sir," she replied formally. "You are the head gardener, I believe? My friend, Miss Sally Lafayette, has spoken of your kindness in showing her the night-blooming flowers."

A smile warmed his thin, creased face, and his head moved gently side to side. "Ah, Miss Sally—she is a rare blossom herself. If you would care to walk with me, I will show you what is in flower. Not so much at this season, but we have some pleasing things. If the path is not too damp for you?"

"Not at all; I'm wearing my sensible shoes." She took his arm.

Knowing that the old man had willingly offered Sally his blood piqued her curiosity—and indeed, her appetite —but she felt oddly reticent, even after they had strolled companionably for a half-hour or so. He was Sally's particular friend; Lucienne didn't want to presume that he was open to the advances of any random vamp. She was tired from traveling and still utterly nonplussed by the disappearance of Natalie's trunk; she didn't feel sufficiently quick-witted to move in nimbly for an impromptu nibble. So, as they came through a leafy arbor into sight of the house again, she yawned, apologized and bid him goodnight.

Lucienne awoke hungry, more than she'd been in a while. She'd left Hyderabad—feeling she couldn't stay any longer—with an uncharacteristic lack of planning. her travel flask was close to empty, and of course (she should have foreseen), the maharani's accomodating cook had departed with the royal entourage. Major Hjalvarsen seemed to subsist on crackers and tinned fish; he had seemed relieved when she declined his offer of breakfast, though he did provide a pot of strong coffee, for which she was grateful.

Wandering the bazaar in the late afternoon proved unsatisfactory. With her Parisian clothes and coiffure, it was assumed she was in search of expensive curios or fashionable dry goods. She eventually had to deploy a sort of reverse glamour to make herself inconspicuous enough to avoid ingratiating merchants and helpful passers-by, so that she could explore the more obscure and humble edges of the market place. Her search yielded only one small meat-stall, unsavory with flies;

none of the cuts on offer were freshly enough slaughtered to yield any decent supply of blood.

As dusk fell and her pangs increased, she turned her attention to the people around her, specifically to their necks. Her plan for the day had included dropping in to the Poonah Club for a cocktail and a genteel nibble, but she needed something immediately if she were not to make an unseemly, ravening entrance.

She half-closed her eyes to allow her sense of smell more primacy. The street was full of people, but many of them were lean, stringy workers: delivery boys, rickshah wallahs, exhausted young clerks heading home after a tiring day. Their blood would taste equally tired. A large bright shape caught her eye, and she focused her attention to see a short, plump, well-groomed man coming her way. His salwar kameez ensemble—its vivid azure was what she'd seen first—was so heavily starched as to remain crisp at the end of the workday, though doubtless it had not been an overly laborious one. The gent was clearly a boss or business owner. His oily skin and pomaded hair gleamed with well-being, and his well-upholstered limbs and unapologetic paunch spoke of a hearty enjoyment of his lunch, his afternoon tea and several additional snacks.

Without hesitation, Lucienne launched herself at him; seizing him in a fervent embrace which placed her teeth against his throat, she held on for a long luscious swig— his blood was as rich as she'd hoped—before coming up for air and licking her lips clean.

"Darling!" she exclaimed in her giddiest voice. "How divine to see you here, isn't it?"

The man blinked in confusion. "Do I know you, miss?"

Lucienne took a step back, fluttering her lashes as if adorably baffled. Then her hand flew to her mouth. "Oh no! Oh my goodness, please forgive me; what must you think? I completely mistook you for my . . . sweetheart. I mean, my uncle; I mean, my friend . . ."

Rubbing his neck with a bemused smile, he answered, "Well well, no harm done. No harm at all. May I . . . see you to a taxi, miss? Or get you a cup of tea?"

"Oh sir, no need. You have already been too kind." She bestowed a ravishing smile and stepped back to melt away into the crowd.

Half an hour later, Lucienne alit from a taxi in front of the white-painted, wedding-cake-tiered main building of the Poonah Club. Comfortably full from her plump benefactor, she was eagerly looking forward to a cocktail, a nibble and (she hoped) a bit of news.

A turbaned doorman showed her in, and she proceeded to the reception desk. "Member or guest?" said a young man, not looking up from his paperwork.

"Good afternoon. I am a guest of the Maharani of Cooch Behar."

"The Maharani is not currently in residence; therefore, Madam's membership is temporarily suspended."

"I beg your pardon." She leaned forward into his sight-line, trying to force him to look up at her. "Are you saying I cannot come in because my hostess is out of town?"

"Club rules, miss," he muttered, continuing to shuffle papers.

"But that's ridic . . ." She broke off, realizing that the young bureaucrat would not respond well to her insulting the sacred rules. "I'm sorry. I really need your help, sir."

He was finally looking at her—progress.

"I'm only here for a day or two. Indira specifically said I could stop off on my way . . . south, to Pondy. But the house is mostly closed up, as you know, and I don't want to put the caretaker to any trouble—you know, Major Hjalvarsen—so I told him I'd just come to the club. Isn't there any way I can come in, for a bite and a cocktail?"

The clerk sighed. "Do you know any other members?"

Lucienne pictured afternoons of dances, card games and idle chatter, but any names attached to the young English social and military set eluded her. With desperate inspiration, she asked, "Is there a young woman with the Christian name of Molly? I'm afraid I can't remember her surname."

The clerk turned a ledger page and then brightened. "Of course, the Honorable Miss Molly Gloucester. And she's here right now, having tea. Would you like to join her?"

"Oh yes, please," Lucienne said with profuse gratitude. The exchange had made her hungry all over again.

Sitting alone near a window, the pale, slender woman raised wide blue eyes as Lucienne was ushered across to her table. She looked about 24, and her blond hair had the crispest marcelle waves Lucienne had ever seen.

"Hello. Do I know you?" The question was not exactly unfriendly, but genuinely curious and a bit challenging.

"Do forgive me intruding on your teatime. I'm Lucienne Leung, Lady Molly, and I'm sure we must have met, perhaps last month? A group of us used to come over from Indira's place, almost every day."

"Oh, of course! You were with that dreamboat, the dark-haired German fellow. Such a good dancer! Where is he? I haven't seen any of your crowd for a while."

"The maharani has decamped to her Cooch Behar palace for the season, so we've all scattered. I'm just back from Paris, and I'm only here for a day or two. Aaron has gone off to Palestine. I think he's hoping to settle there."

"Palestine! Oh—oh dear, I didn't realize. He must be Jewish. What a shame."

"Well, I don't think he'd agree, although things are difficult at the moment. But listen, Lady Molly—I'm so glad to see you here, and not just because I'm famished. I say, shall we have a cocktail? But anyway, I wanted to ask you if you've seen my friend Sally lately? Sally Lafayette—tall French girl, hair . . . about like mine."

Molly laughed suddenly. "Of course! I never quite knew her name, or yours, I'm afraid. We call you the Dolly Sisters, because of your hair, and because you're both so pretty—I hope you don't mind! Yes, I did see her, maybe a week or two ago, just on her own, like you are today."

Tea, cocktails, eventually a light supper and a few sips of Lady Molly—she was so delicately built that Lucienne was afraid to take too much—added up to a pleasant but ultimately frustrating time. Lucienne deployed so much glamour and wit that the young Englishwoman's brittle shell of artifice and reticence cracked wide open; after their second gin sling, they were laughing together like childhood friends. But Molly knew nothing. Sally had clearly not confided in her about her own immediate plans, let alone her history or the dilemma of Natalie's well-being. And Molly had never visited Indira's house, so the boy's naming her remained baffling.

To make matters worse, due to the off-season, it was a quiet night at the club, with no music or dancing and hardly any other guests. After a last, after-dinner ciga-rette, Lucienne cut her losses and said good night. She was still hungry.

Bone-weary, Lucienne alit from a rickshaw cab at the entrance to Indira's grounds. She'd been too tired to try her luck in the bazaar again and didn't really have a clue about how she might be nourished—odd thoughts of rats and bats flitted across her mind.

She was startled enough to jump back with a gasp when a dark figure approached along the path.

"Not to worry, memsahib; it is only I, head-*mali* Ram, at your service. Here, memsahib is faint; allow me to assist." He caught her as she collapsed. It was only for a minute or two, and as she recovered, she was flooded with relief at the old man's kindness, his comforting arm and pleasant smell. And of course! She should have remembered her rudimentary Hindi lessons. *Mali,* sounding identical to "Molly," meant gardener.

"May I bring Memsahib Lucienne to my humble cottage for some refreshment?"

"Please. I would be so grateful."

With perfect tact, he unspeakingly allowed her to feed, and when she was deliciously full, he insisted she take the one comfortable chair—directly opposite the tall, brass-bound trunk, Natalie's trunk.

"I felt, when first Memsahib and then Memsahib Sally went away, that *she*"—he looked toward the trunk—"was lonely. She called to me, in a dream. I went inside the big house and told the boy I had been instructed to store the box." (He pronounced it with two syllables, as the boy had done.) "*So* carefully I brought her down the stairs. I am still very strong." He said it not boastfully but as a simple matter of fact. "Now she stays here with me, until you are ready to bring her where you go. Sometimes at night, she talks to me and I talk to her, so she is not lonely."

"She . . . talks to you. Have you . . . do you . . .open the trunk?" The old man was so calm, she could entertain the idea without worry.

"Once, I open, just to see she is safe after moving. But I do not need to open it. I see her, here--" his finger touched the center of his forehead, "and I hear her, in my mind."

"What does she say to you?" The whole situation was so unreal, Lucienne could only feel curious.

"She tells me her life has been very long, sometimes beautiful and sometimes terrible, and she has been very tired. She rests, and she hopes to become strong again, to spend time with you and with Memsahib Sally. With you, things are beautiful."

Lucienne awoke, the following afternoon, from what felt like the best sleep she'd had in weeks. Well-fed and rested, freshly showered and dressed, with a jaunty new scarf from Paris, she felt ready to face the next dilemma —how to reach Sally.

Unexpectedly, the dour Major Hjalvarsen came to her assistance. Although his greeting when she came down-stairs was hardly reassuring: "Not to pry, miss—and your presence here is no trouble at all—but what are your plans?"

Lucienne explained about how Sally had gone south to Pondicherry, precise whereabouts unknown. "I wrote to her, and she might be returning here even as we speak, so I don't know if I should set out to go there . . . but of course, it's possible she never got my letter . ."

The Swede nodded thoughtfully. "What you need is the *wallah* network. A *chai-wallah* here will know a *chai-wallah* in Pondi—or a supplier, or a cousin of one, or a commercial traveler in tablewares or folding chairs. The point is, once we find a connection to a cafe in Pondicherry, the rest is easy. Cafe proprietors have telephones, and they know everything. A tall, beautiful young Frenchwoman will surely be a source of local gossip. We just ask the *wallah* network to locate her and convey an urgent message for her to call here." He snapped his fingers. "Easy as gingersnaps. Leave it to me; I will make some inquiries."

"I have news," Hjalvarsen said, the very next afternoon. He took the veranda steps in two energetic strides and placed a fresh lime and soda beside Lucienne.

"So soon?"

"I told you the *wallah* network was effective. But the news is perhaps not so good."

Lucienne felt a shiver of alarm. "Tell me."

"They all know her there—her appearance in town was highly noteworthy. For the first two weeks or so, she was seen regularly, sitting in cafes, shopping, strolling the seafront. But lately, she is almost never out before dusk, and she frequents only a rather disreputable cafe. And— this is perhaps most important—she does not come to pick up her mail. There are letters, perhaps the very ones you have sent, waiting for her."

"Oh, no." Deep in thought, Lucienne drank down the glass beside her and coughed. She really didn't care for lime, or carbonated water. "I'll have to go there. You don't happen to have the train timetable, do you? I wonder if I can go today."

"There is a train at 10:15 pm, Miss. An overnight trip, but first-class should be fairly comfortable. I will drive you to the station."

Pondicherry

Anxious and filled with foreboding after a sleepless night, Lucienne stepped off the train and found a pedicab driver who promised to take her to a good hotel. As they rolled through the quiet town, she realized she was in a perfectly charming place—well-kept streets lined with graceful, European-style buildings, painted in candy colors and bedecked with flowers. Not far away, the morning sun was just rising, low over the sparkling blue sea. They pulled up before a door with a French sign; inside the cool lobby, a polite French-speaking woman checked her in and showed her to to a small room with wooden window shutters and a soft bed, where she immediately fell into a deep, dreamless sleep.

In the late afternoon, after a flask in her room and an aperitif in the tiny hotel bar downstairs, Lucienne ventured out. At sunset, the town was just as pretty as in the morning, and was lively with people strolling, shopping and sitting in sidewalk cafes, buzzing in a mix of French, Tamil and other languages.

Strolling the seaside promenade, she glanced over at one of the cafes she was passing and was happily surprised to spot a familiar face.

"Ragesh!" She squeezed between tables, making her way over to where he sat with another man, both of them nursing glasses of red wine.

"Mlle Lucienne!" He sprang up from his chair, as did his companion. Beaming, he took both her hands in his and pressed them fondly as he spoke rapid, effusive French. "I am so happy to see you, you have no idea! Has Mlle Sally summoned you? Thank the heavens, now she can get the help she needs."

"I . . . no, she hasn't contacted me. I came because I was worried; I haven't heard anything from her. Where is she? What you mean about her needing help?"

Ragesh and his friend exchanged a look, and Ragesh quickly pulled out a chair. "Where are my manners—please, sit and join us. And may I present my dear friend, Etienne Dupont."

"Enchanté, mademoiselle," the dark, slender Etienne said with a half-bow.

"*Du vin rouge, s'il vous plâit,*" Ragesh added to a passing waiter. "So . . ." he began, and then trailed off. The waiter brought a carafe of wine and a new glass, filled all three and turned away. Lucienne took a sip and raised an inquiring eyebrow.

"So, you have had no letters at all from Mlle Sally?"

"There was one, when she first arrived. She was ecstatic—delighted with everything: the charm of the town, the beauty of the sea, your kindness, Ragesh, and all the friendly and interesting . . . people she was meeting." She threw an involuntary glance at Etienne, not certain of his affiliation.

Ragesh instantly noticed and smiled. "You can speak freely in front of Etienne. He is, of course, one of us. And one of my very dearest friends."

"Yes, and in the short time I've known Mlle Sally, I have come to think very highly of her. So vibrant, so full of passion and curiosity . . . and of course, so beautiful and charming. And so, like you, I am distressed at what has happened."

Lucienne stared at him, the taste of wine bitter in her mouth. "But what *has* happened? I wrote her several letters after that first one, but got no replies."

"Forgive us, Mlle; we need to give you the full story." Ragesh patted Etienne's hand, cleared his throat and then paused, gazing out toward the tranquil evening ocean. "When Mlle Sally first arrived, she was, as you put it very well, ecstatic. As I hope you are already aware, this is a lovely town, with a very agreeable way of life. Among both the mortal and vampiric communities, there are many artists, musicians, people of culture, making for a lively and ever-changing scene. Sally embraced it all— she was out every night at concerts, plays, galleries and parties—and we all took her to our hearts as well. In a very short time, she made many friends. But then . . ." He stopped, with a heavy sigh. "I blame myself."

Etienne returned the affectionate gesture of a hand pat. "Ragesh, there is no way you could have known."

"I am sorry. I am telling this so badly." Ragesh met Lucienne's gaze, which was almost wild with distress and incomprehension. "To ease your mind, let me say first, Sally is here, in Pondy. She is safe and, I believe, in adequate health. But she is—only temporarily I pray —lost to us, in a sense. She has fallen under the sway of a very powerful and, I would say, malignant personality." Ragesh paused, looked around and lowered his voice. "He is called Shivabai, or Pierre, or the Master. He has disciples, not many, but fanatically devoted to his teachings. I fear our Sally has become one, and I blame myself."

"I don't understand," Lucienne said.

"Of course not. You see, I held a party for her, to introduce her to our local society . . ."

"Yes, she wrote about that; it was coming up and she was delighted."

Ragesh sighed. "If only . . . She had told me of her interest in our Indian classical music, how she had been studying the tabla with a pandit in Poonah. And so I arranged for some musicians to perform, never dreaming . . . One of them invited Pierre to come along with them. He is quite a skilled player, you see—in fact, some call him the demon drummer."

Etienne nodded. "I watched her, watching him play—she was utterly enthralled. After the musical set ended, she went over to speak to him. I should have interrupted them, but then someone asked me a question, and I lost track . . ."

"And I was in another room, arranging the refreshments—we had an array of fresh fruit juices for our mortal guests, as well as various types of blood. Within a few minutes, a few fateful minutes, she had agreed to study with him. And after that, things developed very quickly. She spends all her waking time with Pierre in his compound, 'studying,' if you can call it that—drumming herself into a frenzy, or listening to him going on about his 'philosophy.' He is, as I have said, a very powerful personality, with a mesmerizing effect on some people. We never see her in the cafes or galleries any more—she rarely leaves his side. Except, sometimes late at night . . oh, this is the most horrible part . . ."

Ragesh broke off, took a long drink of his wine and wiped his eyes. "I can't . . ."

Etienne took over. "As you doubtless know, our vampiric community here, as in most of the civilized world, practices modern, ethical vampirism—we take small, non-lethal amounts of blood from a variety of animals and humans. Our human 'suppliers' enter willingly into relationships with us, in a mutually beneficial arrangement.

"But Pierre has, as Ragesh noted, a 'philosophy,' a very evil philosophy. Basically, he holds humans in contempt, although he twists his words to conceal the fact and claims to have their best interests at heart. He has convinced his disciples—whether he believes this himself I do not know—that a significant portion of all humans are suicidal, and that a vampire's role, even duty, is to kill. The hours between midnight and four in the morning are when they hunt, and they consider anyone out at that time to be fair game."

Lucienne gasped. "Merde. And Sally is caught up in that? I have to talk to her. Where can I find her?"

"I will show you where she was staying. I don't think she is often there, but it's a start."

Ragesh accompanied her to the rooming house. Clearly impressed by Lucienne's crisp elegance, the landlady instantly accepted her as Sally's sister, and showed her to the small top-floor room she had been occupying. The room looked lived-in: a novel propped open next to an armchair, make-up set out on the dresser, the closet full of summer frocks, hats and shoes.

"But," the landlady said, "I have not seen memsahib for more than one week. And," she added apologetically, "rental is now due."

Lucienne opened her purse, took care of the nominal amount and arranged to move into the room herself, at least until her friend's return. "No need to pay for a hotel, with this perfectly nice room sitting empty," she explained to Ragesh, who had waited for her at a nearby café. "I'll have my things moved over later."

"Not there for a week. She must be staying full-time at Pierre's compound," he said gloomily. "I cannot tell you exactly where it is; I only know it is on the east side of town. If you go out at midnight, you will hear the drumming when you are near. Perhaps I should come with you."

Lucienne caught his reluctant tone. "No, it's better if I go alone, at least at first. Thank you for all your help. I'll be fine."

Despite her confident words to Ragesh and the peacefulness of the night streets, Lucienne was uneasy as she made her way to the "east side of town," realizing how vague the directions were. But soon she did indeed hear drumming, the rapid beats so much like a rainstorm that she questioned her own perception of the clear, mild sky. The pattering grew louder and the rhythm changed, to irregularly accented beats of increasing forcefulness. "Drumming themselves into a frenzy," she recalled Ragesh saying, as she found herself beside a high wall which supported a profusion of flowering vines. The sounds came from within; she just had to follow the wall until some opening appeared.

An open gate led to a path through the garden, to a door. She waited for a pause in the music before knocking.

The man who opened was strong and well-proportioned, a little shorter than her, with longish hair framing an attractive, ageless face. His wide-set brown eyes took her in with a warm, curious expression, and his mouth widened into a particularly beautiful smile, showing a hint of fangs.

"Sister!" he exclaimed. "Welcome!" He put his palms together in greeting, and then immediately spread his arms wide, beckoning her into an embrace. "I knew you would come. Sally has told me so much about you, I feel we already know each other." He pronounced her friend's name with an accent that turned it into "Sah-lee."

Lucienne stiffened and drew back. "Where is Sally? She hasn't told me anything about you."

"Loulou—may I call you that? Don't be cross. You probably wrote her letters, and she hasn't answered, but don't blame your darling friend, please. She thinks of you constantly, I am sure, but she has been so busy, learning so many new things, beginning a new life. She will be so happy to see you. Only, right now, she is in a special state—you might call it a trance—so we need to give her a little time."

"A new life? A trance state? I don't understand; this doesn't sound a bit like Sally. Who *are* you anyway?"

"Please, come inside, let me offer you our hospitality. Please, follow me, dear sister." He smiled again. "I won't bite."

With a sigh of misgiving, Lucienne crossed the threshold, through a foyer and into a large room lit with glowing lamps and decorated with spare good taste. The floor was a shining expanse of polished wood, as were the paneled walls, with a few cloth hangings and a vase of red lilies adding color. Fragrance too—the scent of the flowers mingled with a complex, smoky incense. Her host gestured to an arrangement of silk cushions around a low table.

"Please, be comfortable. I will return momentarily."

He opened an almost invisible door, set flush with the paneling in the rear wall, and Lucienne again heard drumming, as well as chanting, before it closed. There was no sound though when he returned only a few minutes later, with a tray holding a stoneware ewer and two small cups. After he poured and passed her one, he raised his in a salute. "To a long and beautiful friendship."

Lucienne could think of no reply; she nodded, sipped and suppressed a grimace. "Thank you. What is this?"

"Our special blend—blood with spices and honey."

Lucienne set her cup down. "I'm sorry. Honey has always disgusted me. Processed by insect bodies." She shuddered.

The man gave her an amused look. "Indeed? Well, to each his own." He took a hearty slurp from his cup.

"So . . ." Lucienne said after a pause. "What do you do here?"

Pierre opened his eyes extremely wide, with a look of barely suppressed mirth that she found intensely irritating. "What *don't* we do? We meditate, we play music, we create beauty with our minds which one day will transform the world. And your dear friend, my dear Sally (again, that odd, annoying pronunciation) is destined to be one of the greatest of us. When she is able to fully embrace her Kali nature . . ."

"Her . . . what?"

Instead of answering, he put his palms together and bowed slightly. "I must not overwhelm you with too many details. All in good time, my dear. Sally has said you are delicate."

Before she could reply, the door in the rear wall was flung open, and a noisy, boisterous group of four or five —quite at odds with the studied calm of the place—staggered through, gasping, shouting, stumbling in a state of mingled exhaustion and euphoria.

"Master, did you hear?" a petite woman exclaimed, in English. "We were so close, we are making a real breakthrough!"

All talking at once in a babel of languages, they were running toward him but stopped or fell back on seeing Lucienne. Except for one, the tallest (whom Lucienne at first took to be a young man), who shrieked, staring, and then ran forward, arms outstretched.

"Loulou? What are you doing here?"

"Oh my god, Sally, it's you!" Lucienne stood, eyes riveted on her friend. Sally's hair was unwashed, and her impeccable coiffure had been carelessly, unevenly trimmed. In place of her usual artful maquillage, her eyes were heavily and rather crudely outlined in thick kohl, and a streak of grime slanted across her cheek toward her pale lips. Her clothes—a long, yellowish kurta and a shapeless skirt—hung loosely; she was clearly thinner than usual. Her feet were bare and dirty.

"Cherie," Lucienne said as they embraced, "you smell awful. I mean that in the most loving way. When did you last bathe? Never mind, come with me—I'm staying at your rooming house. We'll sort you out."

Sally drew back. "You shouldn't have come. I don't need your superficial value judgments."

Lucienne stared for a moment. "Basic hygiene is a value judgment? I'm here because you wrote, urging me to come. Swimming in the warm, moonlit sea! The beauty of the town, the kind, cultured society. But Ragesh says he never sees you . . ."

Sally hissed, "Stop it, you don't know anything about my life here. Have you come to take me away? You can't! Don't touch me!" she snarled as Lucienne tried to stroke her arm.

"Sally, please," Lucienne said soothingly. "I came all this way to find you. You stopped answering my letters, and I was worried. But I'm so glad to see you. And . . . you're playing music? That's wonderful! Listen, can we just take a little walk outside? It's a beautiful night."

Sally turned away, shaking her head. "I don't want to go anywhere. My place is here. *You* should go."

Pierre had been occupied with his students, but now he turned to them with a bland smile. "Sally dearest, we mustn't be rude. Our sister Lucienne is welcome to stay with us as long as she likes."

Sally gave him a palms-together half-bow, but continued to glower until Lucienne dropped her eyes.

"All right, another time, then." She stood up quickly.

Lucienne was deeply asleep, but the sound of a key unlocking her door roused her to instant alertness.

"Who's there?"

"It's me." Sally's voice was thickened by a sigh. "Pierre said I must talk to you. Might as well get it over with."

Lucienne arranged her pillows to sit up and switched on the small bedside lamp, frowning. "Darling, I don't understand what's happening. Oh," she added, as her eyes adjusted. "Oh good, you've brushed your hair."

Sally sat stiffly on the end of the bed. "Yes. I washed a bit, too, to spare your delicate sensibilities." She made a face somewhere between a grimace and the ghost of a smile.

"Oh, Sally . . ."

Sally raised a warning hand. "Don't. Please. Things are different now. You must understand, I will never leave Shivabhai. He is my consort."

"Oh! Do you mean . . .are you in love? Oh, Sally, that's . . .that's lovely! He's quite good-looking, really, those intense eyes. I can quite see . . ."

Sally shook her head. "You see nothing, you can't understand. It is a spiritual practice; he is an incarnation of the god Shiva, and I am Kali, his sister, his consort. It is destined; it has always been. Through our drumming we create and maintain the world, we destroy what needs to be destroyed . . ." She sat very still, eyes wide, staring unseeingly inward.

Lucienne leaned forward. "Sally?" she whispered. "Darling, forgive me, but you don't sound like yourself. Please, tell me what's really going on." She reached out and gently touched Sally's knee.

Sally recoiled with a snarl, and at the same moment, there was a knock on the door. It opened a few inches, showing a young man with unruly hair, a crumpled kurta and bare feet.

"Kali, sister. Please come now. Shivabhai wants you back."

Lucienne returned to the walled compound at three the next afternoon ("first thing in the morning" by vamp standards) and was shown into the same room she'd been in before, empty, cool and tranquil, with freshly arranged yellow lilies. The inner door opened.

"Little sister, I am so glad you've come! Namaste, bonjour!" He bowed and came forward to sit beside her in the cushioned alcove.

Lucienne inclined her head slightly. "I am not sure I'm comfortable yet with expressions of kinship. You may call me Lucienne, monsieur . . . ?"

His smile widened. "Please, call me Pierre." Sally's 'consort' was freshly shaven, neatly combed, cleanly fragrant with sandalwood soap and wearing a starched white kurta of impeccable crispness.

"Pierre. Is that your name?"

"It is a name I have gone by. You may find it simplest. Like you, I have spent a good deal of time in France."

Lucienne raised her eyes to his, and he held her gaze insistently until she looked away.

"You should not make assumptions about what I would find simplest," she said lightly. "I would be interested in hearing more of your names." With effort, guesswork and a bit of linguistic glamour, she added, in a multi-lingual sentence, "We can converse in Roma, or Farsi or . . . Croatian, if you prefer."

He laughed. "Very good! But believe me, I am most comfortable in French. *You* learned it as a girl, did you not?"

She ignored the question. "You and Sally have become very close, it would appear."

Again his smile widened, knowing and toothy. "Oh, little sis . . . Mademoiselle Lucienne! How long has it been since you've had real, vamp to vamp sex? You know there is nothing else like it."

"Your question is inappropriate."

"Oho, that long!" He leaned back into the cushions, shaking with laughter and then quieted, sitting forward. "Really, ma petite, you should not deprive yourself. You are so . . . exquisite." Holding her gaze hypnotically, he gently touched the curve of her cheek.

Curious about his intention, she kept herself from flinching as his fingers slid down the side of her neck and came to rest on her breastbone.

"Right there, you had an amulet. Jade. A gift from your first lover. You have not been the same since you lost it."

Lucienne drew back and delivered a quick precise slap to his cheek. She half-expected him to grab her hand and try to wrestle with her, but he only sat back with his infuriatingly imperturbable smile.

"Such spirit! Perhaps you are also an avatar of Kali."

Lucienne frowned. "I'm afraid I am not very much interested in religion. How do you know about my amulet?"

Pierre tapped the middle of his forehead. "I see it clearly here. It has left a shining mark . . ." He broke off with a laugh. "No, Sally told me all about it, of course. Your friend Natalie, the Long Sleep, all of it. You should bring her here, in her coffin; we can all be together. I am prepared to join with any number of consorts . . ."

"Yes, I'm sure you are. But you must let Sally go. Whatever kind of hold you have over her, I ask you to release her. We are on a journey together, and it does not end here."

Pierre raised an eyebrow. "Don't be so sure." He turned to a side table, picked up a miniature brass hammer and struck a small gong three times.

After a moment, the door at the other end of the room opened, and a half-dozen of Pierre's disciples,

Sally among them, entered. Unlike their high spirits of the previous night, they filed in silently, eyes cast down. Crossing the room, each approached Pierre, bowed low and touched his or her forehead to their master's feet. Seeing Sally, disheveled again, perform this abasement made Lucienne feel sick.

No words were spoken. Pierre conveyed with gestures that they were all to leave, except Sally, who seated herself on the floor beside him. After the others had gone, he reached over to stroke her hair, as if she were a pet.

"Your friend wants you to leave me."

Sally looked up at him, eyes wide with alarm, then turned to Lucienne. "Loulou, how can you? You don't understand how happy I am here."

"Are you?" Lucienne stared at Sally, trying to read her closed, almost feral expression. "Maybe you should show me. I really don't understand all this, but perhaps if I were to spend the day with you, you could help me see your . . . happiness."

"Excellent idea, ma chère. Sally, you should show Mlle Lucienne everything—and take her out with you tonight."

"Out . . . tonight?" Sally looked startled, but settled back into a sort of sullenness with a sigh. "All right. Come along, Loulou."

Once through the mysterious flush door, Lucienne looked around in surprise.

Sally grinned. "Ha! I know what you expected—some sort of dungeon. Or at least, bleak, ascetic quarters. Not all this."

"Of course I didn't think you were in a dungeon!" Lucienne protested, indignant and embarrassed. "But I never expected all this . . ."

The space was a beautiful courtyard, filled with soft indirect light, ringed by roofed and screened but open-walled rooms, with the same finely crafted woodwork and serene aesthetic of the reception room. Different areas were evidently devoted to meditation, music and rest. The center of the courtyard was a garden, lush with greenery and fragrant flowers. Narrow, inviting paths led to a moss-edged pool.

"It's so lovely. I had no idea."

"Come, let's visit the fish." Sally took her hand, and they entered a miniature woodland, deliciously shady and refreshing. They followed a flower-fringed path to a wooden bench beside the pool. The water was full of large, healthy koi—golden, white, orange, blue-black— and their movement was hypnotic.

"Oh, they're so sweet. I haven't seen fish like these since I was a child! We had a garden something like this."

"It's my favorite place," Sally said. "I could watch them forever." Her face was peaceful and relaxed as she leaned back and stretched her long legs, pointing her toes.

"Sally," Lucienne said softly after a time, "this is the first time I feel I'm really *with* you since I've been here.

Why have you been avoiding me, trying to send me away?"

"Sshh. Just watch the fish. Don't you want to stay here forever?"

They watched the gliding fish in silence for a long time. Lucienne wanted to take advantage of the quiet and privacy to question Sally, but she found herself lulled into a dreamy, accepting state, where conversation seemed an inessential distraction.

Gradually she became aware of movement and sounds coming from the music studio. The disciples and Pierre himself had appeared and were tuning the instruments, warming up.

Sally stood up. "Music time, let's go."

In the studio, she sat cross-legged and took up a tabla, gesturing to Lucienne to sit nearby. "You can play this small drum. Just tap it every so often, like this—when you feel it's the right beat."

"Couldn't I just listen? I don't want to do something wrong."

Sally flashed a smile. "Don't worry. There's very little you can do wrong here."

The music began with a drone, a small organ-like instrument that produced a steady, see-sawing two-note sequence, and a light patter of drum beats. Pierre spoke a series of syllables that seemed to count off or intro-duce the piece, rapping out a rhythm, and the sound of the group became more definite. Lucienne closed her eyes and let her mind wander.

Everyone was playing, intent on synchronizing their beats. Pierre and one other young man had stringed instruments, and the modal lines of melody rose and twined around each other. After a while, she heard Pierre speaking again, but not the way he had begun the music. She couldn't tell whether he was using his voice or directing his thoughts to her mind. He seemed to be addressing all of them, however:

"In the beginning, children, there was Shiva. He had created the world, with plenty of creatures to feed him, but he was lonely. Then he found you, his children, his friends—you pleased him and helped him, but he was still lonely. He needed his consort, and her searched for her every day—for her or for him, for a divine consort can take any form. He searched for her among you, but none of you was the One. Then one day, one radiant day, she arrived, coming from the North, his eternal consort, his Kali. Now that she has come, his power can grow, *their* power, as a sacred dyad . . . And she must never leave, never . ."

Lucienne didn't realize that she had stood up until she found herself standing over Pierre, looking down at him. She hadn't realized he was sitting right behind Sally, so close . . . in fact, she was on his lap, still playing her tabla, as he played with her hair, squeezed her shoulder and casually cupped her breast, his instrument forgotten.

"Stop." Lucienne spoke so softly, she hardly heard herself above the music. "Stop," she said again.

The music continued to a crescendo, and then one by one, the musicians played more softly and faded out. Sally struck the last beats, eyes closed, and Pierre smiled up at Lucienne.

It was raining when they went out, fat heavy drops that soaked their hair and ran down their faces.

"Ugh, I should have brought my umbrella," Lucienne grumbled.

"Can't hunt with an umbrella," Sally said softly, peering ahead into the darkness.

"Yes, about that, darling . . . Why is it we're out here, instead of in one of those nice, dry cafes where the civilized vamps and their obliging human friends spend the evening? La Mangue Verte, Le Singe Qui Rit; it's really quite a charming scene. We could see Ragesh and . . ."

"Sshh!" Sally was half-crouching now, staring intently. Suddenly she darted forward, and Lucienne saw her seize something which she brought to her mouth—a large rodent with pale fur.

"Mon dieu, is that a rat?!" Lucienne stared, sickened. Sally had killed the creature with a single bite and was drinking avidly.

"Bandicoot," she said thickly, once she'd finished, wiping her mouth. "I'll catch one for you; there are plenty."

"No thanks, I'm really not hungry. Sally, is this what you've been living on?"

"Sure, partly. There's always blood tea available at the compound, but it's invigorating to catch fresh prey. Pierre thinks it's important to maintain our instincts."

"But . . . rats? It seems so primitive. What about drinking from humans?"

"Do you see anyone around? It's well after midnight, everything's closed."

"Is there ever anyone? A solitary person out late?" Lucienne began cautiously. "Ragesh said . . ."

"You can't believe everything Ragesh says," Sally broke in sharply. "He's been horribly jealous ever since I met Pierre."

"Yes, but . . ." Lucienne found herself blinking away tears (blending with the rain) of dismay and frustration, "I don't understand why you've turned your back on vamp society, especially here. I don't understand any of this . . ."

"No, you don't." Sally turned away, and Lucienne thought she was going to simply walk off and leave her. But just as she herself was about to stalk angrily away, Sally turned back. "Loulou, I'm sorry. I *want* you to understand. Didn't you feel it at all today—the garden, the music?"

"I liked the koi pond. The drumming—well, you couldn't really dance to it . . ." She hoped Sally would laugh, but there was no response. "Do you really like Pierre being so handsy?"

Sally ignored the question. "Come on, let's go to the beach. Have you felt the lovely warm water yet? There's no moon tonight, but it will still be beautiful." They linked arms and walked. "Loulou, I'm not explaining it well, but it's more than any one thing—the fish, the flowers, the music, the compound. It's Pierre, and it's more than him. I'm part of something so much bigger, a spiritual breakthrough. We vamps—if we don't have a spiritual life, what are we?"

Lucienne was silent, trying to understand what it was that struck a false note.

They reached the seafront, and Sally led the way down some steps, across a narrow beach of soft sand, gray beneath the starry sky. A light breeze, scented with jasmine, lifted their hair; ahead, tiny black waves lapped gently. Sally slipped out of her sandals and held Lucienne's arm to steady her while she unbuckled and removed her shoes, unfastened and rolled off her stockings. They waded in, knee deep, Lucienne lifting her skirt slightly. The water was warm, its movement deliciously silky and refreshing. Lucienne found the shifting of sand beneath her bare feet had an almost effervescent quality, like bathing in champagne.

"Sally, I know, of course I do, that the spirit is important. It's just . . . I've always felt that *you* found spirit in so many things—in art, in dancing, style, kindness, laughter, language, love. I know I feel that way. This Shiva and Kali business—I know, it's an ancient religion, important to many people but, I don't know, it doesn't seem as if it's *your* spiritual path. Or Pierre's, for that matter. He wasn't born into this tradition; he isn't Indian. What if he's just using these ideas for his own gratification? For power, for attention, for a supply of willing, subservient bodies?"

Lucienne broke off; she hadn't meant to say so much. But Sally stood tranquilly, stretching her arms to the night sky, eyes half-closed, water lapping her legs, as if she didn't even hear.

With a sigh, Lucienne turned away from the sea. "Will you help me with my shoes, darling? I'm tired, I think I'd better go back and sleep."

"All right, I'll walk back with you. But come to the ashram again tomorrow. It's good to spend time with you, Loulou."

Arriving at the ashram the next afternoon at four, Lucienne was surprised to be greeted in the reception room by Pierre and Sally together. More surprising, and pleasing, Sally was clean and well-groomed—tunic and trousers crisply pressed, hair brushed and shining, her eyes carefully outlined in kohl and a dab of lip rouge brightening her mouth. She and Pierre sat companionably side by side, with none of the overtones of dominance and subservience that had troubled Lucienne. They made a handsome, happy-looking couple.

Sally poured tea, and they all drank, an herbal infusion scented with saffron (no blood, or honey) served in an elegant porcelain pot. The lilies on the table today were pink and exceptionally fragrant.

"Ma petite soeur" Pierre began, and then stopped with a rueful smile. "Mlle Lucienne, as always, it is a pleasure to see you." After a few pleasantries, he turned serious. "I would so much like to learn more about your friend Natalie, and about the ritual of the Long Sleep. Can you tell me all about it?" He leaned toward her, holding her gaze with his deep brown eyes.

Lucienne found herself speaking candidly and in detail, starting from the beginning. She told him about the months she'd spent at her Uncle Yu's casino in the summer of 1929, leading a cosseted, sybaritic life, but held against her will by her uncle's power. How, in her time there, she'd secretly studied her uncle's books and papers, learning some of his ancient vampiric spells and practices. How Sally and Natalie had enlisted the Maharani Indira to free her, and of the fateful card game between the two old, powerful adversaries. And then how, back in Paris, Natalie had grown so unutterably weary that she began trying to end her own life. Older than Lucienne and Sally by centuries, Natalie had always been prone to melancholy, troubled by her long and bloody past.

"But, our Natalie—so beautiful, so dear to us, with her lovely deep voice and her lithe movements—we could not let her go like that. We persuaded her—or, I did, since I had read about the technique—to let us keep her with us, in a thirty years' sleep. When she wakes . . ." Lucienne broke off for a moment, taking a deep breath. "If all goes well, she will be rested and strengthened. And we will have found a good place to live, and we can all be together again." She turned to look at Sally, her eyes bright and questioning.

"And the ritual—how is it done, exactly?" Pierre asked.

Lucienne sighed. "I will try to describe it. I have never been quite sure about some of the incantations, whether I spoke them all correctly." She glanced again at Sally. "It troubles me sometimes that I might have made an error . . ."

Pierre placed his hand on hers. "I am sure that if your heart and your intention were clear and pure, that you did everything as it should be done. Tell me, can you repeat the incantations?"

Lucienne shivered. "I would rather not, right now. Perhaps another time. I might wish to go over the words, discuss the language with you."

Pierre dipped his head toward her. "Of course, all in your own good time. But can you tell me—what were the steps of the ritual?"

Lucienne stared into space, seeing the far-off scene. "We fasted. We talked together through the night. I lay with Natalie, head to head, heart to heart, and felt her thoughts and memories, absorbed some of her essence into myself . . . Then the incantations . . . no, maybe some were earlier. It's all a bit of a blur now. Then the ritual touching with the object of power . . ."

"The jade Buddha's hand," Pierre said eagerly, leaning forward. "Yes, Sally has told me of it, how you had to trade your green jade pendant for this strange, misshapen gray thing. And where is this object now?"

"It's with Natalie, in the trunk—isn't it, Loulou?"

Lucienne gave her a sharp look, but nodded. "Yes, it stays with her; it's a sort of talisman, wrapped in silk, wound around her waist."

"Ah . . ." Pierre closed his eyes, sunk deep in thought.

They all sat quietly. The fragrance of the flowers mingled with the saffron scent of the cooling tea.

"Yes, of course!" Pierre said suddenly. "I see it all. We must bring her here."

Lucienne spent most of her time over the next few days at the ashram with Sally. She learned to let go of her thoughts and meditate by the koi pond, and she began to enjoy making sounds on a small drum during music sessions.

She would leave after dusk and spend a few hours at the vamp cafes with Ragesh and his friends and their human acquaintances, socializing and feeding. When she was able to talk with Ragesh privately, she confided, "He doesn't seem as bad as I expected. Very self-centered and a bit of a charlatan, perhaps, but not truly demonically evil. I don't think they actually go out and murder people at night."

Ragesh gave her a skeptical look. "Not that you've seen, you mean."

"True. Still, I don't particularly trust him. And Sally has changed in so many ways, it's a bit disturbing. At least she bathes and brushes her hair now that I'm here."

Later, contentedly full from a warm flask and a nibble or two, she would join Sally for a walk, and would look away while her friend caught a fresh rodent dinner, after which they would ramble to the seafront.

It was there that they'd argue:

"Pierre is right; we should bring Natalie here. This place is as close to perfect as we're likely to find—we could stay forever."

"Eating fresh bandicoots? Living with Pierre and his scruffy crew? I don't think so. Listen, cherie, I'm fine being here for the moment. It has its beauties, of course it does." She lifted her eyes to the pale yellow half-moon and took a deep breath of the scented air. "And I can see how it—he—makes you happy in many ways. But . . . forever? When Natalie wakes up, when we're all together again, we need to be in a metropolis, not a backwater."

Sally looked at her quizzically. "Why?"

"Oh, Sally." Lucienne spoke with heavy sadness. "As long as I've known you, you've had this drive, this need—to know everything you can, to be always learning what's new, to be at the center of things. You are a Parisienne, born and bred. It's what makes you *yourself*."

"Don't you see, Loulou—what's new, what's at the center of things, it's all right here." She rested her hand on her breastbone. "Natalie could find peace here, a respite from all her terrible memories."

Lucienne shook her head and dropped the subject. But later, drifting off after moonset in her soft boarding-house bed, she found herself thinking, 'What if Sally is right?'

"I have something to show you, Mlle Lucienne. Come with me, please."

"Where is Sally?"

"She wished to meditate privately for an hour; she will join us later. Come, please, it's not far." Pierre seemed to be fizzing with excitement as he got to his feet, far from his usual languid tranquility. He led the way out to the entry courtyard and across it to a shadowy archway she hadn't noticed before. Down a short hallway, he opened a door.

Softly lit by a high window, the room was hung with rich silk draperies; more silks covered a sleeping platform, with smaller platforms at its sides and foot. A young woman resting there immediately rose and departed with a bow.

Lucienne stiffened. "This is your bed chamber."

Pierre laughed. "Oh, mademoiselle, I have no designs on your chastity. Only when you are ready, ma chère." As she backed away, frowning, he turned serious. "Please, forgive me, I am only jesting. What I want to show you is here."

He moved to a corner of the room which held a shrine—a low table holding small bronze statues and objects, flowers, fruit and incense, in front of a large, intricate painting.

"The painting is very old; the colors have darkened. Let your eyes adjust, and then look, here, the upper right quadrant. Look at this figure."

Lucienne peered at the painting, a crowded composition full of tiny figures. The central subject was a blue-faced, many-armed deity, but in the area Pierre had indicated, a miniature drama was playing out: a woman wrapped in a red garment lay on the ground, eyes closed, attended by two other female figures. In an adjoining section, the woman in red was standing, eyes open. A man and a woman stood in front of her, holding some kind of object to her chest; they were all surrounded by a rainbow aura.

"Do you see?" Pierre said eagerly. "It is her, your Natalie, I am sure of it. This is a powerful place—Pondicherry, this ashram—surely you must feel it. We must bring her here, heal her troubles. I think it is very possible she could wake sooner than you think."

"Do you really . . . I don't know if . . ." Lucienne was tongue-tied, confused. The room seemed very hot suddenly, and the incense was very strong. She swayed and found herself thinking she might lie down on the cool silken coverings of the bed platform. Shaking her head, she turned away from the painting, the altar and Pierre. "Excuse me, I should go. Thank you for showing me this; it's very interesting. Has Sally seen it? We'll talk it over, later."

Holding her handkerchief to her face, she hurried out of the room, across the courtyard. Sally caught up with her just before she reached the gate to the street.

"You were in Pierre's room. Did you have a good time with him?"

"What? No, what are you thinking! He showed me a painting, the one in the shrine corner—how there's a figure of a woman asleep or dead, and then she's awake, with two people holding an object to her chest. Have you seen it?"

Sally, seeming not to hear, looked at her coldly. "Loulou, in all our time together, we've never poached each other's *amants*. I know he has had his eye on you ever since you came; he wants to make you another consort. But I didn't expect you to let him . . ."

"Sally, you haven't heard a word I've said. He was just showing me the painting . . ."

"Showing you his etchings, you mean?"

"Sally, stop. Honestly. Hasn't he shown it to you? He thinks it's a representation of something like Natalie waking from the Long Sleep. I couldn't look at it very long; the incense made me dizzy, but—what do you think? Should we bring Natalie down here and hope the power of this place, or something Pierre knows, can help her?"

Sally blinked. "You were looking at that picture in the shrine? With all the tiny people in it, really? Hmm. I've never looked at it closely. But do you really think .

. ." She broke off, absently running her fingers through her hair.

"I don't know. He thinks she could . . . wake here. Maybe it is worth a try. I don't even know if it's what she would want, but Sally, you don't know how worried I've been, about whether she's all right." Lucienne had sunk onto a bench, her head in her hands. Sally dropped beside her and after a moment, put her arm around her friend's shoulder.

"Don't worry, Loulou darling. Pierre will help. We'll all be together—and then we can figure out what's best to do."

In the shady, late afternoon, Lucienne rushed across the courtyard and flung open the door to the reception room. To her delight, Sally was there alone. "I've done it, Sally!" she gasped. "I thought it would be difficult, or that I'd have to go there myself to make the arrangements. But I was able to take care of everything on the telephone. Bless that Major Hjalvarsen and his Norwegian efficiency! He's arranged for Natalie's trunk to be put on tonight's train. Your friend the gardener will travel with her, to keep her safe. She'll be here the day after tomorrow!"

"Oh, Loulou!" Sally stared at her, eyes shining, and then enveloped her in a tight hug. "I knew you would come to love it here. And all three of us together! Let's go tell Pierre."

Lucienne spent that night and the next with Sally, lying side by side, sleepless with excitement, in a little room down the hall from Pierre's. "I thought you slept with him, as his consort?" Lucienne asked.

"Oh, we don't consort all the time."

On Wednesday, they rose relatively early and bathed and dressed with care.

"What time does the train get in, again?" Sally asked, roughly every twenty minutes.

"Four-ten," Lucienne answered patiently each time. "We can go to the station at three-thirty."

They were waiting on the platform, sitting on a shaded bench, when a large automobile pulled up on the other side of the small square station building. Sally and Lucienne paid no attention to the cheerful toot of its horn or the sound of doors slamming, but suddenly, they found themselves being pulled to their feet by Princess Annie, in full flying leathers, and Maharani Indira, in a blue and silver sari and sapphires.

"Here you are, you foolish girls!" the maharani said warmly, embracing each of them.

"Oh, you've gone native, I see," said Annie with a laugh, taking in their linen kurta pajamas. "Here, you must meet my friend, Kati." She beckoned to a petite woman who was standing behind them, also dressed in flying gear, and introduced them.

Lucienne (stung by Annie's remark and feeling rumpled, even though her clothes were perfectly well-pressed) looked at the three of them in confusion. "It's absolutely marvelous to see you—and to meet you, Kati —but what are you doing here?"

The maharani looked them over coolly and then smiled. "Oh, we have just come to knock some sense into your silly heads."

"And to fly you back to Poonah. That's why Kati is with us; we've brought two planes. Not this minute!" She laughed at Sally's stricken expression. "We need to rest a bit, and I'm sure you have loose ends to tie up. Tomorrow morning we'll take off."

"But . . . you can't . . ." Sally's outcry was interrupted by the arrival of the train. She rushed forward to stand near the disembarkation steps, while Lucienne found a porter to wait with them. A handful of passengers off-boarded, a mix of locals and European visitors, but none of them was the old gardener, and the luggage being unloaded included no large trunks. Lucienne pressed a few coins into the porter's hands and dismissed him, and they returned to the newcomers.

"I don't understand," Lucienne began. "Major Hjalvarsen said the mali would be on this train, with our trunk."

"Major Hjalvarsen reports to me," Indira said sternly, "and I told him it was out of the question. What on earth were you thinking?"

"I believe I can explain." Pierre, barefoot but impeccable, had crossed the platform to join them. He sank to his knees at Indira's feet. "Maharani, I am at your service.

Would you and your companions do me the inestimable honor of visiting my humble ashram?"

Somehow, everything was different in the maharani's presence. The ashram looked shabby; the lilies scenting the reception room were wilted. The tea was lukewarm; the disciples seemed dazed and exhausted. Everyone's feet were dirty. Pierre talked at length, and jumping up, insisted on leading them all to his chamber to view the painting in the shrine. Indira was mostly silent, listening carefully, raising her monocle to her eye to study the details of the artwork.

Back in the reception room, a gong sounded from the inner courtyard, and Pierre rose.

"You must excuse me; it is time for our daily music practice. Sally . . .?"

Indira, sitting between Sally and Lucienne, placed a hand on each of their shoulders. "You must excuse these two. I need to speak with them."

Subdued, almost cowed, Pierre inclined his head and left the room.

"Come, take a walk with me, please." As the maharani stood, she seemed to glow with power, her brilliant jewelry ablaze. Wordlessly, the four young women followed her.

"I won't say he is, exactly, a fraud. I think he *thinks* he means well. He may even believe most of what he says.

But he understands very little of our mythology, our religion. What a charming place, isn't it?"

She looked around as if just noticing their surroundings. They were comfortably seated on the deep, shaded terrace of a pleasant cafe facing the seafront, sipping cool drinks which an ancient, aproned waiter had just delivered.

"Charming," Indira said again, with a nod of emphasis. "The French influence, the sea breezes. I can see why one might enjoy staying here. But not with that 'Pierre.'" She put his name in audible quotes. "You know that isn't his name. He has been around for quite a while; I believe I've heard of him over the years . . . Well, never mind."

"He wants to help us. To help Natalie." Sally half-muttered the utterance, sounding both defiant and half-defeated.

"He *wants* . . . I wouldn't say 'to help,' exactly, except to help himself. He wants something you have; something Natalie has. Come girls, drink up. I've booked a suite for us all in the best hotel here; we'll get a taxi and stop by your rooms to pack up your things. And you might want to send a message to that nice friend of yours to say goodbye." She had her monocle in and gave them a look that allowed no argument.

Next morning, far too early (it was not yet eleven), they were at the airfield. This time, Lucienne was to fly with Annie, and Sally with Kati, who gave her a huge smile and a wink.

"Annie says you're a bit of an experienced pilot your-self. Wait til you see what I can do!"

Indira took leave of them with maternal hugs. "One time up in this air-machine was enough. I shall take one of our trains. Wait for me at the house; I'll be in to-morrow afternoon. Major Hjalvarsen has orders to keep you under lock and key, if necessary. But I doubt that will be necessary."

Lucienne sighed. "Where would we go?"

"Oh, you *will* go. You've gotten up to enough trouble in my country. The arrangements are all made, for next week: I've booked passage for you on the *Conte Rosso*, for Shanghai."

S.S. Conte Rosso,
February 1935

Installed in their snug stateroom, with Natalie's trunk in the corner and their travel wardrobes unpacked, Lucienne took a piece of paper from her purse, unfolded it and pinned it up between their beds. After giving them a long, stern maternal talking-to, Indira had insisted that Annie type up her instructions for them (which she did, alternately giggling at the absurdity and swearing when she hit the wrong key):

1. Be chic and mysterious. Keep yourselves to yourselves.
2. Do avail yourselves of cocktail bars, concerts, jazz bands and dancing; these are essential to culture. Light flirtation is acceptable, even healthy, but do not form serious relationships at this time. See number 1.
3. The insulated case of vacuum flasks I am sending with you should keep you supplied for the

length of your journey. Should you desire a fresh supplement, seek out crewmen; avoid your fellow passengers. See number 1.

4. Be kind to each other. Neither of you is at fault.
5. Prepare for a new beginning in Shanghai. My dear friend, Sir Victor Sassoon at the Cathay Hotel, will be expecting you.
6. Keep a close eye on your luggage when you disembark. The go-downs of China are not to be trifled with.

Later, they sat in deep armchairs in a corner of the handsome Grand Lounge, sipping expertly-made Conte Verde cocktails (named for their vessel's sister ship and pleasingly tinted with absinthe). They wore Patou afternoon frocks, and the tilt and veiling of their small hats fulfilled the maharani's "chic and mysterious" mandate.

"I must say," Sally said, leaning back luxuriously with a small sigh of pleasure, "the old girl knows a thing or two, doesn't she? I feel better than I've felt in ages. How about you, Loulou?"

"Mm, yes, I feel very well-rested. It's peaceful, avoiding social entanglements." She turned slightly to follow, with an appreciative eye, two passing stewards speaking in rapid Italian.

"Oh really," Sally chided with a laugh.

"We're allowed to sample the crew. And 'light flirtation' is acceptable," she protested. "I wonder how Aldo and Giacomo are doing. Do you suppose they still remember us?"

"They've probably entered a monastery to nurse their broken hearts." Sally toyed with her shagreen cigarette holder. "I wonder what Shanghai will be like. And this Sir Victor character."

"Sally, I've been thinking . . . what if we stop in Hong Kong first? It's on the way; we'll be there in a few days. It's a nice big city, very cosmopolitan—the British run it, so you should love it there."

"That's all very well, but why, darling? Our passage is paid all the way to Shanghai, and we have this introduction. Shouldn't we go on following Indira's instructions?"

Lucienne leaned back in her chair with a deep sigh. "I don't really want to talk about it, but Shanghai . . . has a lot of history for me. Memories I don't want to revisit. I didn't realize until we started getting closer . . ." Her eyes went wide and unseeing; finally, she shook herself. "I just can't, not quite yet. If you want to go ahead with the plan, go on; we can meet up later.'

"Oh Loulou, no! I don't want to be apart from you again, not now. If you want to go to Hong Kong, that's where we'll go."

Hong Kong,
September, 1935

Well past midnight, Lucienne was still agitated, fidgeting with her last good jade bangle, when Sally came in from her shift at the Red Lotus.

Despite a fierce scowl that suggested she would have slammed the door if she wasn't so tired, she looked utterly defeated. Already slumped, she leaned forward limply to slide her dress off over her head before flinging herself onto the cotton mattress. After a few immobile moments, she unbuckled her shoes, unhooked and rolled down her stockings and tossed them away, stretching her liberated bare feet.

Lucienne took two stoneware bottles from the cupboard and handed one to Sally. They both drank deeply, Sally leaning against the wall with closed eyes. Lucienne watched her friend with wordless sorrow: grayish skin, lackluster hair, bruised feet—Sally looked terrible.

"I'm guessing we're not going out tonight."

Sally opened her eyes and groaned. "I'm done in—and I've got to mend this frock. Seam's out again."

"Sally . . ."

"Don't. You know this is the only job I can get here. I'll be fine—just need to rest my dogs a bit—and as long as you keep getting translation work, we'll manage. Really, I'm fine." Her color was, in fact, improving as she drank. "If only the rent for this rathole wasn't so outrageous. But we do need a roof over us, however shabby." She glanced around the room, taking in the clothes hung everywhere, the table cluttered with cosmetics and the large trunk in the corner.

"Sally . . ."

"Loulou, stop. And please, don't ask me to sell any more jewelry. I wish you wouldn't either. We will get out of here, somehow."

Lucienne sat down beside Sally and put an arm around her shoulders, smoothing her silky bob. "You need to get your hair done, darling—your original color's coming through. Anyway, come on, let's find some nice clothes and go out."

"Really, I can't."

"Really, you must. We're celebrating. And you don't have to go back to that foul dancehall tomorrow night, or ever. I've had the most amazing news."

Hong Kong, August, 1935

Hong Kong was, at first, curiously fascinating. They hadn't planned on heading there—they'd been en route to Shanghai, when Lucienne realized she wasn't ready to face the place yet. Once arrived, they hadn't planned on staying more than a couple of weeks, but now more than six months had passed.

Lucienne would never have expected or admitted it—having lived a cosmopolitan, mostly Parisian, life for so long—but there was something comforting about being in a place where she looked approximately like everyone else. She was taller than average, and certainly far more chic, but she didn't automatically stand out in a crowd. She was not exotic.

Sally, of course, *was* exotic in the extreme: close to six feet tall, pale and angular. Not that she minded attention. Head high, she walked the Bund as if she were still modeling couture on the rue Cambon, bestowing an occasional radiant smile if the attention came from someone attractive. Unfortunately, attractive partners were in short supply at the Red Lotus, where her looks had gotten her the job as a dance hostess.

Meanwhile, Lucienne had met Freddy Yang. He worked for a large textile export firm, and after a chance encounter in a French bookstore, where Lucienne spotted him leafing through a copy of Baudelaire's *Fleurs des Mal*, he began to call her several times a week for translating jobs, as well as coffees, cocktails, dancing and concerts.

"I like him so much," she confided to Sally in an almost incredulous tone. "He's handsome, intelligent, worldly—everything but rich, unfortunately. And I love how he tastes. You know," she added playfully, "it's widely acknowledged that Chinese blood is the most delicious in the world."

Sally raised her eyebrows. "Really?"

"No, I just made that up. But he does have a particularly savory flavor. I haven't liked anyone as much since Alain . . ." Her eyes clouded as her thoughts drifted back to the sweet young Frenchman she had inadvertently killed. It seemed so long ago. "I'll never make that mistake again." Lucienne peered closer to the mirror, extending the fine line of her brows with tiny, expert strokes. "What are you wearing tonight, Sally? Can I borrow your peacock blue?"

"Sorry darling, no, I have to mend it again. The punters always swing me too hard; I think they do it to compensate for being shorter than me."

Lucienne frowned. "We've got to find you a better job. Can we try again spending a little time each day on language lessons? I'm sure it will go better, now that we're more settled."

Sally sighed. "I don't think so. We all have our talents, and language facility is clearly not one of mine. All those years I thought I was becoming fluent in English—what a laugh!"

Hong Kong, September, 1935

Sally had bought a battered, second-hand phonograph and a handful of records at a street market within days of their arrival, and Lucienne had frankly thought she was crazy. But she was grateful now, heading back to their room with Freddy's gift, for Sally's jazz-mad obsession.

"Look darling, Freddy's given me some hot new tunes!" she called as she unlocked the door, before realizing that Sally had already left for the club. With a shrug, she opened the player and slid the black disc out of its wrapper.

Bright horns, a quick syncopated tempo, a minor key —Sally will adore this, she thought. But the music faded out, and after a moment's silence, a voice began: a dry, elderly, familiar voice that sent chills down her spine.

"Liu Shien, beloved niece. I apologize for this childish ruse, but I have been desperate to contact you. As you must know, I know that you have left Paris and relocated several times, yet you have sent back all my letters, ignored my telegrams, and I've no doubt you would turn away any messenger whom you knew to come from me.

"The reason I must reach you is simply this: I am dying, my dear, and I need to settle several arrangements concerning you. There is an address printed on the record label; please go there, I implore you. One of my solicitors, Mr. Julius Han, will explain everything and go over the necessary paperwork.

"Liu Shien, I ask you this in honor of your ancestors and our familial bond."

Lucienne heard a cough and a throat-clearing, and then the voice changed, becoming deeper, with rich resonant overtones. "Shien, ma petite, my precious night-blooming jasmine. I know that you will do this for me."

She gasped, still as helplessly thrilled as when she was a girl of sixteen.

"To come to the point. . ." Julius Han, Esquire, had reached this statement after at least a half hour of formalities and preamble, "Your uncle has named you as his primary beneficiary. You will have a guaranteed income, sufficient to your needs, for life." He raised his eyes to hers briefly. "For your lifetime, however long. The funds will become available to you upon Liu Yu's death."

"I see," Lucienne said neutrally. "And how is my uncle?"

"He is quite well, or as well as can be expected. Of course, none of us is as young as we once were." Again his eyes flicked up to meet hers, his expression opaque. "But most likely his health will endure for at least another decade or two."

"So then, we are not talking of any immediate change in his—or my—circumstances. Forgive me, but I fail to understand his urgency in contacting me."

"Ah, I have not conveyed something of importance." Mr. Han leafed slowly through the papers on his desk.

"Your uncle wishes you to take immediate possession of his largest business concern: the Imperial Casino in Shanghai. He considers it fortuitous that you are here."

"What! No. Oh, no. Never."

Lucienne closed her eyes, flooded with images and memories of her time at her uncle's Casino Impériale in France. Glamour and blood, exquisite brocaded gowns, her lavish apartment, spying eyes everywhere, implacable rules, human despair, stifling atmosphere . . . She'd inhabited a luxurious prison, supplied with blood pets to keep her perfectly sated, and she'd watched her uncle's establishment purvey sublime pleasure and utter ruin with equal indifference.

"I cannot possibly accept," she said, opening her eyes to look levelly at Han.

The lawyer inclined his head courteously. "It is, of course, your right to refuse . . . though I assure you, Liu Yu will be devastated if that is your decision. But as you say, there is no great urgency; you may take your time to consider this offer. You should know, also, that the terms of your ownership will be completely up to you. You may take a personal role in the running of the casino—and as he values your talents so highly, that would be Liu Yu's dearest wish. But if your interests lie elsewhere, you may allow the establishment to continue under its present, very competent management, and merely accept fifty percent of the profits, as is due the owner, deposited to your account, wherever you may be. Or, you could even sell the place."

Lucienne shook her head. "I am, unfortunately, too well acquainted with the source of those profits to ever enjoy them."

Mr. Han held up a hand. "Please, Miss Leung. You must take some time to consider. And, let me clarify: if you reject ownership of the casino, you will, de facto, no longer be your uncle's heir and will receive nothing upon his death. Now, I must go north on business for a few days. Please think this over carefully, and give me your answer any time after the end of the week. Good day, miss."

Lucienne sighed, smoothed her gloves and stood up, pushing her chair back with a harsh scrape. "Goodbye, Mr. Han."

Lucienne walked away down the crowded, late-afternoon street, seething. Office workers, students and street hawkers all gave her a wide berth. She had dressed with particular care and knew that her make-up and clothes (even though they were several seasons old and would be hopelessly passé in Paris) gave her an intimidating foreign chic. More than that, if even a little of the rage and shock she felt showed on her face, people must surely see her as mad and dangerous.

"Damn him. How dare he try to buy back my loyalty and affection? Money is always his answer." As clearly as if it were right in front of her, she saw his hand putting a roll of banknotes into hers.

Indochine, 1878

She was sixteen, leaving her home and her parents for the first time, and forever. She had to leave. Luc —her magical, midnight lover, who read poetry to her in his thrumming, resonant voice and crushed jasmine blossoms against her skin—Luc had changed her. She was no longer a docile young girl, ready to marry the merchant her parents had chosen for her; she was a vibrantly aware, sensually awakened young woman—with an extreme sensitivity to light and a taste for blood.

The last time Luc had come to see her, she didn't need to be told it was the last time. His tenderness as he held her, as she sucked sweet blood from his wrist; the look in his gentle, serious eyes; the way he inhaled her fragrance—all spoke clearly. He gave her a gift, too— an oval pendant of lettuce-green jade, covered in exquisitely fine carving. It hung from a fine gold chain which he'd fastened carefully around her neck, his eyes wet.

She did not weep or cling to him when they parted; she only kissed him, and let him kiss her, deeply enough to remember all her life.

The next night, her Great Uncle Liu Yu had summoned her to his wing of the family compound. Though the old man gazed at her with kindness and affection, he told her that she had disgraced her family and must leave immediately.

"Go tonight. Here is some money for your journey; find a ship and go as far away as you can. You are clever and beautiful, my child—you will make your way."

The thick roll of money seemed enormous, so naturally her plan was to go to Paris, the marvelous city of her schoolbooks. She packed a small bundle with some extra clothes rolled around her comb and her three jade bangles; she dressed in simple dark trousers and tunic and made her way to the docks. After several hours of questions and of being laughed at, she learned that the farthest she could reasonably travel was Shanghai.

Shanghai, 1878

The city was huge, hot and far too bright. They arrived in mid-morning, and after she'd stepped, squinting, down the gangplank, she took the first open door she could find into a shadowy warehouse, wedged herself into a corner behind a pile of crates and slept.

Emerging into the more comfortable light of late afternoon, she had only gone a few yards when a sailor fell into step beside her.

"Hello, little girl. Can I help you?"

She looked up at him demurely. "I'm new to this place. Where should I go?"

The sailor, a slim but muscular fellow, puffed up a bit with importance. "You've asked the right man; I know this town very well. Come, I'll show you some of the sights."

"Are you hungry or thirsty?" he asked, after they'd wandered the city for several hours. It was early evening by now.

"Not really. But can we sit down here for a minute?" Shien indicated a tree-shaded bench in a small park.

"Of course we can, sweetie," her guide said with a smile. As they sat, he put his arm around her shoulders and drew her close.

Shien could smell his blood; his throat, in the open collar of his middy shirt, looked smooth and inviting. She'd never drunk from anyone but Luc, but she knew what to do. Delicate and needle-sharp as a cat's teeth, her fangs emerged as she snuggled up to him. She drank gently—he didn't struggle or gasp—and she took what she needed but not more than he could spare. When she was done, he gazed at her with wide, sleepy eyes.

"Little girl, where'd you learn to kiss like that?"

She fluttered her lashes at him, filling his mind with mist and softening his memories, until he closed his eyes.

"Hello, beautiful! Want a cup of tea?"

Shien turned at the sound of a female voice, low and melodic, with what sounded like a trace of her own accent. She saw a gracefully-built woman, extraordinarily pretty and well-dressed, standing beside the brightly lit doorway of an elegant building. She couldn't quite tell what the place was (a hotel? A vastly large home?) and couldn't imagine why someone there would speak to a shabby-looking young creature like herself. But she had been walking for hours now; it was quite late at night, and she had no idea of where she might shelter from the dawn.

"Come in—I won't bite." The woman smiled, and Shien smiled back. Was this a coded message, someone like her?

"Thank you, but I couldn't possibly put you to any trouble," she said politely.

"Don't be silly. I'd like your company; it's the quietest time of night. Come in," she insisted. She led Shien through a huge foyer into a small cozy parlor with European-style furniture. A kettle steamed over a little gas heater.

"Have you eaten? I can ring for some soup and rice."

"No, thank you. I have eaten very well this evening." Shien found herself slightly disappointed that the woman did not appear to know this. "But a cup of hot tea would be nice."

The woman filled porcelain cups for each of them and placed them on a low table, in front of a velvet sofa. As soon as Shien sat down, she sat beside her, very close, and studied her intently.

"Heavens, you're so young to be out on your own. And really very beautiful." She smoothed Shien's hair and put a finger to her cheek, turning her face toward the lamplight. "May I?" Without waiting for an answer, she undid the top, knotted button of Shien's tunic.

"Don't be afraid, I just want to see how pretty you are. Your voice is well-bred. Your clothes are good quality. You come from Indochine if I'm not mistaken, and you can't be more than . . . sixteen?"

Shien nodded, lulled by the woman's kind, warm voice and the fingers gently squeezing her shoulder, stroking her neck.

"Perfect, velvet skin. Fragrant as a lily. So young—but you're not a virgin, are you?"

Shien's eyes widened, and her hand went to the jade pendant resting against her chest, under her clothes.

"It's all right, little darling, don't worry. I know all about it. You had a lover, a wonderful boy, but he's gone. He had to go—who knows why. He gave you this . . ." Her fingers drew out the pendant and she eyed it appreciatively. "This exquisite jade, and you'll always remember him. But you've changed, he changed you, and you can't live your old life anymore, so you're here. You need a safe place to stay, and I can give you that. Stay here, with us."

Shien blinked. She hadn't even noticed how, but her buttons were all undone, and the woman was gazing at her breasts and at the jade plaque against her skin. "Perfect, perfect," the silk-clad, perfumed lady murmured.

"But, what is this place? What do you mean 'stay with us'?"

"This is a house of women, and a house of stories. We all have stories, like yours. I am Madame

Chrysanthemum. You will meet the others, in time. And your name, little one?"

"Liu Shien, Madame."

"Perfect—we will call you Lucienne. Chic, French!"

Hong Kong, September, 1935

Lucienne shook her head, returning to the present. She'd grown up fast in that house of women, especially after hearing some of their stories. Within two weeks, she was Mme Chrysanthemum's personal assistant. She also, in time, vastly increased the house's income, in a way that involved no direct contact with clients, except in the case of a few gentlemen with extremely specialized tastes—with whom she completely enjoyed her encounters. She did not entirely regret the experience. Yet, she knew that Uncle Yu could easily have given her enough funds for direct, first-class passage to Paris, and an elegant townhouse too, for that matter.

But then, I might never have met Sally and Natalie. She sighed, and hurried back along the Bund toward their room. She had to talk to Sally, and to decide what to do.

Shanghai, October, 1935

Sally took in the large, luxe room: modern furniture, gold wallpaper, huge bed in its curtained alcove. And all hers. Lucienne's room, with celadon wallpaper, was next-door; they shared a sitting room, bath and a massive closet, with a nice secure corner for Natalie's trunk.

"Not too shabby. Not bad at all. Oh, Loulou—how can I thank you enough? I know you didn't want to take this on—the casino, the rest of your uncle's legacy—but thank you from my deepest depths. I was starting to think I would actually die, never mind immortality, on that bloody dance floor at the Red Lotus."

"Bloody as in a British obscenity, or as in blood? I thought you didn't do any snacking on the job."

"Bloody as in my poor, blistered, worn-to-shreds feet!" Sally flung herself onto a satin pouf at the dressing table. "I intend to stay off them as much as possible for at least the next fortnight."

"All right, but remember, I want you to help me with the staff interviews. I plan to keep everyone in place, for the most part, but I still want to meet them all and check whether anyone seems off. I'd really appreciate your judgment. We should go downstairs in about an hour."

"Of course, darling," Sally murmured, gazing into the large round mirror, brushing her hair with a silver-backed brush.

"Sally, are you ready? Oh . . ."

Sally still sat at the dressing table, still lightly smoothing the brush over her hair.

"Hey, are you planning to look in the mirror all day?"

Sally blinked slowly and smoothed an eyebrow. "You know, I think I will."

Lucienne sighed, ready to scold her friend, then shook her head and left the room. Sally clearly needed a break.

Always, she had sought the new. As a child, she always felt she could not wait for each next birthday, each year of new lessons and skills. Learning to write, to explore the manifold world of books, to play tennis, to classify flowers, do mathematics, identify the constellations . . . And then the still more exciting realms of adolescence: languages, philosophy, dancing, flirting, kissing.

Her life since the change had been, for the most part, a two-hundred-odd-year adventure. The strong, supportive traditions of her family and circle—especially her mentor, M. Grandin and her beloved *grandmère*—had guided her through the transition, so that she'd been free of the shock, trauma and confusion that were so often the new vampire's lot. Moderation, skill, self-care and ethical blood-letting were all part of her training, allowing her to focus on the pleasures and benefits of a very long lifespan. Keeping up with the latest developments in the sciences, literature and above all, her passions—fashion and music—kept her constantly engaged and excited. True, some eras seemed inherently more or less interesting than others. At the moment, she could not help regretting the end of the vibrantly experimental spirit of the last decade. People at present tended to be less playful, more serious, preoccupied with politics and money.

Apart from jazz and cocktails and delicious frocks, the 1920s would always be dear to her because of meeting Natalie and Lucienne. Not since the 1780s had she had such sustained, and sustaining, friendships with other vamps. She had always sought out interesting mortals and spent rewarding times together; she loved the flutter and frisson of human romantic attachments, too, though they rarely deepened into real intimacy, because of the parts of herself she couldn't share. But her bond with Lucienne and Natalie, despite their differences in taste and personality, was wordless, immediate and unbreakable. Their time together in Paris . . . she thought of them, making an entrance at the Ritz, strolling the grand boulevards, sharing secrets, songs, confidences and clothes . . . had been a rare and special joy. She could only hope it would happen again. Did the Long Sleep really work? Had Lucienne understood the ritual well enough And could they keep Natalie's coffin safe for another twenty years?

"You have got to get a good jazz band in here," was Sally's first comment after their tour of inspection. They were lounging on divans in Uncle Yu's—now Lucienne's—private office, shoes kicked off, swigging from their flasks.

"What do you mean—what's wrong with the band down there?"

"Oh, come on—those arthritic geezers? Sure, they know the latest tunes, but . . . I don't know, they play as if they're translating. You can tell the string bass player wishes he had an *er-hu*."

"I don't want to make a lot of changes until I understand the operation better. Anyway, the band is fine; people dance to it."

"Big-time players and their lovers stagger out and fox-trot just to take a break from the tables, but come on, Loulou, it's dreary. Don't you want the Imperiale to be the talk of the town? If people come for the music, they'll stay and gamble."

"Fine. You want a hot jazz band? *You* find them, audition them—I give you complete authority to hire a band."

"Really?" Sally was beside herself with excitement.

"Yes, really. That can be your project. I'll . . . try to make some sense of these." Lucienne leaned over a number-filled ledger, frowning.

Sally had had what she thought was the brilliant idea of asking each band to play "Dinah," but by the sixth time through the lively but well-worn tune, she wanted to scream. Chinese, American, German, Filipino and French—all the bands she'd heard so far had been at least halfway competent musicians, but all were lacking the spark, the special something she was looking for.

She called a lunch break and went up to Liu Yu's office to drain a flask and rest her ears. When she returned, another band was just finishing set-up: two Chinese guys on trombone and cornet, a European-looking fellow on drums, a Black American bass player and a slim, dark-haired pianist, facing away from her, who seemed to be the leader.

From their opening bars, she was hooked, but when the pianist took a solo, she put down her notebook and cigarette, took off her dark glasses and stared. When they finished the tune, stood and took a bow, she flew from her seat, arms wide.

"Claude! Is it really you?"

"Sure thing, little girl. I might ask the same thing you're about to—what the *hell* are you doing in Shanghai?—but I think I can guess well enough."

Sally stood with her hands on his firm, strong shoulders and pulled him close, nuzzling his coffee-brown neck, inhaling his scent. "That wasn't *my* question. You . . . you're not dead! I wish I'd known! I've missed you so much, I've felt so sad . . ."

"I know, I know . . . Listen, cherie, I'd love to take some time with you. But first, can I tell the boys whether we've got the job? Do you want to hear another song, or do we need to play for the boss?"

"I want to hear all your songs, but I *am* the boss, and yes, of course you've got the job. Eight to one, Sundays and Mondays off, name your price. Give them the news and then come with me; there's so much I need to ask you."

They were settled in a snug, private lounge, normally reserved for high rollers, a decanter of cognac between them. Claude produced a flask and fortified his drink, while Sally raised an amused eyebrow.

"Blood and Courvoisier? Never had those together."

"My drink of choice. Mm, Sally, you are a sight." He looked her up and down appreciatively, from her tiny veiled hat, down the sleek line of her suit, to her ankle-strapped peep-toe shoes. "The new styles suit you."

She shrugged. "I still prefer ten years ago—and of course, I'm freakishly tall for Shanghai—but thanks. So . . . the last time I saw you, that night on rue Cambon . . . What a debacle, but you played phenomenally!"

Claude nodded graciously. "It was such an extraordinary spectacle; I was just trying to keep up. You know, Mlle really is a genius."

Sally blinked. "She . . . what? I've hated her all these years; I thought she had killed you. So, what, was she your mistress then?"

Claude laughed warmly. "Sally, you're jealous, girl! You know I don't swing that way. No, we never had a *relationship*, and I can't say I admire her as a person—I just meant she is a really gifted designer." He paused, eyes unfocused. "It wasn't on purpose, her turning me. No, I believe she meant to drain me, but maybe she got distracted. And then, maybe because of all the times you and I had fooled around, I think I must have had some kind of resistance or something. I don't really under-stand it, but I woke up the next evening in the police morgue—and I knew what had happened. Been living '*la vie de vampire*' ever since—it's not that much of a stretch for a jazz musician. And I have to say, it has suited me very well. Not at all a bad way to meet some well-turned out young gentlemen. But now, tell me about *you*—I still can't believe we've both ended up here! How are Luci-enne and Natalie—you three still hanging together?"

"Well, it's a long story . . ."

Sir Victor Sassoon, elegant and portly, was seated at his personal table, beside a window overlooking the Bund, in the Peking Room restaurant and bar, on the eighth floor of his Cathay Hotel. This early in the cocktail hour, the tables were only half-filled, but an agreeable tinkle and hum came from the assorted businessmen, ladies of fashion, journalists, diplomats and tourists who populated the fabled room.

He turned from the outside view to watch with pleasure the approach of two young women, preceded by the maitre d'.

"Well, well—at last—the Misses Lafayette and Leung!" He put in his monocle to gaze at them with bemused appreciation. The Maharani and I had quite given up hope."

As they began to murmur their apologies, he cut them off.

"No need, my dears—you have obviously made good use of your time. Here I was expecting to take in a couple of stray waifs, and instead, I find myself addressing the new owner of the Imperial Casino," he gave Lucienne a small bow, then turned to Sally "*and* the woman who stole the best jazz band in Shanghai from under my nose! I applaud your taste and acumen, my dears. Come, let's have drinks and you can tell me how it all came about." He signaled to a waiter and ordered a round of Conte Verde cocktails. "Something very special—you'll like it."

"Oh yes, we became quite fond of them on our voyage. Though they ought to create a red drink for the *Conte Rosso*, don't you think?"

"I see I cannot impress you with anything," Sir Victor said equably. "Ah, here we are. To Shanghai!"

After a sip, he set his drink down, took out his monocle, polished it and put it back. "Now then," he leaned forward attentively, prepared to be entertained. "You were on the *Conte Rosso*, due to arrive last February. How on earth did you lose your way?"

Lucienne gave him a cool look. "It's entirely my fault, Sir Victor. I had an appointment in Hong Kong. Sally kindly came along to keep me company."

"An appointment? Oh, I see . . ." Clearly, he saw nothing but the opaque expression Lucienne was using to suggest that their detour was none of his concern. "An assignation, perhaps?" he suggested with slight relish, which faded at her continued lack of response. "Or a family commitment . . .?" He trailed off, looking so disconcerted that Lucienne took pity on him.

"A family matter. Having to do with my inheriting the casino from my uncle." Her smile firmly closed the door to further discussion. "And we are thrilled to be here now, especially in your exquisite hotel. In fact, I'd love to pick your brain on some matters of management—it's all quite new to me." With that tactful move, they were soon engrossed in a detailed discussion of staffing ratios, ventilation systems and other esoterica.

Sally's attention wandered as she surveyed the room. A dark-haired, gamine western woman in a black velvet qipao seemed to be headed for their table, but seeing Sir Victor engaged, she changed course, throwing Sally a smile and a wink. Sally smiled back at her and then started in surprise—what she had thought was a small furpiece on the woman's shoulder turned its head and revealed itself as a capuchin monkey.

"Ahem. Miss Lafayette?" Sir Victor's polite tone indicated he was repeating himself and trying not to show impatience.

"Oh, I'm sorry. I was distracted by . . . is that really a monkey?"

Sir Victor peered short-sightedly in the direction she indicated and then let out a laugh. "Of course. That's my dear friend, Mickey! You must meet her sometime. But not now; it looks as if she's working, chatting up a source. She's a journalist, frightfully clever."

"The monkey?" Sally asked, bewildered.

"Hah! You are a wit, Miss Lafayette. No, Mickey is the girl—Emily Hahn, American. I don't remember the monkey's name. Anyway, what I was trying to ask you was whether we might come to some arrangement, to share the audience fairly between both of our jazz clubs. I'm sure you know that Wednesday is *the* night for Ciro's— you know I own that place too, yes? I've got a pretty hot combo working for me, the Jasmine Jazzmen, hah! We could trade off. What about featuring your fellows on Tuesdays at your casino and Thursdays in my little *boite* here on the ninth floor? Fridays and Saturdays I'd have them for the early show and you the late . . . eh? What do you think?"

"What I think is . . . I've hired Claude and his band; I don't own them and can't loan them out. You're welcome to make them an offer and see what they say." She said this with equanimity, knowing what Claude's answer would likely be. "I look forward to seeing this band of yours. As far as the Shanghai audience goes, I believe we'll just have to let the best jazz-men win." She smiled and stood. "*Pardonnez-moi*. I must go powder my nose." She glanced at Lucienne, but her friend's posture conveyed that she wanted to continue her conversation.

In no actual hurry to reach the ladies' lounge, Sally strolled the wide corridors in carpeted quiet. The light was diffused by translucent panels of pressed glass, embellished with jazzy floral and zigzag motifs, reminding her strongly of Paris. The air, scented with eau de cologne, enhanced the illusion—she could be at the Ritz. She reached up to pat her shellacked finger waves and straightened the crisp organdie flange at her neckline, feeling appropriately stylish. Uncle Yu's—Lucienne's—*their* casino was glittery, expensively built and large, but this place spoke of a cosmopolitan taste far beyond mere money. Sir Victor had initially aroused her amused pity (they'd been told about his crippled leg, of course) with his over-obvious, monocled interest in any passing pretty woman, but now, privately, she admitted to herself, *The man's a genius, and his hotel is magically transported from Paris.*

Just as she thought this, Sally blinked at the vision of a tall, gorgeous young woman coming toward her. Perfect make-up enhanced her exquisite features and tawny skin. Her elongated frame ('I think she's taller than I am!') was snugly encased in a cocktail suit of subtle detailing and sumptuous cloth—a dark lamé with the sheen of polished leather. A lavish brooch sparkled on one shoulder and was echoed by a smaller gem on the elegant turban that wrapped her small neat head. Her ankle-strap shoes had the highest possible heels, yet her gait was comfortable, confident, professional . . .

"I know you!" Sally exclaimed at the realization. "Princess . . . Sumaire, n'est-çe pas? We modeled together at Mlle's atelier! Just one show, I think, and then I heard you'd moved on to Schiaparelli."

"Of course! I remember you." Her arms were out; they embraced and exchanged double air kisses. "What on earth are you doing in Shanghai?"

"Is this Shanghai?" Sally laughed. "I thought we were at the Paris Ritz."

They found their way to the ladies' lounge, and Princess Sumaire shared a soupçon of cocaine from her lacquer cardcase. "So, what the hell have you been up to in the last . . . oh god, it can't have been eight years!"

"Oh, you know . . ." Sally said vaguely, "seeing the world."

Sumaire leaned forward with unexpectedly keen interest. "Let me guess—you're a diplomat's mistress? Banker's wife? No, sorry, nothing so ordinary. But there's something . . ." Her eyes widened. "You're not on the run, are you? From a bad man, or, or . . . the police? Have you pulled off a jewel heist?"

Sally smiled and touched one of her sapphire earrings. "I came by these fair and square, a gift from a lovely boyfriend in Egypt. But what about you? How do you happen to be here?"

The princess sniffed and put her case away, turning to check her lipstick in the mirror. "Oh, I'll tell you my whole epic story . . . but I need to figure you out first. It's just something I do. I can tell you have secrets."

"Who doesn't?" Sally took out her own compact and inspected her maquillage.

Sumaire turned to her again, studying her intently. "Are you a spy? I am. Part-time, anyway."

"No, but they thought I was, in Barcelona. I was almost locked up."

"And you talked your way out of it, I dare say."

"I supposed you could say that. I was so confused by their questions that they concluded I was a perfect idiot! So, how do you come to be a part-time spy?"

"Oh, no." The princess wagged a finger playfully. "Your story first. Where did you go after Barcelona?"

"Hmm. Rome briefly—we didn't stay too long, the political situation seemed . . . unpleasant. Then Cairo., a fascinating place; we were there quite a while. Then India—mostly in Poonah—and a stopover in Hong Kong, and then here."

"Poonah! Great town—did you go to the races? It's a bit off the usual tourist track; how'd you come to be there?"

"Well . . .we'd gotten to know the Maharani of Cooch Behar in Paris, and she always said . . ."

"Ma Cooch Behar! Indira! I know her quite well—how extraordinary! But why Poonah?"

"I believe it's because her great-niece is studying at the university there; she has a house . . ."

"Of course, a winter residence. And then she goes north for the season. So, you didn't get to see the palace, then? What a shame, we used to have marvelous times there . . ."

Sally raised an inquiring eyebrow.

"Oh, you know—all of us royals are like one big, happy family. Or well, not always happy, but still . . . I should explain: my papa is the Maharaja of Indore. Well, he's my uncle, actually, but he's been like a father to me. We were always visiting back and forth among the families. Except for some, like the Nizam of Hyderabad; he's a dreadful snob, won't mix with the rest of us . . ."

"Oh, we met his nephew Ahmed on our boat to Bombay! He's not a bit snobbish—we became quite good friends with him and his wives. In fact, my friend Loulou almost married him too. Or, maybe she did . . .I'm not sure I ever heard the whole story."

Sumaire's expertly outlined eyes narrowed. "Well. You *do* move in interesting circles! Who did you say you were spying for in Barcelona?"

"I didn't. I wasn't!"

"Um hmm." The princess nodded skeptically. "Oh!" She had lowered her gaze to her onyx and diamond watch. "Is that the time? I must fly. See you soon, darling!" She quickly rose, blew a kiss and was gone.

Down the long, luxe hallways, Sally found her way back to the Peking Room, where Lucienne and Sir Victor were just finishing their talk and their drinks, seeming to have hardly noticed her absence. Dinner was being delivered by a pair of elegant waiters.

"I've just had the most extraordinary encounter." Sally was still bemused. "Someone we modeled with in Paris, Loulou—Princess Sumaire. She knows Indira, and Ahmed's uncle."

"I'm not convinced she's really a princess," Sir Victor remarked. "Gorgeous woman, though. They say she's a spy, but I'm damned if I know who for. She comes and goes—don't be surprised if you never see her again."

"Is there an extra flask in our overnight case?" Lucienne asked. "I'm famished."

Sally rose from her angular chair and crossed an expanse of geometrically patterned carpet. After dinner and nightcaps in the ninth-floor club, Sir Victor had insisted they be his guests for the night, and they had selected the Futuristic suite from the deluxe themed offerings.

"Here you go, love. I'm glad I packed us two each. That dinner was a bit trying, wasn't it? All those green bits, and prawns, and rice—not really my cup of tea. And that pale tea wasn't, either! Everything was so carefully arranged; it was hard to hide what one hadn't eaten . . ."

"I know," Lucienne sighed. "The cocktails were lovely, but a few minutes into dinner, I realized that despite all the modern elegance, the glamour, the view . . . it was just a Chinese restaurant. Still, I'm glad we came. Now we know what we're up against."

"Oh? I thought the plan was to be cordial cooperation?"

"Hah, I *don't* think. Why should we share our crowd with his second-rate musicians?" Taking a deep, invigorating swig, she pushed up out of her futuristic chair and bounced over to give Sally a kiss. "Thank you for insisting we get a better band! The nightlife competition is cut-throat here, and Claude is not only our dear friend, he's our secret weapon! With Claude in our club, it doesn't matter that we don't have feline hostesses like the Black Cat, or any of those scandalous acts at the Great World . . ."

"And that brothel in the French concession already has the Voluptuous Vampires of Vladivostok!"

They broke into simultaneous hoots of laughter.

"We should go and meet them," Lucienne said slyly. "Just to compare vamp notes, right? They're Russian— do you suppose any of them knew Natalie?" Her laugh faded. "No, I'm sure they're just posing. I miss Natalie so much . . ." She stretched, staring discontentedly around the room. "I want my own bed, not this 'machine for sleeping.' Shall we just skip out of here and go home?"

"Let's." Sally instantly began re-packing their few effects, surprised to realize that she, too, felt that their small apartment, tucked away on the third floor of the Imperial Casino off Bubbling Well Road in Shanghai, was "home."

"Miss Leung?"

Lucienne started; she had dozed off at her desk. She sat up straight, grateful that her assistant was so respectful and discreet.

"Yes Peony, what is it?"

"There is a guest whom I think you should observe. She is in the Coromandel Salon at present. A European lady, quite distinctive."

"Very good. Thank you. I'll be down shortly."

Peony Chan departed with a deferential bow. Lucienne stood up and regarded herself in the full-length mirror behind the door. As usual, she could hardly believe she was here, here once more—in a perfectly fitted cheongsam of silver brocade, in a luxe casino. It hardly mattered that she owned and ran the place; she still felt Uncle Yu's hand on her shoulder. With a sigh, she retrieved her purse from the desk drawer and touched up her mascara and lipstick.

"So, I went to see what was going on," she told Sally an hour later, "and there was this western lady, betting hugely, winning big. Gorgeous woman—dead chic, absolutely the latest Paris style, looked like Schiaparelli. Exquisite makeup, and beautiful. *Mad* coiffure—her hair was . . ."

"Cerise."

"Yes. It's her."

"I suppose I'll have to see her."

"Cerise."

"Sally, my darling! Oh my god, how thrilling to see you . . ."

"Please." Sally raised her hand in a warning gesture. "I need a moment. I thought you were . . ."

"Of course; you thought I was dead, somehow. But darling, you know I'm immortal. You *made* me."

"Yes, but . . . Garry could still have shot you in the heart. Your body wasn't found. The Grand Canal was right outside your drawing room window; you could well be moldering there. Not a word from you—it's been almost ten years!"

"I've always been rotten at correspondence, my dear; I know I should have written . . . And I so wanted to go to that showing at Mlle's atelier. How I wish I'd been there; it must have been so amazing . . ."

Sally could only stare at her one-time friend, while memories of the spectacle on Rue Cambon, that evening of glamour and blood at the end of 1929, washed over her. That show had changed fashion's direction, sweeping the loose, leggy look of the '20s off the stage, and had ended in a riot of carnage, leaving four men dead. Actually, only three, she suddenly realized.

"Claude is here," she told Cerise. "You know, from the Chocolate Dandies. They used to play all the best spots in Paris. He's got a terrific new band, and they're here at the casino, most nights . . . You don't know what

I'm talking about, do you?" she finished, noting Cerise's blank expression.

"A jazz band? Wonderful. I'm afraid I never really pay much attention to who's playing; it just seems a sort of background to what's really going on. But Sally, truly, I am so glad to see you again. You look marvelous as ever—*toujours chic.*"

"And you," Sally reciprocated. "I love your hair. And you're wearing . . . Schiaparelli?"

"I've got a clever dressmaker who copies my Paris things so they'll stay immortal along with me." Cerise stroked her crisply cut lapel and smiled. "At least, until some new look comes along."

Sally smiled back, but wryly. "I just wish I could have heard from you—or that you could have made some public statement. I spent months in fear of being picked up by the police."

"Oh, a few months, oh dear. Don't you realize I had to keep a low profile for years? I couldn't very well step forward, with my husband dead under such peculiar cir-cumstances, with that stupid suicide-pact note."

"So you dyed your hair a most inconspicuous color." Sally finally had to laugh. "Come on, then. Let's go have cocktails and catch up properly. You remember my friend Lucienne, don't you? She owns this place now; we'll go to the private bar."

"Cheers, ladies." The three of them clinked cocktail glasses and sipped; almost simultaneously, each set down her glass to add a swirl of blood.

"I see you still have your Cartier platinum flask," Lucienne noted.

"Actually, this is a replacement." Cerise set the elegant object on the table. "I lost my original one, intentionally. I didn't want anything with my monogram when I went incognito."

"Oh, of course. So, you don't go by Cerise Callahan Massey anymore?"

"No, I didn't even want the same initials. My new name is Renata—don't you like that, 'reborn?' I thought of keeping Cerise as a middle name, but it seemed unnecessarily risky. The hair color is my private joke, though. Of course, *you* must call me Cerise."

Sally picked up the sleek platinum flask and inspected it admiringly. "So, Cerise—Renata—how did you manage to hold onto Garry's fortune without revealing your identity?"

"Oh, I didn't. I had a few assets—some negotiable bonds, disposable jewelry—that I was able to get ahold of discreetly, to tide me over for a while. But generally, I rely on husbands."

"Plural?" Lucienne raised an eyebrow.

"One at a time, naturally. But they tend to die if they're elderly, or I just get tired of them, or someone more advantageous comes along . . . you're not shocked, are you? Haven't you done it?"

"Actually, no." Sally sounded mildly surprised. "I've never been married; it never really interested me. Don't you have to put a lot of effort into taking care of a husband? Feeding him and all that?"

Cerise laughed. "They're not housepets, silly. No, I find the ones who already have servants and staff in place for their basic needs, and then *they* take care of *me*. Clothing, travel, entertainment, all that. I insist on having my freedom, of course—not to get up to anything improper, just, you know, a vamp needs to go out at night. They've all been quite understanding."

"All? How many have there been?"

Cerise considered briefly. "Jacob Van Houten—he's in Singapore on business, by the way, he'll be joining me next week—is number five. Six, if you count poor Garry, but that seems like a whole other lifetime. Anyway . . . well, I can see you've done quite well for yourself, Lucienne, but if you're ever in straitened circumstances, I do recommend a spot of well-heeled matrimony. Cheers, darlings," she added, as their glasses were refilled.

Weeks later, Sally was pacing irritably back and forth over the thick carpeting of their sitting room. "Cerise practically lives here these days, doesn't she? I wish she'd move on. Do you think that husband of hers will ever show up?"

"Take your shoes off, darling; you'll wear a trail in the Aubusson. It's no surprise she spends all her time here;

she's become a true gambler. And she's lucky enough—and rich enough—to be able to keep it up almost indefinitely." Lucienne blew a thoughtful smoke ring.

"Well, I don't like it. She feeds on most of the staff and quite a few of the guests, and she isn't always particularly discreet. I know she's got plenty of glamour—both kinds—but last night, I saw people staring at her across the roulette table. She was nibbling the man beside her quite blatantly."

"Good thing it was only roulette. If it was a card game, people would have thought she was cheating. I agree, though. It's not seemly. We'll have to figure something out."

Lucienne stayed at the back of the salon for a while, watching the action. Cerise—wearing a strikingly tailored suit of her namesake color—was at the roulette table, betting with unstoppable nonchalance and mostly losing. Twice in ten minutes, Lucienne saw her lean over to the man on her left, nuzzling behind his ear. To her practiced eye, it was clear Cerise was feeding, but a casual observer might have thought the American woman was merely friendly, in an overly demonstrative way.

When the croupier prepared to take a break, Lucienne approached, giving him a nod. While he announced to the players that he would return in ten minutes, she went up to Cerise.

"May I have a word? Follow me, please." Lucienne turned, not waiting for an answer.

In one of Lucienne's several private offices, the small one on this floor, Cerise flung herself into a chair as if just realizing she'd been on her feet too long.

"It was a pleasure to walk behind you, Lucienne darling. No one fills out a cheongsam better." She smiled, with a provocative lift of her eyebrows. "May I smoke?"

"Of course." Lucienne, seated behind a rosewood desk, pushed a silver cigarette box across its surface.

"And to what to I owe the honor of this invitation? Let me guess—I'm being rewarded for being the chump to drop the biggest chunk of change in this joint. Big fish of the month." She filled her long cigarette holder, red amber studded with brilliants, lit up and took a luxurious drag.

"When did you become a gambler? I never saw you indulge, back when we first knew each other in Paris."

Cerise laughed throatily. "When? Why I've always been a gambler. Marrying Garry Massie, back when I only knew he was a good dancer, with money . . . I didn't know he'd turn out to be crazy, but—turn of the wheel —he was. And then, reinventing myself after his death, after he tried to kill me . . . figuring out where to go, how to live, whom to marry . . . it's been one gamble after another. Casino games are just a pastime." Cerise stretched and unbuttoned her suit jacket. "Just as well you interrupted, though—I don't know how long I was at that table. Could I have a glass of water, darling? And what is it you wanted to talk about?"

Lucienne turned to a small table behind her desk, with a tray of glasses, a decanter of brandy and a vacuum ewer of water.

"Cerise, it's been marvelous to see you again, after all these years, but you should really be thinking about moving on. When will your husband arrive? It's just that we don't really encourage long-term . . ." Lucienne had turned to hand her guest the glass of water, and she almost dropped it, her eyes wide. "How . . . where did you get that?"

Cerise's jacket was open on a satin blouse of a matching magenta hue. Above its deep neckline, against her creamy skin, hung a carved antique jade pendant, accented by a modern setting of geometrically arranged pavé diamonds.

Cerise's hand went to her chest, touching the piece as if for reassurance. "Oh, my pretty jade? Hmm, Rome, I think . . . no, wait, it was when I was married to Guillaume. Paris, of course! From that funny old Chinese man in the red pagoda in the eighth arrondissement. I always wear it when I'm in Asia; people respect the quality. It's a good piece, isn't it?"

Lucienne was still staring. "It's mine," she said quietly. "I mean, it *was* mine. I sold it to C.T. Loo."

"Really?" She watched Lucienne's face with a crafty smile. "Well then, there's my collateral, if I ever run up too much debt. I plan to stay on a while—I'm enjoying it here."

Lucienne gripped the arms of her desk chair; she had a strong impulse to lean forward and rip the gem from Cerise's neck. But her voice remained perfectly cool.

"Actually, Cerise, it's not about money. You've been feeding on my staff and on my guests, and you haven't been discreet. We can't afford to let gossip get started. I must ask you to take care of your needs elsewhere."

"Elsewhere?" Cerise sounded genuinely puzzled.

"Your hotel, perhaps? Or anywhere else in Shanghai —just not here in the casino. This establishment can't support another vamp."

"But I'm here—all the time."

"Exactly."

"Miss Leung." Peony Chan spoke apologetically. Lucienne was clearly in the middle of writing in her accounts ledger and disliked interruptions. "There is a gentleman —well, actually I would just say, a *man*—who wishes to see you. He is quite insistent."

Lucienne looked up at her assistant, gauging her expression, and nodded. "All right. You may show him in, in ten minutes. Please ask Miss Lafayette to join me, and—I doubt we will need him, but have Bruno wait near the door."

Lucienne was again writing in her ledger when the man entered. Dressed in her work-day attire of a tailored suit with a brocade, mandarin-collared blouse, she waited a minute before greeting him with a neutral expression.

"How can I help you, Mister . . .?"

"Lu Shien Leung. This is an honor." He made a half-mocking half-bow. Of moderate height and above-average width, dressed in plain dark clothing with an impressively scarred face, the man appeared to intentionally convey menace. "And this must be the famous Mademoiselle Lafayette," he added in his American-accented French to Sally, who stood to one side of the desk. "Well, well." He gave each of them a long, faintly amused stare.

"Excuse me, monsieur . . . I would like to know who you are and the purpose of your visit. You are interrupting our work."

The man clicked his tongue. "Not the most welcoming manners for a potential partner. You asked how you might help me, but you might want to ask instead how I can help you. You've got this beautiful place, bringing in good money, but, well—two young ladies, dealing with this rough town—you need to think about protecting your investment. My boss can help you out with that."

Lucienne exchanged a glance with Sally and frowned. "Our . . . investment?"

"Sure. It's the talk of Shanghai. Buying out the old man can't have been cheap. Though I'm sure you were able to show him some *persuasive* bargaining points." He looked them up and down with a comically stereotyped leer.

"My uncle," Lucienne said sternly, "gifted me with this casino. Against my will, at first, though I now find myself quite interested in its management. A process which keeps me extremely busy," she added, with an obvious glance at her ledger.

"Your uncle, of course, no offense, Miss Lu. But, all the more reason you should have our help—two young women, new to the business, dealing with large amounts of cash, not knowing who to trust . . . I don't want to alarm you, ladies, but this town is full of gangsters and thugs. We'd hate to see you get hurt."

Lucienne put down her pen and leaned forward. "Tell me, Mr . . . you still haven't given us your name. Did you and your 'boss' ever offer your assistance, your protection, to my uncle? He was an old man, after all; you might think he was somewhat . . . vulnerable."

The man looked uneasy. "No, that never came up. Mr Lu was old, but everyone knew he was powerful. He had connections. And you never saw him anywhere without some muscle at his side. Old Mr Lu would never have met me *alone* in his office." He smiled slyly and started to rise from his chair.

"But I'm not alone, and I *do* have muscle at my side," Lucienne said calmly.

Without even seeming to move, she and Sally were suddenly flanking their visitor, fangs bared at each side of his neck.

"You seem to have had some respect for my uncle, but you seriously underestimate him if you think he would pass his legacy to someone who wasn't his equal in power. Go ahead, Sally."

As Sally clamped onto the side of his throat, her prey gasped and began to flail. Lucienne grabbed his outstretched arm, pushed up his sleeve and sank her fangs into an artery.

They released him, finally, and Sally pushed him back into his chair before he fell.

Lucienne licked her lips, straightened her jacket and resumed her seat behind the desk. "So, Mister . . . I shall just call you Mister Man. Please tell your boss we do not require his assistance. We thank him for his concern. Bruno . . ." She hardly raised her voice, but the powerful bodyguard was beside her in an instant, "Bruno will see you out."

Lucienne now knew far more about management, building systems and local politics (whom to bribe, how to negotiate tax assessments) than she'd ever imagined possible. She was unexpectedly grateful to her uncle, on an almost daily basis, for the uniformly high quality of the staff, which allowed operations to run smoothly with very little effort on her part.

Meanwhile, Sally had made good on her promise to raise the club's level of fashionable buzz; there was no establishment more talked-about and sought-after. While Claude and his Syncopaters were the primary draw, Sally had gradually found other acts to round out each evening and to keep the party going late into the night. A local band, the Hangkow Hot Shots, filled in for the Syncopaters on Sundays and Mondays. A chorus line (some of them poached from the Voluptuous Vampires of Vladivostok) flashed their elegant legs twice each night. Sally had also hired (and developed a personal relationship with) a Russian-Jewish comedian, Nathan Minsk. His eccentric, polyglot monologues were inexplicably hilarious even when only half-understood, and after hours, Sally found him infinitely stimulating and delicious.

Finally, there was the gorgeous Ying-Lee Kelly, a red-haired Irish-Chinese chanteuse and vamp. Her rich, husky vocal timbre, combined with her vampire glamour, gave her performances a completely hypnotic effect; there were patrons of both sexes who came back night after night just to see her brief midnight set. She also brought in her own following from the local vamp community, adding to the intriguing heterogeneity of the Imperial's crowd—international and local, fabulously wealthy or moderately well-heeled, dedicated gamblers, bon vivants, trend-setters and trend-followers, jazz-lovers, fashion plates, sensation seekers.

Ying-Lee and her friends had impeccable vampire manners; if they ever fed on the premises, it was so discreet as to escape notice. Cerise, meanwhile, had finally begun to ease off the roulette tables and now spent the better part of her time at Sir Victor's Cathay Hotel and at Ciro's.

One bustling Thursday night, Lucienne idly scanned the casino's main floor from a mezzanine alcove, only half-attentive to the lively, profitable hum of voices, clack of tiles, slap of cards. Hm, there he was again, the young man who interested her. He wore a Japanese officer's uniform—a high rank, as far as she could tell—and while his tailoring was impeccable and his bearing perfectly correct, there was a suggestion of something about him that was . . . just a touch bohemian, a certain softness. As if he were both a soldier and a poet. Perhaps his hair was a fraction longer than the regulation cut, or perhaps it was the gentle, deliberate slowness of his movements. He only played baccarat, and only occasionally, spending most of his time sipping a neat whisky and watching the play. According to the dealers, he was neither a big winner nor loser.

He was watching the table now, as was she, when he suddenly looked toward her and their eyes met. She felt an unexpected frisson as he smiled, set his drink down and headed up the staircase toward her. She knew she carried an aura of being in charge that tended to intimidate men, and she was pleased to note that his walk was confident but not arrogant.

He removed his cap and bowed in greeting. "Good evening. I thought I should pay my respects," he said in English. "You are, I think, the manageress?"

"The owner-ess, actually." She raised an eyebrow in amusement. "Lucienne Leung."

"Enchanté, mademoiselle." He switched smoothly to French on hearing her accent. "Je m'appelle Yoshirou

Watanabe, but I hope you will call me Yoshi, as my friends do."

She smiled; there was a quality she liked in his manner. "I need to take a break—come with me to my office, if you like."

He declined spirits, accepted tea. It turned out that Yoshi *was* both a soldier and a poet. The military was a family tradition, and he was effortlessly skilled at doing all the things necessary to rise through the ranks. But he felt himself at heart to be a "man of the pen." He had worked extensively in all the Japanese poetic forms ("I can't say that I am a master, but I am at least a journeyman"), but he was most interested in writing in English. He was obsessed with Noel Coward's play, "Private Lives."

"He wrote it here, in Shanghai, you know—laid up with the 'flu in the Cathay Hotel. Wrote it in a *month*, and it's the most perfect thing; they ought to make his room a shrine."

"I've never seen it—what makes it so good?"

"The characters, Amanda and Elyot." (He said the English names with practiced accuracy.) "They're the ultimate sophisticates, deeply cynical, and they fight like cats and dogs, but they truly love each other because they *know* each other. Does that make sense? Do you say, 'to fight like cats and dogs' in French?"

"I don't think so . . ."

"But it's also the language, the rhythm of the dialogue. Elyot has been traveling around the world—to forget, after their breakup—and Amanda says, 'How was it, the world? How was China?' And he says, 'Very big, China.' 'And Japan?' she asks. 'Very small, Japan.' Very small! Hilarious! It's my favorite joke in the world."

Lucienne smiled politely, not quite seeing it. But she liked his earnest silliness in telling it. "I have to go back to work now, but come and say hello again, next time you see me. I'll make time for a break."

The next time Yoshi greeted her, two days later, Lucienne took him to her larger office on the second floor, the one with a large silken divan, where she embraced him, loosened the high, tight collar of his uniform coat and pounced gently on his throat.

"Mmm, just as I thought. You have an exquisite taste," she murmured.

He gazed up at her with wide, peaceful eyes. "I have the taste to appreciate an exquisite like you. I can't resist a modern woman, a *moga*. Don't stop."

"I'm a vamp, not a *moga*. I have to stop before I take too much." She smoothed her hand across his forehead, closing his eyes, causing him to forget what she'd said, and eased into conventional kissing.

The third time Lucienne and Yoshi met, he had two gifts for her. One was a phonograph record.

"Shizuko Kasagi—the very latest jazz from Tokyo. She's a fantastic singer."

"Sally will love it; I'll be sure to show her. And what is *this*?" She hefted a light, elegant package. "It's too beautiful to open."

"Oh, it is nothing. I like to practice wrapping things, but it is . . . nothing. In fact, I am embarrassed by it."

"All right, now I'm curious." Carefully, she slid the scarlet silk ribbon aside and unfolded the gold speckled paper. Inside was a moss-green paper box, decorated with gilt motifs. "Little bats! What are these—cigarettes?"

Yoshi nodded. "I should not have wrapped the box; it is not a personal gift. I am actually asking if you would do me a small favor."

"I don't understand."

"My superiors—my government, in fact—have asked that I try to promote this brand, Golden Bat, here in Shanghai. It would be good for our economy and perhaps even for Sino-Japanese relations. I can bring you as many cases as you like. If they can be available, given away, in a fashionable place like this, people will have positive associations; then perhaps they will continue to buy this brand."

Lucienne opened the box, took out a packet, and shrugged. "I don't see why not. The packaging is pretty; they would look nice on our tables. And bats are lucky, aren't they?"

He smiled. "So they say. And they are magical creatures of the night—like you." He came over and took her hands; she quickly stood up to embrace him and sank her fangs gently into his neck. She led him to the chaise.

Soon, Yoshi was in an affectionate, drowsy daze, and she'd had her fill. She kissed him again, clouding his memory, and gradually began bringing him back to the moment. She stood, straightened her qipao (a jazzy print in black and willow green), picked up a modernist Bakelite cigarette holder from her desk and opened a pack of Golden Bats.

"Better sample these before I put them out for my guests."

It had been a few weeks since Lucienne started seeing Yoshi, and since he adored Claude's band, Sally often kept them company in the jazz club.

"Yoshi, you have great taste in music. That record you brought—the arrangement of 'St. Louis Blues' is phenomenal!"

Yoshi nodded, pleased. "I'm glad you enjoy it. Excuse me a moment, ladies."

"I like him a lot," Sally whispered, as he left their table.

"I didn't ask—but I'm glad. I think he's rather special. I haven't felt so close to a man in a long time." She frowned. "Or maybe ever."

"That's lovely. Is it because . . . because he's East Asian?"

"What? No! He's Japanese. His culture is nothing like mine—well, nothing like what mine *would* be, if I had a culture any more. I mean, I've never really thought about it—what is our culture, as globe-trotting, century-spanning vamps? Or is it just me? You are so essentially *française*, and you've lived a huge chunk of your life in France—like Natalie, with her centuries in Russia. But I left my homeland so long ago, when I was really still a child, and just when I became a vamp . . .Is there really much Indochine left in me?"

Sally looked around the room, with its harmonious golden tones and huge bouquets of red chrysanthemums. It had been freshened but not substantially changed from Liu Yu's tenure.

Lucienne followed her gaze and laughed. "Oh, all right, I suppose I am my uncle's niece."

Yoshi returned from the men's room, and Sally was charmed to see him place an affectionate kiss on Lucienne's cheek before sitting beside her. Loulou looked different these days, she reflected—softer and fresher, glowing with a warmth that was not simply vamp glamour. She's in love! Sally realized, opening her eyes wide. Sally herself had always had amours and infatuations, sometimes quite serious ones. But in the years she'd known Lucienne, she'd seen her friend entertain dalliances, playmates—but always with a certain core of herself held in reserve, safe inside her own shell. Even when Lucienne had contemplated marrying Prince Ahmed, it seemed to have been a sort of bemused experiment or game. Now Sally watched as the couple rose to dance, melting tenderly into each other to the haunting strains of "You Do Something to Me."

Sally startled as someone slid into the seat next to her, touching her arm."

"Cerise!"

"Hello darling." She leaned in and gave Sally a double cheek peck. "I'm just taking a quick break from the tables."

"You look spectacular." It was true. Her outlandishly bright hair piled in curls atop her head was set off by a black satin gown, with a striking jade pendant nestling in her decolletage.

"That pendant . . ."

Cerise smiled and placed a hand on it. "My lucky jade."

"It's . . . it was . . ."

"Lucienne's. I know, she told me." The song was ending, dancers returning to their tables. "Hm, I hear the roulette wheel calling me. I'd better go."

"What was Cerise doing here?" Lucienne slid into her seat.

"Saying hello, I guess. Showing off? Did you know she has your jade?"

"Yes, I know. She bought it from C.T. Loo, and she's had it re-set. And she's playing our tables again, a few days a week. We're keeping an eye on her." She frowned and then turned to Yoshi, patting his hand. "Sorry, darling, it's rude of us to talk shop. But I should probably get back to my rounds. Don't get up . . ." She glanced toward the stage. "It looks like Claude is about to take a solo. See you later." She gave him a quick kiss.

The band was playing a wonderful Fats Waller tune. Sally watched Yoshi listen; he sat tense in his seat, drumming the rhythm soundlessly on his knee, occasionally nodding his head as if in approval. When Claude finished his solo, Yoshi gave a few quick beats of applause—Sally saw Claude glance toward their table with a smile—and when the number was finished, Yoshi was on his feet.

Though it happened frequently, Yoshi was always visibly thrilled when Claude came to join them at their table during his break. As usual, he greeted Sally with a French-style double cheek kiss and then extended a hand to Yoshi.

"My man—my main fan! How'd we do tonight?"

Yoshi shook the pianist's hand carefully, aware of the value of his fingers. "The whole set was fantastic. But 'Ain't Misbehavin' was the most hot ever. I feel honored to have heard it."

Claude laughed genially and sat down, cradling a glass of cognac. "Lucienne picked a good fella when she found you. Why can't you be a record company executive instead of an army officer?"

Yoshi bowed slightly, with a pained look. "I often wish I had been able to make a different career choice."

Early evenings before the club opened, the human dinner hour, Sally usually took a stroll along the Bund to clear her head, while Lucienne had a short nap to be ready for the long night. On this breezy April day, she was enjoying the debut of a new suit, tailored in a light wool perfect for the weather, an interesting shade of willow green. After several years of living out of suitcases and on a tight budget, relying on clever accessories to freshen their minimal wardrobes, Lucienne and Sally now took huge delight in having money to spend on new clothes, in a city full of skillful tailors and dressmakers —as well as having ample closet space in their comfortable, increasingly permanent-feeling suite.

Sally was particularly pleased at having found Janet Lee. She'd first spotted the woman, who appeared to be in her thirties, buying a magazine at a corner stand, and was struck by her up-to-the-minute style: a simple but perfectly proportioned crepe day dress with subtle detailing that spoke of haute couture, lovely shoes, precise make-up, a witty small hat at just the right tilt. Curious, Sally wanted to know where she was headed: a fashionable restaurant? Or perhaps she was going to a smart shop, where Sally might find clothes like hers.

Discreetly, she kept the rich russet color of the woman's dress in view and followed for one block, two, and then many more. Her quarry headed out of the French Concession, skirting the International Settlement, and on into the old town. Sally began to feel more conspicuous, though people on the streets paid her little attention. It was late afternoon, shady enough for her to be out safely, but she was beginning to feel both uneasy and foolish, about to head back, when she saw the woman had stopped up ahead, unlocking the door of a modest building and letting herself in. Frustrated and at a loss, Sally hurried to the door and found it had a small, hand-painted sign in Chinese and—helpfully—in English: "Janet Lee, Dressmaker."

After a brief hesitation, she rang the bell, introduced herself . . . and thus began a rewarding friendship and collaboration. Janet Lee spoke excellent English and a bit of French, self-taught from her constant reading of fashion magazines. She seemed gratified but unsurprised that Sally had been struck by her style enough to follow her, and she was genuinely pleased to meet someone who shared her obsession with *la mode*. If Sally had not been conscientious about getting back to the club on time, they might have talked the whole night, that first evening. Janet was eager to show off page after page of her own designs—Sally often latching onto a drawing, wondering if the pattern could be made for her. Janet also wanted to hear everything Sally could remember about Mlle's Paris atelier—her working methods, her favorite materials, her innovations. Sally tended to be wary of revealing that she'd been in Paris in the 1920s (not to mention a few centuries previously . . .) but somehow it seemed not to matter with Janet. She turned out to be older than she looked, closer to fifty than thirty, and assumed that Sally was, like her, a well-kept mature woman.

Over the next few months, Sally found herself at least a few times a week at the dressmaker's studio—sometimes for fittings, but other times just to sit, sipping tea and talking about fashion and about Shanghai. While they talked, Janet sewed hems or pressed seams, routine work which she did for her parents' cleaning and tailoring shop on the ground floor. Outside the rarified world of the international zone, Sally found herself discovering a whole new city, as Janet gave her new perspectives on this fascinating metropolis where she'd landed. While Janet valued Shanghai's cosmopolitanism, she saw things differently, with an often critical view of the way many foreigners had appropriated the city as their personal playground and income source.

"Mind you, Sir Victor has done a lot of good things, and he's better than most about recognizing Chinese contributions. We certainly can't complain about the flow of international currency . . . but we ought to have a bigger piece of the pie, don't you think?"

Janet's studio was on the top floor of a four-storey building. On her way up to visit her friend, Sally learned to greet the women in the kitchen, chopping vegetables and gossiping; the scholarly, sleepy grandfather drowsing over his books; and the gaggle of children who inevitably surrounded her, showing off their latest toys or drawings, practicing the "Good morning, Miss" which Aunt Janet had taught them.

The family was originally from Hunan, and while they had been Shanghainese for two generations, they maintained connections with family in the country, who still farmed an ancestral piece of land and occasionally visited the city with gifts of seasonal produce. Janet's passion for food and cookery was one of the interests they did not share; Janet, on the other hand, had no ear for music and found jazz baffling, as Sally discovered when she invited her to visit the club. But their shared language of fashion—seams, color, nuance—kept them always engaged, and the hours flew pleasurably in the airy room on Woochang Road. It had been so long since Sally had had a new friend.

One May evening, Sally found herself having a cocktail with Cerise in the casino's main floor bar. Sitting by a window overlooking the glamorous spangled lights of Bubbling Well Road, they clinked their vivid Negronis and each took a moment to doctor the drink with a few drops from a flask.

"What a smart hat—I love her look," Sally remarked as a svelte woman passed their table.

Cerise followed her gaze. "Oh, I know her. She's American—Jordan Baker, the golf champion." Cerise's expression was vaguely disapproving. "She grew up in St. Louis. Adopted, obviously . . . I suppose she feels more at home here, among her own kind."

Sally frowned and turned to gaze at the view, changing the subject, which seemed to be the always tiresome American preoccupation with 'race.' "I really do love it here. It's the only place except Paris where I feel I could stay indefinitely."

Cerise raised one of her perfectly plucked eyebrows. "Really? It's all right, I suppose—nicer than anyplace else I've been out here but . . . all these Chinese people. I've never gotten used to the taste. Have you ever heard the joke, 'Drain a Chinaman, and you're hungry again in an hour'?" She started to laugh, but stopped at the flash of Sally's eyes. "Oh, sorry, darling. I didn't know you'd be sensitive. Have you got a special pet too, like Lucienne's little Jap? And then there's your chocolate friend, Claude—I suppose you've always had a taste for exotica . . ."

Sally set her half-full glass down hard and stood. "I believe you've been asked not to frequent our casino, Cerise. Even if you've become more discreet in your feeding, I don't appreciate your prejudices. Please leave after you finish your drink. Goodbye."

Hours later, talking with Lucienne before bedtime, Sally was still bothered. "I don't know why I felt so shocked. Cerise has always been a silly, shallow woman since we first met her—she only wanted to become a vamp so she wouldn't lose her looks—and since she's turned, she's never really felt that humans were anything more than walking snacks."

"A lot of vamps feel that way—but it's one thing to disdain humans in general and another to single out certain kinds of humans for mockery or insult. Thank you for telling her she's not welcome."

"The other thing I minded was how she spoiled my mood. It was such a beautiful evening—I hope you got to see it. The sky was this soft sapphire, and the city looked just exquisite, and I was thinking about how much I love it here, how at home I feel. It's like Paris, the vibrant energy; everyone's always meeting new people and launching new ventures . . . Do you know, Janet has a new commission, dressing the showgirls at the Savoy cabaret? She's hilarious talking about it, she says, 'If every job paid what this one does per square inch, I'd be a millionaire.'"

Lucienne, slipping into silk pyjamas, smiled. "Janet's so much fun, and her frocks are brilliant. I'm so glad you found her, and it's wonderful you've gotten to know her better too. I do believe you've even learned a bit of Chinese?"

Sally nodded shyly. "Thank you, *xie xie*. I'm trying."

"I didn't have a chance to look out at the view tonight, but I know just what you mean. I really feel at home here too. Who would have thought Uncle Yu's stupid casino would be such a good thing? It's just enough work to be interesting, but it mostly runs itself, and it gives us this wonderful, comfortable base. And with Claude and the band, plenty of amusing punters . . . and Yoshi . . ." She trailed off dreamily, then took a sip from her nightcap bottle. "I think Natalie will like it here, too."

Lucienne and Yoshi were lying on the wide chaise in her office, her head pillowed on his shoulder. She'd had just enough of him to feel perfectly content, drowsy and dreamy.

He usually seemed to feel that way, too, after she'd fed, but she became aware that he was holding himself stiffly, frowning, his eyes fierce.

She pushed herself up. "What's wrong, darling?"

Yoshi sat up with a heavy sigh and turned to face her. "My dear one." He put his hands on her shoulders, leaned close and kissed her. "Lucienne, cherie. I am so sorry. In a better world, we would be together a long, long time—perhaps all our lives."

Lucienne looked away a moment; when she turned back, she was shocked to see tears in his eyes. "Yoshi! What is it, love?"

He was silent a long time before he spoke. "I cannot tell you much, but . . . there is a war coming. There will be fighting, terrible battles, here in Shanghai. You should liquidate your assets, if you can, and make plans to leave."

"What! No, surely not! The French Concession, all the international zones, are safe. No one would dare to harm us here."

"Perhaps not. But your safety cannot be guaranteed. There will be chaos, shortages. Your clientele will fall away—they will be frightened, and they will have less money to spend."

Lucienne shrugged, with a small smile. "Oh, is that all? We can weather a few storms, if necessary. We can close for a while, lie low. Business will always pick up again after things calm down. People need their diversions, after all." She stood and stretched, lit a cigarette and offered it to Yoshi. He shook his head, and she fitted it into her jade holder. "Please don't worry, darling." She touched his cheek.

He pulled away, shaking his head. "You don't understand. My country—my stupid, beautiful, arrogant, ruthless country—is going to make war on China. It will be horrible. And if anything were to happen to you, I couldn't bear it." Yoshi stood up, took her hands and kissed them feverishly. "I must go now. We will speak of this again."

There was a situation at one of the roulette tables—a stout Frenchman accused the croupier of nudging the wheel off its position. Sally noticed the slight commotion as she crossed the room and looked around for Lucienne; normally, she was on the spot in an instant if any problem arose.

She checked the adjoining salon and scanned the mezzanine but, seeing no sign of her friend, she hurried over to calm the agitated customer. Chatting him up smoothly in French, she led him away for a drink, signaling over her shoulder that the employee should take a break.

The man was so well-nourished and characteristically French-smelling that Sally quite enjoyed spending a half hour in conversation and discreet feeding. "Ah, you remind me of home," she told him appreciatively, as she left him to his cognac. Then, seeing that Lucienne was still absent from the main floor, she went in search of her.

If Loulou and Yoshi were together, she'd have left them to their amorous devices, but having confirmed with the doorman that Major Watanabe was not on the premises tonight, Sally was concerned. She peeked into the tiny main floor office and then took the back stairs, two at a time, hurrying down the corridor to Lucienne's more lavish hideaway.

Dressed in silver, eyes half-closed, Loulou lay on her chaise, smoking with an extravagantly long holder.

"Salut, cherie," she murmured dreamily at Sally's arrival.

"Darling, are you all right?"

Lucienne opened her eyes and turned to Sally with a radiant smile. "Perfectly. Why wouldn't I be?" As her gaze focused on Sally's expression, she sat up. "What's wrong?"

"Nothing much, I hope—but you've been gone from the floor for over two hours. I had to deal with a cranky punter. You might want to reassure Francois Lam that he hasn't done anything wrong." She briefly explained the events.

Lucienne frowned. "I couldn't have been gone that long! I just came up for a cigarette and ten minutes off my feet."

Sally glanced at the ashtray which held two gold filters, as well as the holder Lucienne had set down. She picked it up, took a puff and coughed. "Ugh, what are these? The taste is odd."

"They're called Golden Bats—Yoshi brought them from Japan. I suppose they're not the best tobacco, but they make me feel closer to him. And look how pretty the box is."

Sally shrugged. "*Chacun à son gout*, I suppose. I just had a long drink of a rather obnoxious businessman because he reminded me of France. Anyway, hadn't we better get back to work? This place doesn't *completely* run itself."

"You're right, of course. Give me a moment." She slipped her feet into the shoes discarded at the end of the chaise and tottered over to her dressing table to retouch her eyelashes, finishing up quickly before Sally could hurry her.

Flying like a witch through the night sky, a cold gibbous moon high overhead. Below her, snow, scattered villages, wolves prowling the woods . . .

Sally awoke with a start. What *was* that? The scene seemed like Russia. Was she receiving dreams or memories from Natalie? She reached out and tugged at the curtain of her sleeping alcove. Cool light outlined the shuttered windows. Late morning, far too early to be awake. She turned over, snuggled into her pillow and returned to strange dreams.

"I'm going to fly, one of these days soon. I've hired a private charter—it's costing me an arm and a leg, but I need something big enough to cross the Pacific safely, not some little aero-flivver. You should come with me, you and Lucienne." Cerise was back. Sally wasn't entirely pleased about having drinks together, after their last encounter, but she'd promised Lucienne she would keep an eye on her.

Sally took a careful sip of her cocktail. "Would you have room for us? What about your husband?"

Cerise laughed throatily. "Jacob? You know, as soon as I settled here in Shanghai, I wired him saying he should join me. And have you seen a hair of him? He's in Australia, with a new sweetie, but my divorce lawyer will sort things out in due time; I should get a good deal out of it. No, Jacob is history—time for fresh fields and pastures new."

"Where will you go?"

"Buenos Aires, darling! In the Argentine. I've been studying up—elegant architecture, bloody steaks, beautiful sophisticated people from all over, all mad for the tango! Doesn't that sound divine? I need to learn a bit of Spanish, but they'll understand my money well enough.

Do come along—there's a place called the Café de los Inmortales; it's made for us!"

"Thank you for the offer. I'll talk to Lucienne and we'll think it over."

"Do, and don't take too long. This place is getting to be more of a *trou de merde* every day, n'est-çe pas?"

That night, Claude stepped to the front of the stage and announced, "Ladies and gentlemen, we have a special treat for you tonight—Miss Cassandra Jones! Please give her a warm welcome, and enjoy!"

The singer wore a gold satin gown that hugged her curves and brought out honey highlights in her rich brown skin tone. Her shining marcel-waved coiffure caught the light; her smile was generous and mischievous. The audience, captivated even before she opened her mouth, was all hers once she began to sing. And to scat. And to crack jokes, and to step to the piano and take a solo while Claude smoked a cigarette at stage left.

Sally sat rapt with Yoshi, forgetting to keep her usual eye on the house or even to sip her drink. Lucienne joined them near the end of the set and snuggled up to Yoshi, eyes wide as she watched the stage.

When Claude and Cassandra arrived at their table during the band break, Yoshi stood and bowed low over her hand. "Miss Jones, it is a true privilege to be in your presence."

"I'd have to agree," Sally enthused, stepping forward to give her the firm handshake that she thought of as

English and modern. She was aglow with the pleasure that good jazz always gave her. "I would . . . we would . . ." She glanced at Lucienne, who seemed a bit cool and remote. Was she jealous of Yoshi's attention to the singer? After just a moment's hesitation, Sally continued, "We'd love to offer you a performance spot in the club, at least a few nights a week. Wouldn't we, Lucienne?"

"Oh, yes, of course. I just caught the end of your set, Miss Jones; you were marvelous. Sally manages the jazz club, so I'll leave the details up to her. Forgive me, I have to attend to something upstairs. You stay, Yoshi," she added, as he stood. "Enjoy yourself."

After the last set, Sally invited Cassandra and Claude back to her office to discuss terms.

"Actually," Claude said, "you don't need me there. I'll grab a bite to eat. I know you'll give her a square deal, Sally. Just don't let her take my job completely—damn, girl, when did you learn to play piano like that? I mean, I *might* ask you to fill in for me if, say, I got a chance to go play with Bo Diddley in Batavia—but I *will* be back."

"Go, get a bite." Cassandra winked at him. "We'll be just fine."

Cassandra accepted a glass of whisky and one of Sally's Egyptian cigarettes and settled herself comfortably, slipping out of her shoes, while Sally filled out a contract.

The singer's eyes widened a bit as she read it over. "This is almost twice what any other club in town is paying."

"Then they're fools and cheapskates. I believe in paying fairly for talent and commitment."

Cassandra shrugged. "I'm not complaining. And Claude says you have the best taste in music of anyone he knows, so I'm flattered. You sure it's okay with the boss lady?"

"This place was dreary when we first took it over. I said I'd make it chic and lively, and I have. Lucienne is the owner—she inherited the casino from her uncle—but I have carte blanche in the jazz club."

Cassandra nodded. "How did you learn about jazz, Sally?"

Sally took a deep drink from her flask, leaned back and smiled. "It was love at first hearing. This American band had come to Paris—this was before the Chocolate Dandies, and honestly, they weren't nearly as good—but it was so different from the music I'd grown up with, so exciting! It made me feel so *alive*. It's one of the things I love most about being here now, this century . . . I mean . . ."

"You don't have to cover up. I know you're a vampire. Like Claude. Quite a bit older than you look. Considering the music you must have grown up with—like what, Mozart?—it's impressive how you love jazz so much. But tell me something, Sally. How long has your girl Lucienne been a junkie?"

"What!?"

"Sorry, is that too American? You know, a hop-head. Opium."

"I don't understand. Lucienne doesn't do anything like that."

The singer raised her eyebrows. "We all have our vices. I don't judge—you don't have to protect her."

Sally could only stare. "But, it's impossible. I'm with her every day—we work together, we share a suite. I would have noticed . . . anyway, vamps don't use drugs."

Cassandra took a big sip of her whisky and smiled. "Claude sure likes his cognac. And he wouldn't say no to a bump of *whatever's* around. But okay, you know her. Has she always been so dreamy? Distracted? Have her eyes always looked like that?"

"Like what?" Sally began to be indignant, but fell silent, thinking. "She *has* been acting a bit different lately, spending more time napping . . . or something . . . letting things slide. I thought it was because she's in love with Yoshi, but . . . ." She put her flask down, needing to end the conversation. "Well, if the contract is acceptable . . ."

"Very much so." Cassandra signed with a flourish and slid the document back to Sally. "Thank you. I mean it. And I didn't mean to say anything out of line, but if you care about your friend . . ." She trailed off and left.

The dream began again with flying, but it was Shanghai below her this time, the curve of the Whangpo, the oval of the Hippodrome. Gardens and parks, crowded lanes, modern buildings—the Cathay Hotel and Embankment House forming the shapes of Sir Victor Sassoon's initials.

The view was engaging, but she began to hear strange, disturbing sounds—wails and screams, sirens, booming explosions. Then, there were things falling all around her, dropping onto the city and bursting into blossoms of flame. She could smell the smoke.

Sally opened her eyes with difficulty and sat up, gasping. Another strange dream, and this one couldn't have come from Natalie. And, she could still smell smoke.

She opened her bed curtains and swung her feet to the floor, pausing to steady herself. It was still dark, just a bit of pre-dawn gray outlining the shutters. She padded across the carpet to the connecting door to Lucienne's chamber. (After years of sharing a room, she found it both luxurious and lonely, now that they each had their own space.)

"Loulou, are you awake?" Sally whispered as she opened the door.

There was no answer. She waited a moment for her eyes to adjust; this room faced north and was darker. Lucienne's bed curtains were open; she had heaped up her pillows and reclined on her back, her mouth slightly open. Though her breathing was visible, there was a deep stillness about her. A gold-tipped cigarette smoldered in an ashtray on the bedside table and was the source of the smoke she smelled.

Instantly furious, Sally hurried to the bedside. She grabbed Lucienne's shoulders and shook her awake. "Loulou, what are you doing, are you insane? We don't smoke in bed. You could set yourself on fire, burn the place down. What's wrong with you?"

"Mmf, leave me alone, I'm sleeping." She turned on her side and tried to burrow into her pillows. Sally reached across and snatched up the ashtray, taking it to the bathroom. She returned with a glass of water and gently sprinkled a few drops onto her friend's forehead.

"Open your eyes, darling. I'm worried about you."

Lucienne sighed heavily and rolled over, glaring at Sally. "What are you doing? You should be asleep."

"I had a bad dream. And then I smelled your cigarette. You mustn't smoke in bed, Loulou, it's dangerous. We never do that—what were you thinking?"

"I . . ." Lucienne sat up against her pillows. "I was missing Yoshi. The Golden Bats help me feel close to him, and I was just having a last one. I must have dropped off."

"Yes, and you could have dropped the 'Bat' in your bedclothes and gone up in flames! Promise me you won't ever do that again. Please."

Lucienne nodded, contrite but not altogether convincing.

Sally frowned. "You've been smoking a lot more than you ever have before; I don't think it's healthy. You even said yourself, it's not very good tobacco. I notice Yoshi has his own brand. It's odd that he . . ."

Lucienne yawned hugely. "Sally, it's the middle of the night. We need our sleep. Can we talk about this tomorrow?"

"All right, darling. It's just . . . never mind. Good night, sweet dreams."

"Mmm."

Sally was awake quite early, noon, the next day. She phoned Janet to cancel an appointment and waited until it was a decent hour, close to three in the afternoon, before knocking at Lucienne's door. She felt a bit ragged from her bad night, but she had bathed and dressed with care, and she was relieved to see Lucienne looking fresh and rested, showered and alert, in a pretty Japanese dressing gown. The smell of smoke had dissipated; Loulou was sipping from a flask and reading a two-month-old *Vogue* that had just arrived.

"Good morning, darling. Cheers!" Sally toasted with her own flask. "I thought I'd join you for breakfast, so we can talk about things."

Lucienne put her magazine down. "Cheers, cherie. What do you mean, talk about things? Is there a problem?"

Sally sighed. "When I was in Pondicherry, you got worried about me. With good reason, as it turned out."

"Hah. I am glad we got out of there—the clothing was atrocious. And all that drumming . . . sorry, darling, I know you liked the music . . ."

"Yes, but . . . it wasn't worth living like that. Anyway, what I wanted to say is, I'm worried about you. Not in the same way, obviously, and not all the time, but there are times when . . . you don't seem like yourself. You go off and leave things—things you were always so attentive to, like the tables, that unhappy punter the other night."

"I *am* entitled to a private life, you know. I don't mind when you go off to see Janet, or Princess Sumaire, or hang around with Nathan Minsk or Claude, or Cerise."

"Cerise! You know I hate spending time with her. *You* asked me to keep an eye on her."

"You looked cozy having Negronis with her yesterday. Very interested in what she was saying."

"I *was* interested. She has invited us to leave Shanghai with her, share an aeroplane she's chartered."

Lucienne sighed lengthily. "Leave Shanghai. Everyone keeps saying we ought to. Even . . . even Yoshi." She turned away, her shoulders shaking.

"Oh, darling, don't cry!"

"I . . . I don't want to go. Damn it, I actually seem to care for that man. It hurt so much, when he told me we should leave."

"I imagine he cares for you a great deal too. I'm sure he just wants you to be safe."

"Safe! I'm immortal. What's the point of worrying about safety?"

They were both silent for a minute, until Sally spoke cautiously. "You know, we're not completely immune to danger. If there is a war, if there's shooting and bombing and fires . . . I'm just saying, we could be hurt. We could lose things. I don't like the thought of leaving either—I really have come to love it here too—but we should probably think about our options."

Lucienne sniffed and dabbed her eyes, then got up and went to her dressing table. "Fine. We'll do that," she said in a flat voice. "Was that it? What you wanted to talk about?" She rummaged through a drawer and retrieved a box of Golden Bats and her jade holder.

"It's . . . no. It's everything. Those cigarettes. All you do is smoke and forget about things. Cassandra asked if you were a dope fiend!" Sally covered her mouth. "Sorry, that was out of line, I'm just . . ."

Lucienne's eyes flashed. "*Cassandra* said? That American singer, who has seen me exactly once? If she doesn't want to work for me, she can leave. I know I gave you complete authority over the jazz club, but your musicians should know their place, and if they don't, I will tell you to drop them."

Sally stood up. "I'm going now."

The Syncopaters were always superb, but they were jumping tonight on "Burning the Iceberg." Sally sat riveted to her chair, hardly able to believe what she was hearing. The cornet player and clarinet were in a manic, fabulous dialogue; the drummer had taken leave of his senses; Claude himself was holding onto the keyboard for dear life, bursting out now and then into crazy handfuls of rhythm. They crashed to an ending, and the room exploded.

The chair beside her was empty. If Yoshi knew what he just missed, he'd commit *seppuku,* Sally thought with a smile.

And then Cassandra came to the stage and cast a spell of silence. Slowly, delicately, Claude touched the piano keys.

She began the song with its intro, in French: *"Comme le roulement du tamtam, quand la jungle s'obsourcit/ comme le tic-toc d'horloge majestueuse, près du mur/ comme la goût d'eau qui tombe, quand un orage est fini/ une voix me repette constamment, un mot—toi . . .*

"Nuit et jour, tu est mon choix . . ."

Sally was lost at sea, dazed in a dream, deep under crystal waves, sailing in a starlit sky—as far out of herself as a song had ever taken her—swimming naked in the music and lusciously entwined with each of the players. Cassandra! Sally saw the two of them embracing, felt the singer's velvet skin, shivered at the timbre of her voice.

Was it just because she sang in French, the language of Sally's birth, Sally's heart?

But at some point, she had finished the verses in French and was now reprising the song in English: "Night and day, under the hide of me / there's an oh such a hungry yearning burning inside of me . . ."

Yearning . . . oh so hungry. She wanted to feed on Cassandra. Burning . . .

Sally opened her eyes wide, nostrils flaring, turning her head to locate a faint, unmistakable smell. She bolted up the stairs. Reaching the second floor, she heard Lucienne's screams. And Yoshi's.

Yoshi had been lounging in a light cotton yukata, printed in indigo and now orange with fire. Lucienne was hitting at the flames, ineffectually grabbing at unsuitable objects—a scarf, a book. An overturned ice bucket and an empty water carafe lay nearby.

"Sally! I can't put it out! Get water, get help, he's going to die!"

"Get his robe off!" Sally gasped. The air was growing hot.

"I can't, it's too hot!"

"Yoshi, you have to roll on the floor! Throw yourself down. I'm getting water."

Yoshi flung himself to the carpet with a groan. Yelling for help, Sally grabbed a large vase of chrysanthemums that stood just outside the door. She snatched the flowers away and emptied it onto him; his garment still smoldered and produced clouds of smoke.

Two maids rushed in with large buckets, and finally the fire was fully drowned, leaving a sodden charred mess.

Lucienne, pale and wide-eyed, knelt at Yoshi's side. He lay gasping for a moment, but then reached out a hand to the more sturdily-built of the maids, who helped him to stand.

"Do not distress yourself, my love. I will be fine. I will call a taxi."

"You should go to a hospital," Sally said. "Those burns could be dangerous."

"It is nothing, really." He was strangely calm.

"Loulou, what should we do? I think he's in shock." Sally bent down to whisper to her friend, who had covered her eyes.

"I don't know! It's all my fault. My damned cigarette. How could I do this? I don't know what he needs now." She began to sob.

Yoshi was gathering his effects—his hat, wallet, the evening clothes he had been wearing earlier. "Might I borrow a valise? I don't want to put these on right now. And my coat, I need a hand, please, Miss Lafayette . . ." He broke off with a gasp of pain. "Ah. I had better sit down for a moment."

Sally quickly helped him to a chair and brought him a glass of whisky, which he took with a shaking hand.

There were unfamiliar voices in the corridor, and two uniformed Japanese soldiers entered with a stretcher. Sally realized one of the maids had left and must have passed on the news to the manager. The soldiers' voices seemed brusque and disapproving as they spoke to Yoshi, but Sally couldn't tell how much of this was due to the inflection of their language. Yoshi seemed, at first, to be declining their help, perhaps dismissing the men (who appeared to be his inferiors in rank), but after a few moments, he complied with their wishes, and they bundled him efficiently, yet gently, onto the stretcher.

Lucienne spent days weeping. She stopped smoking, stopped feeding, stayed in her bed but barely slept. Her excellent staff kept the casino running smoothly, and Sally tipped a flask to her lips twice a day. After two weeks, she received a letter from Yoshi. Sally found her reading it, over and over, dry-eyed but a picture of despair.

"What does he say?" she asked, when she finally dared speak to her friend.

"He is in Japan, recovering. He has been placed on leave from the army. He says we should leave Shanghai."

"He's right about that. It's worse each day."

"Fine." Lucienne was expressionless. "You can make the arrangements."

Sally didn't normally spend much time in her small office, but she felt the need to gather her thoughts in a quiet spot. Cerise had announced a departure date, and again had urged them to accompany her. Buenos Aires sounded promising, though she was filled with regret at the thought of leaving Shanghai. A few weeks ago, it would have been even more difficult—practically un-thinkable—for Lucienne to leave, but now she was numb with her sorrow, ready to passively accept whatever Sally proposed. Which, of course, left Sally to take care of everything. The travel arrangements and packing she could manage, but she felt sorely in need of Lucienne's recently discovered business acumen, to organize the casino's operations in their absence.

There was a knock at the door, and Peony Chan put her head in. "Mlle Lafayette? Miss Janet Lee is here to see you, if you are available."

"Janet! Of course, show her in."

Janet, in a cream-colored suit and a dashing scarlet hat, was as impeccable and unruffled as always, despite entering with a large, heavy-looking canvas carryall. She set it down with a thump as she took a seat, and accepted a glass of water with a smile.

"I'm sorry to come without 'phoning—thank you for seeing me."

"Of course! I always have time for you, Janet. What's happening? Luggage—are you going somewhere?"

Janet took a long sip of water. "I've brought your wardrobe, everything we planned. Two suits, four dresses, that lace evening gown and the two satin ones. I finished everything." She set down her glass with a slightly shaking hand, and Sally realized that, under her perfectly groomed facade, she looked exhausted.

"I don't understand—you were going to work on those for the next two months. How did you . . .? You must have worked round the clock! Janet darling, you look done in; let me ring for some tea, some lunch."

She smiled and shook her head. "I can't stay. I just wanted you to have everything I promised you. If it's not convenient to give me a cheque now, I understand completely; I will give you the address to mail it to. We are leaving, my family and I, going to our village. It will be safer there. And you should leave Shanghai too, as soon as you can. You heard about that bombing, day before yesterday?"

Sally nodded. "I'll write you a cheque right now. And yes, we are also leaving soon. A friend has chartered a plane."

"Good." Janet gave her a long look and then stood up, her hand outstretched. "Goodbye, Sally. I will remember you."

Sally took her hand, and then pulled her into a hug. "And I you, Janet. Stay safe."

"Mlle Leung. Sorry to bother you, but that man is back." Lucienne knew immediately whom her assistant meant.

"Thank you, Miss Chan. I will see him in ten minutes —no, better make it fifteen. Give him tea or something; don't let him come in sooner. And please ask Mlle Lafayette to join me, and . . . if you can locate Claude, the bandleader, ask him to come up here. Also, if by any chance Mme Cerise—oh, what is her new surname, you know who I mean—if she is here in the casino, I'd be grateful if she would join us . . . And have Bruno stand by, of course."

"I understand completely. It's early, but I think a few of Miss Ying-Lee Kelly's friends may be about also; I will send for them. I should have mentioned, the man in question is not alone—there are several others with him. They appear to have weapons. I will advise them that bringing firearms into the casino is forbidden."

Lucienne raised her head, meeting the other woman's eyes with alarm. "Please, be careful, Peony. It's probably best not to engage with them."

Lucienne was in red today, a powerful hue she didn't often wear. Sally, at her side, wore a tailored black suit studded with gold.

Sloppy and slouchy as before, the man entered, followed by a pair of muscular thugs, followed in turn by two tall and well-dressed businessman types, and finally a black-clad, glowering presence who could only be the "boss" himself.

"Gentlemen?" Lucienne raised an ironic eyebrow—the greeting was also a question.

Their previous acquaintance spoke first. "Your girl out there said we should lose the hardware. So we left all the fire-power in your foyer." He raised his empty hands. "That's fine—we want to have a civilized meeting, you know?"

"And what did you wish to discuss, Mister Man?"

"Haha, that's good, you called me that before. As a matter of fact, I go by Manny. Emmanuele Borsalino. But my boss here—you don't need to know his name. All you need to know is he's prepared to make you a very generous offer for your casino property. Gentlemen," he beckoned the two business suits forward, "show the lady our offer."

Blue Suit first presented a one-page document, with a purchase price prominently printed, and a line for Lucienne's signature indicated. Then both he and Gray Suit opened attaché cases filled with bundled stacks of currency.

Lucienne lowered her head, appearing to carefully read the document, and spoke to Sally silently, mind to mind. *This is a pathetic offer—less than half of the casino's worth.*

If you decline . . . I have a bad feeling.

Agreed. I suspect they still have guns, even if they left some outside.

The cash will be useful. We should appear to accept. Then we'll see what happens.

Lucienne looked up and cleared her throat. "I am in-clined to consider your offer. It is by no means a fair price, but we have few options at present."

The faces of the visitors darkened and then cleared, as they processed her words.

"I am glad you are planning to be reasonable, Mlle Lu. As soon as you sign the contract, the money is yours, and we will be on our way."

Lucienne rang a small bell on her desk; the six men tensed as Peony Chan opened the door.

"Miss Chan, we require witnesses to the signing of this contract."

"Yes, madame, right away."

The group remained alert and grim-faced, but seemed to relax as the 'witnesses' arrived—slender Claude, chic Cerise and two chattering, frivolous-looking members of Ying-Lee Kelly's crowd.

Manny chuckled. "I didn't realize we were putting on a show here. But you ladies have a flair for the theatrical; I'm sure that's why you've made the casino so successful. We'll try to keep it up—though I can't guarantee it will have the same . . . elegance. The boss likes things a little more straightforward."

The boss spoke just then, jerking his chin toward Claude and growling something in Chinese.

"You're the bandleader, right?" Manny turned to him. "Consider this one week's notice for you to clear out. The boss doesn't want dark people in his club."

Sally shot Claude a fierce look, but he only shrugged. "No problem. We never play where we're not wanted."

"Your loss," Sally muttered under her breath.

Lucienne cleared her throat again and picked up a green-enameled pen. "Friends, we've asked you here to witness this transaction. As we all know, the situation in Shanghai is becoming increasingly unstable. These gentlemen have made us a very gen . . . have made us an offer for the casino, an offer which it would be imprudent for us to refuse. Cerise and Claude, you both have a great deal of experience with contracts—would you come and look this over, please?"

They stepped forward, and Lucienne briefly locked eyes with each. Claude on her right, Cerise on her left, they leaned over to read the document. Claude only shook his head, but Cerise spoke up immediately:

"You call this a contract? Even my first divorce lawyer did better than this, and let me tell you, he was pathetic. Of course, I didn't know better then, but if any of my subsequent . . ." she broke off to count on her fingers, ". . . six divorce attorneys did a piss-poor job like this, I'd have had their heads."

She glared around the room and fixed her eyes directly on the boss himself. He looked daggers back at her and shouted a gruff command to Manny.

Lucienne spoke levelly. "Unfortunately, we do not have many options at present." She raised her pen and set it to the paper with a conspicuous gesture. "As sole owner of the Imperial Casino, of my own free will, I am signing this contract granting transfer of ownership to . . . the purchaser and his associates. I am accepting full payment in cash, in the presence of these witnesses. Sally, will you take the cases, please?"

Sally held out her hands and the money men, somewhat reluctantly, gave her the attaché cases. As she bent to place them in a locked compartment of the desk, the gray-suited one gave Claude a shove.

"Out of my way, jazzbo. You don't belong here anymore."

Claude caught him by the arm, twisted it back and delivered a sharp punch to his jaw before attacking his neck.

His blue-suited colleague nearby went wide-eyed, exclaiming, "He's a fuckin' vam . . ." before Sally smothered his cry with her attack.

With a huge grin and a snarl of relish, Cerise flung herself at the nearest muscle-man. He grabbed at her, knocking her Schiaparelli hat to the floor.

"Oh, no. No, no, no." She seized him by his burly shoulders and lifted him into position for a draining bite. Ying-Lee's friends meanwhile pounced on the second thug and took him down.

Lucienne was grappling with Manny Borsalino. "Mister Man, I didn't know you cared," she said tartly, as he tore at her blouse. He was a fast and wily fighter who knew how to use his weight, and she found it hard to get a grip on him. Sally finished with blue-suit and moved to help, but Lucienne glanced toward the door. "I'm okay, Sally. Better try to stop the boss before he gets a gun, or hurts Peony."

"Right. Oh!" Manny had pulled a wicked-looking knife from his boot and now held it to Lucienne's chest.

"Better hold it right there, or your friend—lover—boss—whatever she is to you—gets a stake through the heart." He flipped the knife around to reveal a sharpened wood grip.

"Sally, I'll be all right! Get the boss!" Lucienne urged, as Manny called out in Shanghainese to his master.

But there was no answer from the back of the room. Peony Chan had attacked the figure in black with such ferocity that she had completely torn his throat out. Covered in his blood, she was draining the rest.

Sally managed to grab Manny's knife as he stared, and after that, she and Lucienne made quick work of him.

Minutes later, seven vamps were brushing themselves down, assessing each other's minor injuries, gazing around the bloody, body-strewn office.

Lucienne crossed the room to where her assistant stood, wiping her mouth and hands with a handkerchief.

"Miss Chan—Peony. I had no idea! I thought you were an unusually intelligent and astute mortal. I don't know why I never realized . . ."

Peony smiled, her fangs gleaming in her still bloody face. "I guess I'm a very private person; I don't give out the usual signals. But I don't think your uncle would have trusted me with so much responsibility if I weren't one of you. He turned me himself."

Lucienne couldn't help staring. "That makes us . . . sisters, in a way. I'd hug you, but we're both a mess! I'll let you go wash up and change, and we'll talk later. And could you. . ." Lucienne paused, suddenly uncomfortable giving orders or even requests.

Peony nodded. "I'll send the cleaning crew up."

"Do you think we . . . over-reacted? Were they just proposing a bad deal, in good faith?"

Peony shook her head emphatically and indicated the doorway. "Take a look at the weapons out there. There were a few more gang members about to join in, too, but they ran away when I attacked the boss. He was planning a massacre."

Lucienne shuddered. "At first I just thought they were ill-mannered and sleazy, but they started to seem pretty vicious."

"The boss-man is—or *was*—head of one of the largest criminal organizations in Shanghai. I guess they are headless now." She grinned. "Listen, I have to go burn this frock. I'll see you later."

Bathed and changed (without consulting each other, they both chose virginal white), Lucienne and Sally emerged from their suite in the early evening to make their usual rounds of the casino. It was surreal, but deeply reassuring, to see how normal operations carried on—cashiers changing money, croupiers dealing cards, bartenders shaking cocktails, guests chatting and laughing. The senior staff had all been briefed on the afternoon's occurrence, and of course the cleaning crew had been busy for a few hours, but nothing disrupted the smooth functioning of the Imperial's complex organism.

Lucienne took Sally's elbow and smiled as they descended the grand staircase. "Uncle Yu trained them well. When we leave, Peony and the others will take care of everything."

They parted ways at the bottom of the stairs with a quick cheek kiss. Lucienne drifted over to a roulette table and watched for a while, soothed by the spin of the inlaid wheel and the click of the balls.

Sally went down another flight to the club, where Claude and the Syncopaters were just setting up. She caught his eye and could immediately tell he was busy but that they'd catch up later. She circled the room, greeting a few regulars, smiling a welcome to some newcomers and checking in with the barman, before she settled into her usual booth at the back.

She was just sinking into the delicious opening strains of "Jubilee Stomp," when she looked up and saw a figure in white standing by her table—Cerise. Sally gave her a quick nod to indicate she should sit, and then turned her rapt attention back to the music. Cerise was in the habit of talking right over the band, but this time, she did not speak until the number ended.

"Hello darling. And thanks for waiting," Sally said, as the band moved into a more conventional tune. "There's some music I hate to miss a note of."

"Especially since we are leaving soon?" Cerise smiled, arching an eyebrow.

"There is that. Although . . . will a war be any worse than what we went through today? Cerise, *thank* you. You were magnificent."

"Pure pleasure, darling. So . . . I want to fly next Thursday. It will have to be noon, I'm afraid—you know what pilots are like, that's the absolute latest I could talk them into. The airfield is out of town a way; I can come by here in a charabanc for you and your luggage." She paused to accept a Negroni from the waiter.

Sally took her own drink with a nod. As they touched glasses, she took in Cerise's extremely low-cut cream satin gown and the large cabochon pigeon's blood ruby gleaming at the center of her diamond necklace. She laughed, flicking the flutter sleeve of her own more modest ivory crepe gown. "Lucienne's in white tonight, too. We must have all gotten the same, subliminal memo."

"Our innocence? We were merely defending ourselves from those who wished us harm." She touched her jewel lightly. "Just one symbolic drop of blood."

"Your jade pendant would look spectacular with that dress."

"Actually . . ." Cerise opened her evening bag and pulled out a slim leather case. "I've tried to settle up my debts here, but I suspect I'm still in considerable arrears, and it's such a bore getting it totted up. And then, I promised Lucienne, and I've really tried, not to feed on the guests here too openly . . . although there *was* this afternoon . . ."

Sally swatted playfully at her hand. "You helped save us all today! Don't worry about the accounts."

"Well, regardless . . ." She slid the case across the table. "I want Lucienne to have her pendant back. I only paid money for it, but she gave her blood—it is truly hers. Will you give it to her for me? I wouldn't know what to say."

Sally nodded. "She won't know what to say either. But she will be so grateful. Thank you. Again."

Cerise drained her cocktail and stood up. "I think I hear my favorite roulette wheel calling. I'll see you both on Thursday."

Late, after hours—after the Syncopaters' last set, the bars' last calls, when all the gaming tables had shut down except one baccarat game in the private, high-rollers' suite, Lucienne joined Sally and Claude in the downstairs cabaret. Claude had a bottle of cognac; Lucienne and Sally started with a large shaker of Hanky Panky cocktails, which the bartender had mixed for them before leaving. After they finished those, Lucienne fetched another bottle of cognac from the bar, and they joined Claude in his drink of choice. All three took healthy swigs from their flasks now and then, to accompany the liquor.

News of the impending war sat heavily on them. They traded desultory bits of information, smoked and spoke quietly, with long intervals of silence and sighs.

"Mortals! Don't they know they will die soon enough? Why are they doing this?"

Clicking footsteps startled them, and they all swung around from their huddle in the corner booth.

Peony Chan wore a pale gold damask qipao with— shockingly, for her—the collar closure undone. Her always sleek hair was very slightly mussed, and she carried a bottle of baijiu.

"May I join you, Miss Leung?"

"Stop right there. No more 'Miss' from you. We are all sisters and brothers here. And you, Peony, are our hero." Lucienne stood and wrapped her arms around Peony in a long embrace. "I still can't believe I had no idea. You are truly remarkable, my dear."

"Hear hear!" and "Lord, yes!" came from Claude and Sally, saluting the young woman as she sat down.

Peony smiled widely at all of them and took a long swallow from her bottle. "I have been waiting a long while for an occasion like today, I have to say. Those gangsters have been throwing their weight around in the quarter for too long." She opened her evening bag, brought out a gold flask—Lucienne recognized it as one that had belonged to her uncle—and took a small sip. "Miss . . . I mean, Lucienne, Sally—you will be leaving soon, I believe?"

Lucienne sighed. "We really don't want to. We feel so much at home here, we'd like to stay, but everyone has been saying . . ."

"You should, yes, definitely. It is good that your friend . . . that Miss Cerise has offered you space in her aeroplane. Ship passage is impossible to get, these days."

"I didn't know that. I'm not thrilled about spending a long trip with Cerise, but I guess it is lucky that she has offered."

Peony nodded. "It's the wisest course. We will all be doing things we prefer not to, for a while. If you will allow me, I am prepared to manage the casino for the foreseeable . . ."

"Of course!" Lucienne said quickly. "No one is better qualified. But, what will you do if . . ."

"Not if, *when.* Before the war begins, we will secure all the valuables in your uncle's secret vault, board up the windows, lock the building and slip away. I have been talking with all of the staff—we all have villages we can go to that will be much safer than here. The only thing I don't know is . . ." She turned to Claude with a troubled expression. "Where will you go, Monsieur Claude? And all the musicians?"

"Don't be worried about us, Miss Chan. We're all good at layin' low. Part of a jazz-man's life—being quick on your feet, knowing when to leave a place you're not wanted."

Sally laid a hand on his. "Claude, come with us. Buenos Aires sounds like a pretty good place. Do you know, there's a Cafe . . ."

"Des Inmortales. Yeah, I've heard of it." Claude shook his head. "No, I'm not ready for *any* of the Americas yet. I've got connections here, got some gigs lined up already —Kuala Lumpur, Siam. We'll be fine."

"But. . ." Sally locked eyes with him. "I don't want to lose you again."

"Now now, little girl." (He remained the only man who could call her 'little' without infuriating her.) "We will always find each other, I promise. And I will come to see you off, help you with all that luggage and such." He winked and squeezed her hand.

"The docks are madness—go a different way," Cerise directed their driver. He took an abrupt turn, and they all lurched against each other.

Natalie's trunk was up front. The rear of the vehicle was piled with a huge mountain of trunks, valises and the other assorted luggage pieces of three well-dressed women. Claude, Sally, Lucienne and Cerise were crammed, hip to hip, in the passenger seat.

Cerise continued to issue instructions in her high-pitched voice, occasionally adding a word or phrase in poorly pronounced Chinese. Lucienne closed her eyes, wondering whether she'd be able to endure traveling with the American woman. Even her perfume, Jicky, was overpowering. But, she *had* returned the jade amulet. Lucienne fingered the stone and dozed.

It took over an hour to reach the airfield. Tired of the stuffy charabanc but reluctant to step out into the bright midday light, the four vampires waited in the vehicle while crewmen began unloading the luggage and carrying it to the waiting plane.

Natalie's trunk was the last piece to be taken out, and Sally, Lucienne and Claude quickly climbed out to make sure it was being handled properly, while Cerise settled with the driver. The men carrying it were moving fast and had already set the trunk down—not gently enough

—by the cargo hatch before the three vamps caught up. They could see two men in uniform frowning and shaking their heads.

"This yours, Miss?" the taller and blonder of the two men asked Sally. He was American, with 'Hansen' on a pin on his lapel, and he seemed to look right through Claude and Lucienne.

"It is ours, yes. It is fragile and absolutely essential." Sally used her crispest, most British tone.

The two airmen looked at each other. "Nope, can't put it on the bottom then, even if we shifted everything around," the shorter one said. His lapel read 'Wilson.' "Sorry, ladies, no can do." He jerked his head toward Claude. "*He's* not coming, is he? 'Cause we do not have an extra seat, especially for a . . ."

"Our friend is here to see us off," Lucienne said quickly. "What do you mean, 'no can do'?"

"That trunk, Miss—it just won't fit. It's extra-long, you see, and everything's fitted in like puzzle pieces. It just won't work. The only way it could fit is if we took everything out—which would make us even later than we are, by the way—and put it in the bottom of the hold. But if it's fragile, as you say, then all that weight on it . . ."

"No," Lucienne said.

"What'd she say?" Hansen turned to Sally.

"She said *no*, we cannot do that. Please unload all our pieces—I'll show you which ones. We are not going."

Hansen let out an exasperated breath, while Wilson turned away, muttering, "Son of a . . ."

"Listen, Miss." The taller man approached Sally, taking her arm and drawing her a little way away. "Your maid is upset, but I'm sure you can be reasonable. We've got a schedule to keep, weight restrictions, a whole lot of rules we need to follow to keep you ladies safe . . ."

Sally had gone pale, hardly hearing anything beyond the first sentence. "Did you say my *maid*? Do you realize that my dear, lifelong friend here is the owner of the Imperial Casino and probably the wealthiest woman in Shanghai? She could buy your precious aeroplane and find a new crew for it—but I doubt she is interested. If you cannot accommodate us, then please unload our luggage at once."

Cerise arrived, freshly made-up and thoroughly confused. "What's going on? Are we ready to go?"

"Cerise, we can't go with you. There's no room for our big trunk."

"Is that all? Honestly! Can't Claude take care of it? Or your capable young lady at the casino? Really darlings, we must get going; we don't want to miss our tide . . . or whatever it is. Isn't that right, Captain Hansen?" She turned to the tall man with a brilliant smile.

"Exactly what I've been trying to tell your friends here, but . . ."

"But we can't do that," Lucienne said firmly. "Please, ask them to unload our things."

Cerise sighed and turned to the workmen milling around. "All right, then. All of my luggage is bright pink—

it stays on the plane. The rest—all those brown cases—unload and put back in the charabanc. On the double!"

Claude moved away to supervise the luggage handling, and Cerise turned to Sally and Lucienne. "You're being tremendously foolish. I don't know how you're going to get out of Shanghai now, and you really must. But I know I'm not going to change your minds, so all I can do is wish you well. Sally, you changed my life—you gave me immortality. And Lucienne, you may not have always realized it, but I have the utmost respect for you. *Tu es formidable, ma chère.* I hope you'll come find me at the Cafe de los Inmortales."

Returning to the vehicle, now fully loaded with their baggage, they found Claude and the driver smoking on the shady side of the cab, deep in conversation. Claude was apparently fluent in Shanghainese.

Lucienne raised an eyebrow and asked him a question, then translated for Sally.

"He was here for three years before we got here, so of course he picked up the language. He's got a good ear, you know." She smiled.

They climbed into the seat, Claude in the middle.

"What now?" Sally sighed. "Back to the casino, I guess?"

"Not much point in that; they've already started shutting the place down," Lucienne said glumly. "Cathay Hotel, maybe?"

Claude put his arms around both of them and gave them a squeeze. "Don't worry. We've got you covered, my boy Chow and I. But first, I just want to say—I *would*, you know. Take care of Natalie, keep her trunk safe and get it to you somehow. Be a hell of a surprise for her if she woke up—I was never her favorite person. But we'd work it out, I'm sure . . . But the thing is, being a traveling jazz-man, it's hard on one's luggage. So really, it will be much better this way."

"What are you talking about? And where are we going?"

"The docks, little girl. It's true what everyone's been saying—there's no passage out of Shanghai on the big liners for love or money. But if you only need a boat to Hong Kong—not a problem."

Lucienne and Sally looked at each other. "We *could* go back to Hong Kong, I suppose. At least we'd have the money for a better class of rat-hole, and I wouldn't have to work at the Red Lotus . . ."

Claude laughed richly. "Oh Sally, I wish I could have walked in there one night and danced with you, to some terrible band! But, no, I wasn't suggesting you should stay in HK. They've got these new big, comfortable aircraft out of Hong Kong, cross the Pacific to Hawaii or even San Francisco—the China Clippers. Make Cerise's charter look like a toy! If you've got the fare, Miss Moneybags, they've got plenty of room for you and *all* your trunks."

"But Claude, America? Ugh, that American pilot . . . I can't believe you're suggesting it. You know I've never wanted to go to the place that treated you so badly . . ."

Claude shrugged. "Well, stay in Hawaii, then—supposed to be a tropical paradise, with folks of all colors. Might be tasty. But San Francisco is probably more your style—fashion, restaurants, jazz clubs. It's different from other places in the States—different *enough*, anyway. The important thing is to get out of here, go somewhere safe."

The driver pulled the bulky vehicle skillfully into a parking place and, after a brief confab with Claude, went off to make inquiries. He was back within minutes, just as they were climbing out to stretch, leading a pair of porters who began to load their baggage onto carts. Claude spoke to them forcefully, indicating they should take great care and come back to get the big trunk in a separate trip.

"Your flight is first thing tomorrow morning. Your bags will go direct to the Pan Am terminal once you dock in HK—except for that trunk, of course! Natalie can stay with you at a hotel tonight."

"We've been preparing for weeks, it seems, but this is all so sudden now," Lucienne said.

"At least there isn't a big metal bird with its wings spread hovering over us, and Cerise buzzing around like a queen bee."

Sally lunged toward Claude and wrapped him in a fierce hug. "I am going to miss you so bloody much! I can't believe we have to part after finding each other again. You're sure you won't . . .?"

Claude pulled back just enough to put his hands on each side of her face. They stood eye to eye, exactly the same height. "Little girl," he said softly, wiping a tear from her cheek. "You know we are friends forever. And as vamps, we can *mean* that. We will be together again. Probably in the States. I'm not ready yet, but I'll give them some time to get better . . . And then I'll find my-self a good jazz club, and there we'll be. Hey, how about a nibble for old times' sake, like in those sweet Chocolate Dandies days in Paris? Come here, Mlle Lucienne."

In the shade of the charabanc, they shared a deeply comforting, three-way hug, nuzzling and nibbling at each other's necks. When they separated, they couldn't help their radiant smiles.

"All right then. You take good care of each other, and of your gal Natalie. You're going to do just fine."

"You too, Claude. Safe travels, wherever you go."

Sally and Lucienne smoothed their suits and adjusted their hats. Lucienne directed a few words to the returned porters, who handed her the claim tickets for the rest of their luggage and hefted Natalie's trunk with great care.

Hong Kong

They checked in to the posh Peninsula Hotel and had a much-needed nap. In the evening, they headed out and, at Sally's insistence, peered into the doorway of the Red Lotus.

"Ugh, it truly is a low dive, with a terrible band. I'm so sorry, darling." Lucienne squeezed Sally's shoulder.

"Oh, it's not that bad. But let's *not* go in."

They found a chic cocktail bar, picked up a pair of charming cousins and spent a pleasant couple of hours. Eventually, since their flight was so early the next day, they decided to stay out most of the night, wandering and feeding on random, agreeable citizens. Just before dawn, they returned to their hotel to bathe and change into their travel suits, and then summoned a bellman to carry down their trunk.

Well protected by both veiled hats and dark glasses, they staggered out to their taxi. "Ugh, I feel like a zombie," Lucienne murmured.

The baggage limit turned out to be fifty pounds per person, but a combination of vamp glamour and judicious bribery made the matter manageable.

And then it was time: "All aboard the China Clipper! To Macao – Guam – Wake Island – Midway Island – Honolulu – San Francisco!"

San Francisco, March, 1942

Lucienne, brushing her hair, paused to touch the jade pendant nestled in the neckline of her navy blue crepe blouse.

Sally, also getting ready, smiled over at her. "I'm so glad Cerise gave it back to you. And it's been lucky, don't you think?"

"It has," Lucienne agreed. "I'm sure it got us our jobs."

At loose ends, shortly after their arrival, Lucienne had wandered into an elegant shop, oddly named Gump's. A gentleman,who turned out to be a manager, greeted her cordially and complimented her beautiful jade.

"I think he saw that before he even looked at my face. Then he asked if I was Chinese—well, close enough; I said yes—and next thing I knew he was asking if I wanted to work there."

"And you said, only if I can bring along my lovely and talented friend."

"*Exactement!* Pass my flask, darling."

Sally passed Lucienne's blood over and picked up her own, leaning back in her chair and looking around the room. It wasn't bad, she thought—spacious and warm, with shabby but comfortable furnishings. The rent was low, because it had only one small, north-facing window —gloomy for humans, but suiting them perfectly. The huge closet made a cozy sleeping chamber, big enough for both of them and Natalie's trunk, while a small wooden armoire held their current daily wardrobe: six tailored suits shared between them. Lucienne was wearing the gray wool today.

"People here are trying to be very nice to the Chinese," Sally mused. "And meanwhile, the poor Japanese citizens . . ." She sighed. "Funny how everyone told us we could escape the war by coming here. It's everywhere."

Lucienne nodded absently. "I wish we could have stayed in the Hawaiian Islands. The flowers, the lushness . . . those warm nights. And the people were delicious."

"Mmm. But it's just as well we left when we did. Who would have thought the Japanese air force would fly all that way?"

"Poor Yoshi. He just wanted to live quietly and write poetry. I wonder what he's doing now, if he is alive . . ."

Sally came over to embrace her. "Loving mortals—it's hard, even without a war."

San Francisco,
March, 1946

"I like it here, I really do." Lucienne made some version of this statement to Sally almost every day.

"I know, I like it too. Are you trying to convince me?" A smile, a shrug and a kiss would end the conversation.

Their apartment on Sutter Street was comfortable, and their jobs at Gump's (Lucienne in Asian antiques, Sally in fine jewelry) remained agreeable, requiring little more than showing up at two o'clock, four days a week—a compromise, as they would have preferred two days a week at four o'clock.

In the serene atmosphere of the store, they posed elegantly, answered questions about the beautiful wares and occasionally charmed a customer into a sale. In the shop and elsewhere, they met pleasant, interesting men and women—socialites, collectors, artists, writers. They were invited to the theatre and the opera, and to Pacific Heights cocktail parties (they tried to avoid dinners).

They went to poetry readings in North Beach, where red wine flowed agreeably. Sally adored the Dawn Club, where the band played the "old" style jazz of the 1920s. For dancing and a dressy night out, there was the Top of the Mark and, amusingly, the Forbidden City night-club, whose all-Asian-American entertainers made them nostalgic for Shanghai.

On a cool March afternoon when they had the day off, they walked down to the Rincon Annex post office, where they had a General Delivery account. Often there was no mail for them, but this time, the clerk handed over a fat brown envelope covered in Chinese stamps, addressed to Lucienne.

She stared at the stamps, the penmanship of the address. "Let's go home, Sally; I don't want to open it here. Let's get a taxi."

Back in their flat, Lucienne took a gulp from her flask, sat down and carefully opened the envelope, pulling out the folded sheets of yellow paper.

"It's dated October 16; it took almost six months to get here."

"Is it . . .?" Sally leaned forward.

"It's from Peony. She's re-opened the casino. Things are going well—people are eager to forget their troubles. Hah! She asks my permission to rename the casino 'Hai

Pai.' It means . . . Shanghai culture, East meets West. I love it!"

"I do too! What else does she say?"

"Most of the staff have returned. And as soon as I telegraph our bank account number, she'll wire some funds. She says Claude is back and doing quite well; his band broke up, but he's working with a new Chinese group, and they're not bad. The drummer is a special friend of his. Oh, and Cassandra Jones came around for a while, but she's left for New York. And, she enclosed this. It's from Yoshi."

A smaller, square envelope of thick, cream-colored stock held several sheets of matching paper. The writing was in English, but the bold black ink and stylized calligraphy suggested Japanese aesthetics. Lucienne read and re-read, her eyes filling with tears. She handed the letter to Sally.

'November 2, 1938

My darling, most luminous Lucienne,

I trust this letter will reach you someday. I have been told, by my contacts in Shanghai, that your casino has long been closed and shuttered. I am relieved and grateful that you were able to leave that beleaguered city.

Still, knowing that you are the owner of the property (or "owneress," as you so charmingly put it when we first met), I have faith that correspondence addressed to you at No. 74, Bubbling Well Road will somehow, some day, be held in your exquisite hands and be read by your precious eyes. Such is my faith in the power of postal delivery, and of love.

My darling, I want you to know that I recovered from my burn injuries without undue physical suffering. But suffering takes many forms.

By now, the imbecilic war that threatened for so long is well underway. I regret deeply that I was so misguided by thoughts of duty and family honor as to have been part of this senseless aggression. But all things end, and I feel certain that China will recover. After all, as dear Noël Coward so wisely said, "Very big, China. Very small, Japan."

It pains me to think that you, my dear lovely one, might feel remorse, might feel you had been careless and thus caused the firey accident—which has been, in fact, my salvation. I assure you, my darling, you have no cause to seek my forgiveness. Rather it is I who, unwittingly but no less hideously, wronged you.

The Golden Bat cigarettes, which I brought as a pathetic "gift" at the behest of my superiors . . .the Golden Bats, which you so charmingly and innocently enjoyed . . . They were a cynical, wicked plot. The golden tips were filled with opium, deliberately included to addict the smoker and thus induce "loyalty" to the brand. The casual evil of this plan—purely a money-making scheme, and predicated on my country's contempt for the Chinese—fills me with disgust. And to think how it harmed you, the most precious being ever to enter my life—it is intolerable!

I mentioned that my accident was fortunate for me. Indeed, since that time, I have been able to sit quietly in my garden, recuperating and watching the seasons unfold. I have found peace here, among the birds and leaves, but I cannot forget or forgive the evils I have been privy to. I will not return to the army, but there is only one way to remove myself from my post. Not the melodramatic sword, but the convenient cyanide capsule which was issued to me long ago, when I became an officer.

Goodbye, my darling, my precious love. I wish we could have had a long and beautiful life together. I hope that you have escaped to a place of safety, to a good life, and that you will kindly remember

Your Yoshi'

Sally put her arms around her friend, and they sat quietly for a long time.

"I should have turned him," Lucienne whispered. "If I'd only known . . ."

Finally, she wiped her eyes and stood up.

"Eight years ago! All this time . . . I imagined he was there. I hoped he would avoid having to be in the war. I imagined he was, somehow, sitting in his garden, writing poetry. And, well . . . he did it. He found a way to stay out of the war. It's just . . . I realize, I was hoping all this time I might see him again. I think that's what has kept me here, in San Francisco; I wanted to stay 'close.' But now . . ." She opened the closet door, went to Natalie's trunk and ran her hand over it, turning to Sally with a curious look.

"What do you think, Sally? Once Peony starts sending wire transfers, we'll have plenty of money; we can go anywhere. We've had some good times here, but you know—the art set, the social set, the bohemians—we keep seeing the same people. And everything closes so early! In Paris or Shanghai, we could stay out all night. Here, there's no one on the street but the damned fog." Lucienne shivered. "When Natalie wakes up, this town will not be big enough for her. I think we need to take her to New York City."

Sally stared at her friend. "Claude said once it was the world capital of jazz. I wonder if that's still true." She began to pace the room, eyes far away. "I think it could work, Loulou! I think it could be the best thing. Let's go down to Western Union and wire Peony right away—the sooner we get some funds, the sooner we can start planning our trip. And maybe I can get a message to Claude, too." She had her coat on and was fluffing her hair in the mirror. "Ugh, I'm sick of this poofy hairstyle. I'm going to get a bob again—I don't care if it's not this year's look. I'll be . . . avant garde. Where's my green hat? Let's go, Loulou—are you ready?"

"Just a moment, darling. I'll be right there." Putting Yoshi's letter back into its envelope, she saw that the last page, which she'd thought was a blank cover sheet, had a few lines of writing.

Precious piece of jade
Engraved with a bird in flight
Wing to freedom, love

She folded the page small and tucked it next to her heart. "All right. I'm ready."

FIN

It was so hard to leave the 1920s . . . to leave a time when people could hope that war was in the past, that the future held modernity, progress and more and more marvelous parties!

But, with my characters being immortal (and having burned quite a few of their bridges at the end of *Vamps of '29*) they had to move on. (In fact, my working title for this book was 'Vamps Go On.') I have enjoyed their journey, even if the decade they traveled through grew somewhat darker.

Every vampire fiction has its own rules, and I have shaped the genre to suit my own needs. My vamps are immortal, and they live by ingesting blood, but they are able to survive on a mixture of bottled animal blood and (for the most part) gentle, nonlethal tastes of humans. They avoid exposure to direct, strong sunlight, and they are basically oriented to nightlife, but are able to be more-or-less active during daylight hours. Traveling widely, they cannot be bothered with eschewing garlic or running water, but they will wait to be invited in before entering dwellings; it's only good manners! And as young women of fashion, they absolutely must be able to be reflected in mirrors.

A few other notes:

(1) The story of Golden Bat cigarettes is, essentially (if improbably), true.

(2) There is a lot of smoking in this book. Most adults in the 20th century smoked cigarettes, and there were a great many fashionable accessories involved. My vampire characters, of course, did not experience any health risks (which were, in any case, largely unknown at the time). This is in no way an endorsement of tobacco consumption.

(3) The reference to Jordan Baker in Shanghai ("adopted, obviously" as Cerise notes) is a shout-out to the incredible Nghi Vo's version of Great Gatsby, *The Chosen and the Beautiful*, a book I deeply admire and envy.

ACKNOWLEDGMENTS

This is a work of fiction, much of which stems from a fascination with the sometimes stranger-than-fiction byways of history. I am deeply grateful for the work of historians who have delved into detailed research on the period and places I have written about.

In particular, the following authors have written so vividly and beautifully about some of my vamps' destinations as to bring the settings alive, and I highly recommend their books:

Midnight in Cairo: the Divas of Egypt's Roaring 20s, by Ralph Cormack

Maharanis, by Lucy Moore

City of Devils: The Two Men Who Ruled the Underworld of Old Shanghai, by Paul French

Shanghai Grand: Forbidden Love and International Intrigue in a Doomed World, by Taras Grescoe

Any errors or misunderstandings of historical fact or context are my own. My intent has always been to entertain and appreciate, not to appropriate or offend.

I am lucky to be part of a circle of friends who share my fascination with historical styles in fashion, architecture and music—thank you all for your kindness and inspiration. I can only name a few, but:

Sally Norton, you are still the one who started it all, and I hope you enjoy your namesake's latest shenanigans.

Sara Klotz de Aguilar, whenever I need to picture the most elegant 1930s looks, I just think of you. Thank you for so many years of loveliness!

Kimberly Manning Aker, my fellow writer and dear friend—I can't wait for your next book and our next adventure!

Lastly, my dearest love, Charles Aitel: constant reader, consultant, enabler, researcher, mixologist and sine qua non.

ABOUT THE AUTHOR

Alice Jurow has written and lectured on Art Deco architecture, art and fashion. She is the author of *Vamps of '29,* and lives in Berkeley, California, with her human and feline family.

www.ingramcontent.com/pod-product-compliance
Lightning Source LLC
Chambersburg PA
CBHW030928120726
47906CB00002B/540